D0108781

ABOVE

ABC

DVE

ROLAND SMITH

SCHOLASTIC PRESS · NEW YORK

Library of Congress Cataloging-in-Publication Data

Names: Smith, Roland, 1951– author.
Title: Above / Roland Smith.
Description: First edition. | New York : Scholastic Press, 2016. |
Summary: Pat O'Toole, his brother Coop, and their new companion, Kate,
have narrowly escaped a cultlike community below New York City but must
try to stop the cult's leader, Kate's grandfather.
Identifiers: LCCN 2016019874 | ISBN 9780545564892 (hc)
Subjects: | CYAC: Brothers — Fiction. | Adventure and adventurers — Fiction. |
Cults — Fiction. | Underground areas — Fiction. | Portland (Or.) —
Fiction. | BISAC: JUVENILE FICTION / Action & Adventure / General. |
JUVENILE FICTION / Family / Siblings. | JUVENILE FICTION /
Nature & the Natural World / Environment.
Classification: LCC PZ7.S65766 Abo 2016 | DDC [Fic] — dc23
LC record available at https://lccn.loc.gov/2016019874

10 9 8 7 6 5 4 3 2 1   16 17 18 19 20

Printed in the U.S.A.   23
First edition, October 2016

The text type was set in Garamond.
The display type was set in Impact.
Book design by Phil Falco

FOR ALL THE TEACHERS, LIBRARIANS, AND READERS,
YOUNG AND OLD, WHO HAVE KEPT ME ABOVE
ALL THESE LONG YEARS

NATIONWIDE MANHUNT FOR THE POD CONTINUES
FBI TASK FORCE SEARCHES WIDELY

Members of the domestic terrorist group known as the Pod remain the target of a comprehensive FBI nationwide search.

"They've gone to ground," FBI agent Tia Ryan stated during a brief press conference earlier today.

The Pod is thought to be composed of former members of the Weather Underground Organization, a radical group active in the late sixties and seventies. Their alleged leader is Dr. Lawrence Oliver Dane. Dane was taken off the FBI's Most Wanted list decades ago, after he was presumed dead in an accidental bomb explosion at a safe house belonging to the group, also known as the Weathermen.

The FBI has been reluctant to release any details of their ongoing investigation of the Pod, but a source close to the investigation confirmed that Dane is indeed believed to be alive.

Following his reported death, Dane led a group of radicalized followers, including some family members, to a top-secret, abandoned nuclear fallout facility beneath the borough of Manhattan in New York City. There, the group built a self-sustaining community that they called the Deep and lived undetected for decades.

Dane, considered by many to be a genius, received his first university degree at the age of fifteen. Other advanced degrees quickly followed. He has master's degrees in business administration and agriculture, and PhDs in computer science and psychology.

It is possible that Dane's degrees in agriculture and business administration inspired him to found the gourmet mushroom wholesale business Cloud's Mushrooms, which investigators believe was created as a means to keep the underground group solvent.

Executives of the now bankrupt global company issued a statement categorically denying any knowledge of Dane or his underground followers.

"We had no idea where the mushrooms were grown, or who the owner of the company was," ex-CEO Paul Pence said. "I've never met Dr. Dane. I was told that the unnamed owner was very reclusive and wanted to remain completely behind the scenes."

When asked if this unusual way of doing business raised any suspicions, Pence claimed that it did not.

"We were selling mushrooms — not arms, sarin gas, explosives, or anything else the Pod has been associated with. I will admit that it was a strange way to operate a business, but in the twenty-plus years I worked for Cloud's Mushrooms, it was a well-oiled machine. The mushrooms went out and money came in."

Pence indicated that profits were in the millions.

"But I'm unemployed now," Pence said. "All of us at Cloud's Mushrooms are unemployed. I left work on Tuesday evening with tens of millions of dollars in our account. When I returned on Wednesday morning the money had vanished."

So too have Dane and several of his followers. The FBI is warning the public not to approach suspected members of the Pod and they are asking anyone with information to contact local law enforcement immediately. The Pod are believed to be armed and extremely dangerous.

BENEATH

the newspaper article are police sketches of Lawrence Oliver Dane, aka Lod, aka Lord of the Deep, and several of the original members of the Pod, the so-called Originals.

I'm sitting inside Union Station in Portland, Oregon.

I need a shower.

I need a Laundromat.

I need a real bed.

I need a hot meal.

I haven't seen Coop and Kate for five days.

I'm not sure why we're running.

The train station is crowded because all the trains are late.

Snow all across the country, blocking tracks.

It's snowing outside right now.

Twenty-eight degrees.

I came in from Salt Lake City.

Kate is due in any minute from Seattle. I hope.

Coop is coming up from Los Angeles in a couple hours. Maybe.

The stationmaster just gave me a look the last time I asked him when the LA train would arrive. I'm guessing it's because the answer is the same as the first five times I asked.

The waiting area is packed because of the delays. We're all sitting on these long oak benches, guarding our gear. All I have is a small backpack with a change of clothes; a laptop, which I haven't used since we left DC; and an iPhone, also unused except for a couple texts from Kate several days ago.

Oh, and this journal, and a couple of pencils, which I bought in DC just before I boarded the train. I bought journals and pencils for Coop and Kate too. I wonder if they will use them.

Kate's friend the Librarian gave us the packs and the electronics after we escaped from the Deep. The Librarian's real name is Alex Dane. He's Lod's younger brother. *Younger* is a relative term. They're both in their seventies, though you wouldn't know it by looking at either of them. Good genes, I guess.

Alex said that he would let us know when it was safe. He hasn't called, texted, or emailed. He said we needed to change our appearance. Stay off the grid. Travel separately, because Lod and his people would be looking for three kids traveling together.

I cut my hair.

Ridiculous.

Because it's been so cold I've worn a sock cap since I left DC.

I quit shaving.

Ridiculous.

Because it would take me about a hundred years to grow a beard.

People are starting to get up from the oak benches. Picking up their packs and bags, they begin lining up at the door leading out to the tracks.

The Coast Starlight Number 11 is pulling into the station from Seattle.

Between people trying to board and people detraining, it's impossible to pick Kate out of the crowd. I'm making a minor spectacle of myself standing on tiptoes and craning my neck trying to spot her in the mass of colliding humanity until I realize that's exactly how one of the Pod people will end up spotting me.

Kate is either on the train or she isn't. If she is on it she'll find me. Most of the people inside the station are boarding the southbound Coast Starlight. Those who have just detrained are hurrying toward the station exit.

I sit back down on the hard oak bench.

It doesn't take long for Kate to appear.

She sits down twenty feet away.

She's cut her hair and dyed it blond, but she is perfectly recognizable.

She's wearing sunglasses, which is the last thing anyone needs inside the dimly lit station. She might as well have had a sign around her neck that reads: HI, MY NAME IS KATE DANE. THE REASON I'M WEARING SUNGLASSES IS BECAUSE I WAS BORN AND RAISED UNDERGROUND AND MY EYES ARE SENSITIVE TO LIGHT, EVEN DIM LIGHT, WHEN I'M ABOVE.

I doubt it matters though. We're nearly three thousand miles away from New York City. From the sound of things, Lod and the Originals have more important things to worry about than three kids — like every law enforcement officer in the world trying to find and capture them.

Kate seems to be looking everywhere, and at everyone, but me. I want to jump up and shout: *I am right here!*

But I don't.

It must have been so strange for her to see the country for the first time on that long train ride. She's never been outside of New York City before, and most of that time she was living underground.

Traveling cross-country by train can be deceiving. Railway tracks do not run through the nicest parts of cities. If Kate was judging the country by what she saw clacking through the run-down parts of towns and cities, she might be thinking she made a big mistake surfacing and blowing the whistle on her grandfather.

Minutes pass.

I open my multi-tool pocketknife and carefully cut out the newspaper article. I've been snipping articles about the Pod at every stop and sticking them into the back of my notebook. I'm putting together an epistolary journal — from the Latin *epistola*, meaning letter. The author uses diaries, letters, and newspaper articles to tell the story.

Coop and I are no longer using digital recorders to communicate, but I still keep my recorder in my pocket out of habit. There could come a time when I might need it again.

It's interesting that none of the newspaper articles have pointed out that Pod stands for People of the Deep, or that if you reverse the words in Cloud's Mushrooms you come up with the symbol of a nuclear bomb explosion. Not that they have a bomb; at least I don't *think* they have a bomb, and that's the problem. We don't know what they have, where they are, or what they're planning. All we know is that they are planning *something*, because, according to Kate, "Lod always has a plan."

I WATCHED PAT

out of the corner of my eye, writing in his little pocket note-book. He had given me one just like it in Washington, DC, and I'd been using it.

I took off my sunglasses, squinted against the light, then slowly scanned the thirty or forty people left in the station one by one. Satisfied that there was no one in the station that I knew, I got up and walked over to Pat and sat down next to him.

"I think we're clear," I said. "I don't recognize anyone. But let's move over to the other bench so we're facing the entrance in case somebody I do recognize comes in. Is that the only entrance?"

"I think so." Pat stuffed his notebook into his pack and followed me.

I did another visual sweep, then turned to him and said, "How have you been, Pat?"

"Fine. I could use a shower and a hot meal."

"Me too. I'm starving. Is there a restaurant here?"

"There's a place called Wilfs. I haven't checked it out, but I looked at the menu outside the door. I've been here for hours."

I squinted at him, still bothered by the light. "You don't look that different."

"You do," Pat said. "At least with the sunglasses off. By the way, you need to keep them off."

"Really?"

"I don't know if you noticed, but it's gray outside and snowing. The lights inside are barely bright enough to read by. Nobody is wearing sunglasses. I doubt anyone in here is even carrying sunglasses."

"My eyes hurt even in this dim light," I complained. "When I crossed North Dakota a few days ago I thought my eyeballs were melting even with my shades on."

Pat shrugged. "It probably doesn't matter anyway. I doubt the Originals are looking for us."

"You're wrong," I said.

Pat retrieved his notebook and pulled a newspaper article out of it. "I think they have other things on their minds besides us," he said. "There's a massive manhunt for them."

I looked down at the sketches. I'd read several articles as I crossed the country, but I hadn't seen this one. "The sketches are accurate," I said. "Very accurate. But of course they don't look like this anymore."

"What do you mean?"

"My grandfather and the Originals are experts at disguise." I pointed at one of the sketches. "This is Bill Ord. He has brown eyes and gray thinning hair. Now he has a full head of black hair and a carefully trimmed black beard. His eyes are blue now. The same shade as mine. He looks twenty years younger."

Pat grinned. "You act like you've seen him."

"I did see him. He was in Sandpoint, Idaho, yesterday."

11

"It must have been somebody who looked —"

"It was Bill Ord," I insisted. "I've been making sure to get off the trains with the crowd. I saw him before he saw me. I slipped into the women's restroom and hid." I pointed at another sketch. A woman. "That's Bella. Bill's girlfriend. They've been together for decades. She was at the station too. In a wheelchair."

"How did she get out of the Deep? It isn't exactly handicapped accessible."

"Bella is as handicapped as you are. The wheelchair is a disguise. In the Deep she was our BJJ and yoga instructor. All Shadows are required to have black belts in BJJ."

"What is BJJ?"

"Brazilian jujitsu. I've been practicing it since I could walk."

"Did you use martial arts to get away from Bella and Bill?"

"Of course not. They didn't see me. I hid in the restroom custodian's closet while Bella checked the stalls; then I slipped by them while they searched the rest of the station. I took a bus to Seattle and caught the train down here."

"Maybe they were just catching a train. They're on the run too."

"You don't need to check toilet stalls to catch a train."

"'You don't need a weatherman to know which way the wind blows,'" Pat said. A quote from Bob Dylan's song "Subterranean Homesick Blues," which is where the Weathermen got their name.

I gave him a smile. "You're kind of funny. Let's get something to eat."

WILFS RESTAURANT

was even darker than the station. Kate checked out everyone in the restaurant as we walked in. The hostess took us to a table, which Kate rejected, pointing at another table in a dark corner where she could watch the entrance.

I had the pacific prawns with roasted jalapeño peppers and celeriac, which turned out to be root vegetables sautéed in fresh herbs and butter. Kate had the Steak Diane, which she regretted because the waiter brought it to the table flaming, or flambéed, in an iron skillet. Everyone in the restaurant, of course, watched the spectacle. For a second I thought Kate was going to jump up and make a run for it, or hide under the table. Instead, she put on her sunglasses.

"Don't worry," the server said. "I have yet to splatter anyone with hot grease."

Which caused the people at the two closest tables to laugh.

The flaming beef incident took less than a minute, but that was more than enough time for Kate to suggest that we leave.

"We'd have to wait for the check," I said quietly. "The waiter would want to know why we didn't like our food. And I'm hungry."

Kate took off her sunglasses and put them on the table. "I've never eaten in a restaurant."

I shouldn't have been surprised, but I was. I've eaten in thousands of restaurants. My parents are two of the most undomesticated humans on the planet. The kitchen in our house in McLean, Virginia, functions as a kitchen in name only. The fridge isn't there to keep food chilled. It's a magnetic bulletin board for take-out and delivery menus.

"Where did you eat when you were traveling cross-country?"

"Train station convenience stores."

"Did you know you could eat in the dining car? The food isn't that good, but at least it's food."

"Too exposed. I picked my seats carefully. Window seats at the front of the car closest to the dining car, with the restroom forward. People going to the restroom, or the dining car, had to walk up from behind me."

"What about when they returned to their seats?"

"I sat in window bulkhead seats. They'd have to turn their heads to see me. People walking down a narrow aisle tend to look straight ahead. People exiting restrooms generally don't look at anyone. Don't tell me you didn't know this."

"No. I didn't."

Who thinks like this? People of the Deep. That's who. When Kate was Beneath she was a Shadow, kind of like a cop whose job it was to keep an eye on other Pod members. Paranoia runs deep Beneath, but if there was a nuclear holocaust you would want to have a Shadow at your side. They can see their way in the dark, and they're expert trackers and scavengers.

I forked a spicy prawn into my mouth.

It was delicious.

Kate started in on her steak.

"Did you talk to anyone on the trains?" I asked.

Kate shook her head. "I put my backpack on the aisle seat. If the car was full I put the pack at my feet and acted like I was asleep. Did you talk to anyone?"

"Of course. How can you not talk to anyone for five days?"

"By not talking to anyone."

I ate my third prawn.

Three to go.

I thought about ordering another plateful.

"What did you talk about?" Kate asked.

"Nothing really. Just strangers-on-a-train things. 'Where are you going? Where'd you come from? Cold enough for you?' That kind of stuff. I lied about most of it, of course. Parents divorced. Going to see my mom, or dad, or uncle, or aunt, or grandparents. Told them my name was Jack, when they asked, but most of the time no one asked. So you never went to a restaurant when you were on top?"

"Never. We weren't up top often, and when we were, it was usually very late, or very early in the morning. Most things were closed. And when we were up top we were always working — shadowing people, mostly Originals. If they had to go inside a building, we waited outside for them. Not much risk of an Original running. We were more like security than shadows. Lod liked us to spend time up top so we'd be used to it in case there was a runner."

"Did you ever have a runner?"

"Twice. Caught one Beneath. The other managed to make it up top, but he was only up for ten minutes before we ran him down. Very nice guy. His name was Bob Jonas. Some kind of computer genius. He was going to be promoted to Original. We were all shocked that he ran."

"What happened to Bob?"

Kate slowly chewed a piece of steak, which she seemed to be enjoying, before answering. "Lod said he sent him to the mush room. He said he would return as soon as he was back in sync with the group." Another bite of steak. A sip of water. "I never saw him again. No one did."

Coop and I had been sentenced to the mush room before Kate had helped us escape.

I scarfed down another prawn.

Two to go.

"Up top," I said. "That's where you saw Coop. I mean, the first time."

She nodded. "I was up top with Lod. He had some business to take care of. He went into an apartment building to talk to someone. I was standing on the stoop, waiting. Coop walked by with another man. They stopped under a streetlight and started tap-dancing. It was so weird. I was mesmerized by the strangeness of it."

Another piece of steak disappeared.

"The following week I was up top again for a drill. We had a lot more of them toward the end. That's how I knew something was up."

"What kind of drill?"

"Retrieval. Lod would send someone up top and the Shadows' job was to find them and bring them back down."

"And you saw Coop again?"

"Three more times. Once on his own, tapping in a tunnel.

Twice with Terry Trueman when they were Dumpster diving. That's when I first thought that Coop might be trying to join Terry and the others Beneath."

"Were you looking for him?"

"That's the strange thing. I wasn't. I just kept bumping into him in completely different parts of the city. It was like he was a magnet."

More like a lightning rod, I thought, eating my last prawn. Coop had been attracting people to him from the moment he was born. Complete strangers. Rich and poor. From every walk of life.

"Somehow I knew," Kate continued. "I would meet Coop in the Deep."

The server brought the check. I paid him from the pile of cash Alex had given us in New York. We had divided it three ways. I still had several thousand dollars left.

The station had gotten a lot more crowded. I was trying to figure out where we were going to sit when Kate grabbed my arm and yanked me into the tiny convenience store near the restaurant.

"I've already been in here," I said. "They don't have anything I —"

"Bella," Kate said.

There were windows in the store looking out into the waiting area. I peeked out past the potato chips. Fifty feet away was a woman sitting in a wheelchair. She was facing the boarding doors.

I couldn't see her face.

"How do you know it's Bella?"

"Because Bill Ord is standing fifty steps to her right, facing the opposite direction, holding an open paperback like he's reading. But what he's really doing is scanning the crowd."

Bill Ord. Black hair. Black beard. He was too far away to see the color of his eyes. He looked nothing like the sketch in the newspaper.

"How did they get here?"

"Train? Car? Bus? Airplane? Who knows."

People were gathering their things.

Standing up.

A train was pulling in.

I walked over to the counter and asked the woman which train it was.

"Los Angeles," she said.

Coop's train.

Kate came up behind me. "You can leave the station through the restaurant."

I stepped away from the counter. "Me? What about you?"

"Someone has to intercept Coop before he comes into the station. Someone has to warn him."

"And that someone should be me. Not you."

"You have no idea who these people are. What they're capable of."

"Exactly," I said. "They've never seen me. I could walk over and offer to push Bella's wheelchair, or ask Bill what he's reading. Neither one of them would look at me twice. My disguise is that they don't know who I am."

She stared at me for a second, then gave a reluctant nod. I followed her back over to the window.

Bill and Bella had not moved from their positions.

"What's your plan?" Kate asked.

I grabbed a bag of Cheetos. My third of the day.

"I'll get in line like I'm catching the train. Hopefully I'll spot Coop before they do. He and I will figure out a different exit strategy. There has to be another way out of the train yard other than through the station."

I hoped there was another way out of the yard.

"And what am I supposed to do?" Kate asked.

"Voodoo Doughnuts."

"What?"

"I just read about it. It's not too far away. It's just the kind of weird place that Coop would like." I showed her the newspaper advertisement with directions. "We'll meet you there."

BELLA AND BILL

looked as innocent, and as common, as all the other train watchers. They could have been grandparents waiting for their grandkids. They might have been a little paler than those around them, but I'd noticed earlier that almost everyone in the station looked like they could use some sun. They weren't wearing shades, though they were squinting a little in the dim light. To be honest, I'm not sure I would have noticed this if I hadn't known who they were and where they had lived for the past forty years.

I got in the disorganized line and tried to work my way to the front without being too pushy and drawing attention to myself. I'd been watching the detraining and boarding process for hours and had a good idea of how it worked. Most of the people waited politely for the arriving passengers to get into the station before rushing the train, but there were always a few jerks who couldn't wait to find a good seat and pushed through the incoming crowd.

I needed to be a pushy jerk. I didn't expect Coop to detrain first. The only time his feet ever moved quickly was when they were tapping. He was always the last to arrive and last to leave. Going for a walk with him was a form of torture. A fifteen-minute stroll could last an hour or more. For him, getting there was a lot more interesting than being there.

But I couldn't be sure of that now.

Coop might have changed since leaving home over a year ago. I'd barely gotten a chance to talk to him in New York. For all I knew he might jump off the train while it was still moving and sprint into the station. Finding Kate in the Deep might have changed him.

Coop believed, and it might even be true, that he had been heading into the Deep and to Kate his entire life. And I had to admit that there had been some very strange coincidences.

Like Kate's parents being murdered and tossed into a Dumpster at the exact moment that Coop was born, during a lunar eclipse.

Like FBI agent Tia Ryan being the lead New York City detective for Kate's parents' homicide case before joining the FBI and busting Coop for blowing up our neighborhood.

Whether it was fate, predestination, or some kind of cosmic spiritual collision, two things were clear: Coop was smitten with Kate, and Kate was smitten with Coop, even though they barely knew each other.

Which is why I was rudely pushing my way to the front. I had an image in my head of Coop running in slow motion to get to Kate like they were in a sappy movie, only to have Bella wheel up and shoot him in midstride.

It seemed that after the long wait, everyone wanted to get onto the train as soon as they could. I blundered out to the tracks, fending off elbows and shoulders as I searched the incoming faces for Coop's, hoping he hadn't already hurried past me into the station.

I didn't find him. He found me.

"Hey, Meatloaf."

One of his many nicknames for me.

Mom is a former astronaut. Dad is a Nobel laureate. Here's how Coop put it: "With their combined DNA, they expected filet mignon. When they opened the oven, they got two pans of meatloaf."

Coop had done a much better job disguising himself than Kate or I. He hadn't just had his hair cut. He'd had it dyed blond, like Kate's, and styled. The scraggly beard he'd grown Beneath had been replaced by a trimmed, blond goatee. He was wearing round eyeglasses. His green eyes were now brown. He was wearing a suit and tie, an unbuttoned camel-colored overcoat, and a black muffler. He looked like a young banker. The only thing missing was a copy of the *Wall Street Journal* tucked under his arm and a leather valise in his hand. He had the backpack Alex had given him slung over his shoulder.

The only thing that was the same was his grin. He was obviously enjoying my complete shock.

"You changed your hair," he said.

"And you changed everything."

"During my last walkabout, before I got to New York, I met a stylist in Los Angeles. He always wanted to do a make-over. This time around, I let him. Where's Kate?"

I told him about Bella and Bill. He didn't seem surprised or upset about it.

"You think they'd recognize me?" he asked, still grinning.

"Mom and Dad wouldn't recognize you," I said. "But Bella and Bill might wonder why I fought my way out to the train, then came back into the station." I looked up and down the tracks. There was a ten-foot chain-link fence topped by razor wire for as far as I could see.

"You thinking of scaling it?" Coop asked.

"No. I was hoping for an open gate, or a tear in the fence." I was still having a hard time getting used to his new appearance.

"I think I know someone who can help us."

We walked along the length of the train, away from the station entrance.

Stragglers climbed aboard.

Snow fell in big swirling flakes.

Coop waved at a conductor.

The conductor waved back. A big friendly smile on his face.

The conductor had been *Cooped*.

That's what I call it when someone meets my brother and falls under his spell. I've seen it a thousand times before. We walked up to him.

"Otto!" the conductor said.

Apparently Coop's nom de guerre was Otto, which happened to be the first name of the main character in Jules Verne's *Journey to the Center of the Earth*, one of Coop's favorite books.

"This is my kid brother, Axel," Coop said.

In the book, Axel was Otto's nephew.

"Pleasure to meet you, Axel." The conductor shook my hand enthusiastically. "I'm Darien."

I could see that by the nameplate on his uniform.

I could also see that he was completely enamored by his new friend Otto.

"I'm wondering if you can do me a favor," Coop said.

"Sure. Anything."

"Axel has been a train nut his entire life. Is there any chance you can take us through the back entrance to the station and show us around?"

"Not much to see anymore. Train travel is nothing like it used to be in the old days, with baggage, cargo, mail, and porters. But I'd be happy to walk you through." He pointed at a small door next to the station entrance. "Wait for me over there. I'll get this train on its way, then give you a little tour. My shift is over in a few minutes."

The train pulled out. Darien punched a code into the door lock and took us inside. He was right. There wasn't much to see in the cavernous building adjacent to the station. It was empty except for old, dusty baggage carts. It turned out that Darien had been working for Amtrak for nearly thirty years. He began recounting his long career, and it was interesting, but we really didn't have time to stick around and listen. Coop appeared to be hanging on to his every word though, which is one of the reasons people fall in love with him.

After about twenty minutes Coop glanced at his watch (a technological breakthrough for him) and said, "I hate to cut this short, but we have a friend waiting for us outside."

"Of course, of course," Darien said. "I get carried away reminiscing about the old days."

"It was fascinating," Coop assured him. "I'll look for you when I come back through. We can pick up the story where you left off."

"I look forward to it. You have my email and phone number?"

Coop pulled a piece of paper out of his pocket. "Right here."

"If you find yourself with nothing to do while you're in town, I'm just a phone call away. It was a pleasure meeting both of you."

He shook our hands.

I walked out the employee door first, looking right and left for Bella's wheelchair. I didn't see it.

"It's clear."

The snow was sticking to the sidewalk.

BILL WAS WATCHING

the main entrance, so I exited through Wilfs Restaurant.

The front of the station was crowded with people jumping into cabs and cars. A perfect cover to slip away unnoticed.

I started down the snow-covered sidewalk. It felt good to be outside, stretching my legs, breathing in the cold air, but I was worried about leaving Pat and Coop inside the station. They had no idea what they were up against. The Pod had always been dangerous, but they were even more so now that they were on the run. I was tempted to turn back, but Pat had a good point. Bella and Bill were Originals and former Shadows. They would recognize me as easily as I had recognized them. I was lucky to have spotted them before they spotted me.

Still, I wasn't at my best. I was exhausted from lack of sleep, but it wasn't just paranoia and tension that had kept me awake on the long train ride west. It was the land and cities rushing past the windows. For the first time in my life I was going someplace. I was free. I didn't want to miss anything.

The bright snow on the ground hurt my eyes. I reached for my shades, then changed my mind. I was above now. This is where I lived. I needed to act like a normal person. I needed to get used to the light.

After a couple of blocks I started to relax. I passed the

bus station, tensing a little as I walked by the people at the curb waiting for rides, or getting dropped off. No one looked familiar. No one paid attention to me. I was just a girl with a backpack. A fellow traveler on a wintry day.

My eyes stopped watering. I began to smile. I was on my way to a place called Voodoo Doughnuts. Soon I would see Coop. Everything would be okay...and that's when he stepped out in front of me.

"You!" I shouted.

He took his pipe out of his mouth.

"Good to see you, Kate. We need to talk."

HALFWAY

to Voodoo Doughnuts, Coop stepped into a Chinese restaurant, saying he needed to use the restroom.

I waited outside. People walked past, bundled up, hunched against the blowing snow.

Ten minutes later Coop came out looking halfway like himself. The suit and tie had been replaced by jeans, a black hoodie, and a down coat. He still wore the round glasses, but he had removed the brown contacts. His green eyes were back. And there was a new addition, which had been previously covered by the black muffler.

A tattoo.

On his neck.

A colorful bird flying up from under the hoodie.

"You got a tat," I said. "Pheasant?"

"Phoenix."

"Mythical bird that recycles itself every fourteen hundred years."

Coop nodded. "Emerging from the Deep into the light. Seemed appropriate. And it's a good disguise. The Pod isn't looking for a guy with a phoenix tattoo. People tend to focus on the bird and not on me."

Coop had an odd way of looking at things. Sometimes very odd. "I think they look at the bird, then focus on you . . . closely. I don't think this is what Alex had in mind when he said we should disguise ourselves."

Coop shrugged. "Alex isn't our dad."

"Since when did we listen to Dad, or Mom, for that matter?"

Coop grinned. "Good point. But Alex isn't out here with us. Don't get me wrong, I appreciate him getting us out of the Deep, but once we got up top he kicked us out into the cold."

"Yeah," I said. "With forty thousand dollars."

"It wasn't Alex's money. It was Terry Trueman's."

"What are you saying?"

Coop shrugged. "It's just that I don't know about Alex. We're on our own now. We need to do what we think is right, not what Alex wants us to do."

There was no point in arguing with him. The ink wasn't going anywhere.

Coop grinned and wrapped the muffler around his neck. "Better?"

I returned the grin and nodded.

"Did you get the tat done in Los Angeles?"

"Albuquerque. I got hung up there for a night. No place to stay. The tattoo parlor across the street was the only thing open, the only place that was warm."

Only Coop would think to take shelter in a tattoo parlor.

"I was able to lie down, but I didn't sleep. The tat took nine hours. It hurt."

"I bet."

Coop pulled his hood over his head and we started out again.

"How's Kate doing?"

I couldn't believe he had managed to hold off asking for this long.

"A little paranoid, but good."

"*Paranoia* is just another word for heightened awareness."

"Then Kate is very aware."

"Sounds like she has good reason to be, with a couple of Originals scoping out the station."

"But why?" I still didn't get it. "We're not a threat to the Pod. We don't know anything about what they're doing above."

"Did you ask Kate about it?"

"I wanted to, but Bella and Bill showed up.".

"I guess there's not much to discuss. Two Originals showing up at the station means they are after us. Why they are after us doesn't really matter."

"Did you meet Bella and Bill when you were in the Deep?"

"No."

"So they might not know what you look like."

"There were surveillance cameras all over the place, including the infirmary where they had me cuffed to the bed."

I'd been in the infirmary.

I had unlocked Coop's handcuffs.

I hadn't noticed the cameras.

Maybe I was wrong about them knowing what I looked like.

"Uh-oh."

"What?"

"Nothing."

Coop stopped and looked at me.

"You're wondering if they saw you on the surveillance cameras."

Coop was not clairvoyant, but he had always been a good guesser. Perceptive, I guess you would call it, at least when it came to me.

"While you were in the infirmary springing me, they were out looking for you. Slim chance an Original was paying attention to the infirmary cameras. And there's a good chance that the infirmary cameras were broken. Lod hadn't done any maintenance in the Deep in over a year, according to Kate. Why fix things if you know you're leaving?"

"But why did he and the Originals leave?"

"Good question. I don't have the answer." Coop picked up his pace as we crossed Burnside Street, weaving our way through slow-moving cars on the snow-slicked pavement. On the other side he pointed at a group of people standing on the sidewalk about a block away.

"Voodoo Doughnuts," he said.

"You've been there?"

"A couple of times."

"Why are they standing outside in the snow?"

"Because there isn't any place to sit inside. No tables. You walk in, order your doughnuts, and get out. I don't see Kate. Do you?"

"No." Now that we were there I could see that Voodoo might not have been the best place to meet her. "Are the doughnuts that good?"

"They're okay. Voodoo is kind of the cool thing to do. People who work at Voodoo are cool, just like people who work at Powell's City of Books up the street, or Trader Joe's, are cool. In Portland it's not necessarily about the money you make, it's what you do to make your money."

"How long were you here?"

"Six weeks. Thought about staying, but something told me to move on."

"The Deep?"

"Maybe. Weird, I know." He changed the subject. "You say Kate left the station as my train arrived?"

"I think so."

We peered through the Voodoo window. People were lined up at the counter waiting for their pink cardboard box filled with doughnuts.

Kate was not among them.

"Maybe she already got her doughnuts and took them someplace else to eat."

This was a dumb thing to say, but Coop didn't get on me for it. He just grinned. "I doubt she went inside. Kate doesn't seem like a doughnut person."

I was pretty sure I had spent more time with Kate than he had, but he was probably right. Even if she was a doughnut person she couldn't possibly be hungry after devouring a flaming steak and everything that had gone with it.

"Maybe we should call her," I suggested.

Coop looked confused for a second, then said, "Oh, the phones. I'd forgotten all about the phones."

I wasn't surprised. Coop's idea of high tech was a flashlight.

"Do you think Kate has her phone on?" he asked.

"Only one way to find out," I said, thinking she had probably forgotten she had one, just like Coop had.

"Give her a call."

I took my smartphone out of my pocket. "Remind me again why you're anti–cell phone."

Coop pointed at the line of doughnut seekers. "They all have their phones out. It looks like everyone in line is with somebody, but they're not talking to whoever they're with. They're talking or texting people who they aren't with, which is insulting to the person they are with. They aren't living in the present. They aren't even living in the presence of the person they're with."

Quintessential Coop. I was happy to see it. I had been wondering if his year away, or his brutal stint in the Deep, had changed him. Apparently he was no worse for wear. He has a lot of quirky behaviors, but he can explain all of them if you take the time to listen. Sometimes his explanations even make sense.

There were only three numbers saved on my cell phone. Coop's, Kate's, and Alex Dane's. I was about to hit Kate's icon when a hand reached out of nowhere and grabbed the phone from my hand.

"Compromised," Alex Dane said.

I was too stunned to speak.

"Mr. Dane," Coop managed to say, although I could see he was as surprised as I was.

"Better call me Alex. *Dane* is a bad word these days."

"We were supposed to meet Kate here," Coop said.

Alex took his pipe out of his mouth and tapped the ashes out on a lamppost. "I just saw her," he said. "She'll be along soon."

"What do you mean by compromised?" I asked.

Alex threw my expensive smartphone into a trash can filled with pink doughnut boxes.

"Does that answer your question?"

"Not really," I said. "I haven't used the phone. Neither has Coop."

"But Kate has. She sent me a text when she was in Chicago. Three minutes later I got a text from my brother saying that I was an idiot and that he knew where I was and where Kate was."

"You said you thought the cell phones were secure," I said.

"The key word is *thought*, which is not fact. You'll need to toss your laptops as well. We'll be operating completely off the grid from now on."

I glanced at the trash can. Coop noticed, because Coop notices everything, and said, "It's going to be a huge haul for a cold garbage picker tonight."

In New York, both of us had spent time picking through Dumpsters and trash cans. Coop more than me.

He was right. Someone was going to score two cell phones and two laptops.

"I don't see how the laptops can compromise us if we

don't use them for email or texting. What if we need to look something up on the Internet?"

Alex didn't say anything for a few seconds, then shook his head. "We're going old-school. Toss them. And be quick about it. We need to go. Follow me. But keep your distance. The Pod is in town."

We threw them into the garbage can.

"Where are we going?" Coop asked.

"The library."

I wasn't surprised. It was probably where he felt safest, since he worked as a researcher at the New York Public Library for decades. It was probably also the first place the Pod would look for him, but before I could point this out, Coop asked about Kate.

"She'll meet us at the library," Alex answered.

He handed me his backpack, which felt twice as heavy as mine, and started down the sidewalk at a fast clip.

"He could have asked," I said, slinging the pack over my shoulder.

Coop grinned. "He didn't ask because he didn't want to hear no. Don't worry, I'll take over his pack in a couple of blocks."

We followed Alex with a half a block between us, bundled up, leaning against the snow.

Except for the slight limp from when his brother had shot him years earlier, Alex moved well for someone in his seventies. Gray coat, pants, muffler, sock cap, hair.

Follow the gray man.

THE GRAY

granite and red brick three-story Multnomah County Library is on Southwest Tenth Avenue, taking up an entire city block.

We weren't the only ones inside sheltering from the snow. The coffee shop on the main floor was jammed. I found a table at the back. Alex found another, three tables away from me. He was reading a newspaper, or acting like he was reading a newspaper. I was writing in my notebook, trying to catch up.

Coop was on the other side of the coffee shop. He had sat down alone, but within seconds a man joined him. The man talked. Coop listened.

Alex watched them from across the room, frowning. He didn't understand that Coop has no control over the people who approach him. Alex got up from his table and sat down next to me. I guess we were no longer worried about being seen together. I put my notebook away.

"What does he think he's doing?"

"It's not his fault."

"Who's he talking to? What's he saying?"

"If you look close, he's not saying anything."

"Well, we shouldn't be talking, or *listening*, to strangers. We need to keep a low profile."

Alex stared at me in silence for an uncomfortable amount of time.

"What?"

"You don't look much different than you did when you were in the Deep."

I shrugged, not mentioning that he looked exactly the same as he had when I'd met *him* in the Deep. "I don't think they know what I look like."

"Ever been arrested?"

"No."

"Are you on any social networks?"

"A couple."

"Ever posted a selfie?"

"No. I think selfies are stupid."

"Have you ever been tagged in a post?"

"Yeah."

"Is your photo in your school's yearbook?"

"Yeah."

"Then they know what you look like. Do you realize that when you were in New York you were videotaped from the moment you stepped off the train until you went to the airport in New Jersey? It would take some time to find that first glimpse, but once they find your face, they can find it again and again."

"The Pod can do that?"

"If the government can do it, the Pod probably can too. It would be difficult while they're on the run, but I wouldn't put it past them. I think they're capable of just about anything." Alex pointed a finger up at the ceiling. "We're being videotaped right now, which is not to say that the Pod is watching us, but the digital recording stream flows continuously, whether anyone is watching or not. They can stop the stream and dip in for a closer look anytime they like."

I looked up at the ceiling feeling pretty stupid.

"Don't feel bad," Alex said. "They know what I look like too. I should have Tasered the Rottweiler and shot the mush room man."

Back when we were in the Deep, one of Lod's Guards had sicced his dog on us. Alex had shot the dog and Tasered the man.

"Lod must have known you were still alive before we met you," I said.

"Let's just call him Larry," Alex said. "He's no longer Lord of the Deep. When we were kids he was Larry, and I still think of him that way. But to get back to your question. He didn't know I'd been watching him all these years until our confrontation with the Guard in the Deep. I'm sure he's as mad about that as he is about Kate going above."

I looked out the window. It was almost dark. I wondered how late the library was open. People were getting up and putting on their winter coats. But not everyone.

Coop had a new guest at his table. A young guy with long hair and a stack of books.

Alex glanced at his watch, then looked at the entrance to the coffee shop.

No new people were coming in.

"Are you worried about Kate?"

"A little," Alex said gruffly.

He always had a little growl in his voice, but this was different, dismissive, like he didn't want to talk about Kate.

I wasn't about to let him off the hook. "What's she doing?"

He stared at me for a moment, then said, "She's following Bella and Bill."

It took me a couple of seconds to wrap my mind around this.

"How do you know that?"

"Because I told her to follow them."

"You were at the station?"

"I was there before you were. I flew into Portland yesterday."

"From where?"

"New York. I told you I had to take care of some things before I could leave."

"I didn't see you at the station."

"That's kind of the point. Was the shrimp good?"

"Yeah. Wait, where were you sitting?"

"Dark corner about five tables away from you. I thought Kate was going to jump out of her skin when her steak came to the table."

That was funny, but I didn't laugh. In fact, I stopped myself from even smiling.

"I have some questions," I said.

"I'm sure you do. I probably don't have the answers."

I ignored this.

"Do you think it's a good idea for Kate to be following the people who are trying to find her?"

"They certainly aren't expecting her to be following them, so that's on her side. And she's a trained Shadow. Probably the best the Pod ever had."

Except at the restaurant, I thought. When she missed Alex sitting five tables away.

"Why follow them at all?"

"Because in order for me to figure out why they've surfaced I need to know something about their setup above."

"Why don't you call the FBI and let them take care of it?"

"For the same reason I didn't call the police when Larry murdered my nephew and niece, shot me in the leg, and kidnapped Kate. Just because I left the Deep doesn't mean I disagree with Larry's political philosophy. I've softened my beliefs a little over the years, but I'm still with him in a lot of ways. And don't forget, as twisted as he can get, Larry is still my brother. I don't want to see him executed."

"Even though Larry and the Originals tried to release sarin gas into New York City and blow up the followers he left behind?"

"But it didn't work," Alex said.

"Only because we got the information to the FBI before they pulled it off."

Alex leaned forward across the table. "Which I told you to do. The FBI didn't know that Larry was still alive, or that the group had been thriving for decades in the Deep."

"They know now," I said.

"But they don't know my brother. Even if they were to catch him, which is unlikely, his plans, whatever they are, would be carried on without him. Larry has contingency plan upon contingency plan, dozens of them. It's how he thinks. He might have stayed in the Deep for another year, or more, if Coop hadn't shown up."

"Are you saying this is all Coop's fault?"

Alex shook his gray head. "No more than it's my fault for making contact with Kate and giving her books to read to broaden her thinking. No more than it's your fault for going into the Deep to find Coop. All I'm saying is that Larry is the most methodical and patient human on the planet. Think about it. He stayed in the Deep for decades, creating a multimillion-dollar business without anyone knowing that the owner was a dead man. He kept the Pod together, relatively happy, and completely unknown above for more than twice as long as you've been alive. The sarin gas and the explosives had been in place for decades. I helped Larry set them."

"You what?" The few people remaining in the coffee shop turned to look at us.

"Keep your voice down. I was an Original before I became a librarian. If we got caught, Larry wanted to blow the compound and gas people up top. I was the only person he told about it. None of the other Originals knew about it. I helped him set it up because I was afraid he'd botch it. I knew more about explosives and gas. I defused it before I left New York. I would have defused it years ago, but I was afraid he would discover it and reset the gas and explosives in a way that I couldn't sabotage it. By now the FBI knows that it wasn't going to blow. Larry's goal is to take down the United States government and corporations, by any means necessary, including the death of innocent people. He'd like to see this country go back to precolonial times. I wouldn't mind that either, but not at the cost of millions of lives. That's where his and my philosophy diverge. We split apart long before he murdered Kate's parents and shot me."

"He's a maniac," I said.

"Maybe," Alex admitted. "But more pertinent to the current situation is that he is completely committed to his cause. The only way to stop him is to find out what he's planning to do before he does it. If you go to the FBI now, they might catch Bella and Bill, who I guarantee will not give up Larry. They're Originals. They'll never rat him out. And even if they did, they don't know what the ultimate plan is. The only person who knows that is Lawrence Oliver Dane."

"I didn't say I was going to the FBI," I said. "I asked why *you* don't go to the FBI."

I'd thought a lot about Alex during the long trip across the country. I promised myself that if I ever saw him again I was going to thank him for saving us in the Deep. If it weren't for Alex, Coop and I would be dead or stuck in a dark, dank room tending mushrooms forever.

"I'm not going to do anything you don't want me to do," I said. "You saved our lives in the Deep."

Alex didn't deny it.

Or say aw shucks.

Or that we would have been just fine if he hadn't shown up and shot the dog and Tasered the mush room guard.

Instead, he shook his head and gave me a rare smile.

"The reason I hung around New York after you left was that I wanted to try to pick up Larry's trail. I hoped you and Kate and Coop would be able to simply disappear until all this cooled down."

42

"You didn't find the trail."

"Not even a whisper. Larry and the others vanished as if they had never been in the Deep or anywhere else."

"Poof," I said.

"Exactly. One of Larry's magic tricks. His exit from the Deep, hurried and unexpected, was perfectly orchestrated. Not a trace until Kate told me about Bella and Bill."

"Which is why you had Kate follow them."

"Yes."

"So we're not running anymore?" I asked.

WE'RE FOLLOWING

Alex said, and pointed at my notebook.

"Are you keeping a record of this?"

"Something to do," I said. "Helps to keep me focused."

Actually it had kept me from going out of my mind from dread and loneliness as I click-clack-clicked my way across the country on the train.

I looked over at Coop.

He was listening to his third complete stranger.

I smiled.

"What?" Alex asked.

"I remember something Coop told me when I was a kid. He said the word *listen* is an anagram of *silent*."

A young guy came into the coffee shop and scanned the thinning crowd. I didn't know how, but I knew he was looking for us.

Apparently, Alex thought so too.

"Too young to be an Original," he said. "And I doubt he's from the Deep, but you never know. The Pod's being helped by people from above. They wouldn't have been able to disappear otherwise."

"We'll know in a few seconds."

The guy headed directly toward us. He stopped a couple of feet away from me.

"Are you Jack?"

I was about to tell him no, but then I remembered that I had told Kate that I had used the name Jack on the trains.

"Yeah, I'm Jack."

The guy nodded. "I have something for you." He took out a short stack of notebook paper from his coat pocket.

It was the same kind of paper I had in my pocket notebook.

"The girl told me you'd give me twenty bucks if I gave this to you."

I reached down for my pack, but Alex beat me to it and gave him a twenty. The guy put the pile on the table, then hurried out of the coffee shop with his cash.

We looked down at the pile. Neither one of us picked it up.

"Is that from Kate?" Coop asked, suddenly appearing at our table.

"Yeah. She must have torn it out from the notebook I gave her."

He sat down, grabbed the top sheet, read it, frowned, then passed it to Alex.

Alex swore.

He passed it to me.

> They're traveling in motor homes and trailers. Meeting others at Nehalem Bay State Park on the Oregon coast near Manzanita. Caught 6:00 p.m. bus to Cannon Beach north of Manzanita. Bus full. Bought ticket from kid who

gave you this note. $100 plus $40. Not
sure how, but I'll be in touch if I can.
Kate

The note did not surprise me. I'd spent only a few hours with Kate in the Deep, but that was more than enough time to know that she was fearless. Alex had asked her to shadow Bella and Bill. And that's exactly what she was doing.

"Why did she tear out the other sheets from the notebook?" I asked.

"Maybe as a precaution in case she gets caught," Alex said. "Whatever she wrote down was probably incriminating."

I looked at Coop. "Aren't you going to read them?"

"Sure." He picked up the pages.

"Later," Alex said.

Coop shrugged and put the pages in his pocket.

"How far away is this Cannon Beach?" Alex asked.

"A couple of hours," Coop answered. "I stayed there for a week the last time I was in Oregon. Manzanita is about a half an hour south of Cannon Beach. Tiny beach town. I only spent a few hours there."

"We need wheels," Alex said.

"Darien," Coop said.

"Who?"

"A train conductor I met," Coop answered. "He fixes up cars on the side. He has several for sale." He pulled Darien's phone number out of his pack.

All we had to do now was find a pay phone.

IN THE BACK OF THE TAXI

on the way to Darien's, Coop let me read Kate's journal entries. There weren't many.

> It is nearly impossible to capture my feelings in this little notebook. In the Deep we were taught to ignore our feelings, to hide them from others, to avoid conflict and corruption of the group.
>
> I feel fear, anxiety, joy, and wonder.
>
> Confused, vigilant, and lonely.
>
> All at the same time.
>
> Out of control.
>
> Adrift.
>
> \------------------------------------
>
> I watch everyone on the train.
>
> Threat?
>
> Safe?
>
> I listen to their conversations and make up stories about who they are. I

wonder. what stories they make up about me. Can they even imagine?

I miss Coop. I worry about him. What is this feeling I have toward him? Love? But how could that be? I barely know him. What does he feel toward me? I suppose I'll find out soon. We are all headed to Portland, Oregon— different trains, different routes. Will Coop be there? Will Pat? Ha. Will I?

Chicago. Alex texted me back. Compromised. Lod knows where I am. Or where I was. I threw out the computer and cell. Off the grid. My comfort zone. I'm moving west again. Will he follow me? Wisconsin, Minnesota, North Dakota, Montana, Idaho, Washington, Oregon. At which little station will he or a Pod member be waiting for me? I will not get off the train unless I have to transfer. This way I will not lose my bulkhead

48

seat. I have everything packed. Ready to go. Ready to run.

More vigilant now. I'm no longer making up stories about the people I see. Instead, I evaluate their threat level. But this does not stop me from looking out the window. The views are breathtakingly open, nothing but land for as far as I can see. I knew some of these places. When I was younger Lod and I would pore over nature photography books. We had hundreds of them in our apartment. It seemed there were very few places he hadn't been to before he went underground. He spoke of these wild places with love and devotion.

I once asked him why he didn't revisit them. He told me that it would be too sad. "These are just snapshots. Moments in time, carefully choreographed to please the eyes. Most of these wild places no longer look this way. They have been corrupted by our government, corporations, and

people. But perhaps one day they
will be restored to their former
glory."

    I hope one day that Coop and I
(did I just say Coop and I?) can visit
some of these places for a closer look.

Bella and Bill in Sandpoint, Idaho.
Searching. Presumably for me. I will
not be keeping this journal. I will be
keeping an eye out for the Pod.

I handed the sheets to Coop. He put them into his backpack.

"What do you think, Lil Bro?"

"We have to find her," I said.

Coop nodded.

IT WAS AFTER 2:00 A.M.

by the time we drove away from Darien's.

A 1996 Ford Taurus.

$1,500.

Cash.

I think Alex paid too much.

I'm sitting in the backseat with a flashlight writing this.

Darien threw in a set of snow chains in case we needed them going over the coast range. He also showed us how to put them on.

I wish he'd shown Alex how to drive. He hasn't been behind the wheel of a car in decades.

I'm pretty sure we're going to crash and die.

He's swerving all over the road, driving about 40 miles an hour in a 55-mph speed zone. He's leaning over the steering wheel as if he is having trouble seeing through the perfectly clear windshield.

"Road's slick," he says.

Then why is he the only one swerving? Why is everyone passing us?

Coop is sitting next to him.

He doesn't appear to be upset about the swerving, or our speed. He rarely gets upset about anything, although while Alex was looking at the car with Darien, he admitted he was worried about Kate and wished she hadn't gone after Bella and Bill on her own.

"The least she could have done was to come to the library and talk to us about it before she took off after them," he said.

I reminded him that she was eager to catch the last bus and went so far as to pay a fortune to buy the ticket from the guy who gave us the note and the papers.

He gave me the grin. "You're right, Meatloaf. I guess I just miss her. I'm the only member of our ragtag group who hasn't seen her yet."

"Maybe tonight," I told him. "Maybe tomorrow."

Or maybe never, the way Alex is driving.

I can see the headline in the *Oregonian*: "Three Found Dead in Ditch on Highway 26."

I'm getting a little sick to my stomach bouncing around in the backseat and writing by flashlight. I haven't lain down in almost a week.

I wonder what that would feel like.

I think I'd rather die dreaming than seeing the crash coming.

It was a little cramped in the backseat of the car, but I must have slept. Just before I closed my eyes I saw giant fir trees and swirling snow racing past the rear window at 40 miles an hour. When I opened my eyes I saw streetlights inching past at 20 miles an hour.

I sat up and looked at my watch.

5:34 a.m.

"Cannon Beach," Coop said.

It had taken us a lot longer than two hours to get there.

There were shops on both sides of the street. Art galleries. A kite store. Clothing boutiques. Restaurants. A bookstore. A grocery store. All closed. No one on the foggy sidewalk. No cars driving on the wet street.

"Take a left up ahead," Coop said.

Alex swung too wide, missing the curb by an inch.

I'd driven a car only a few times, but I was pretty sure I'd be better at it than he was.

"Stop up ahead."

Alex did hit the curb this time. We were parked next to a bus shelter.

"This is the bus station?" I asked.

"Cannon Beach is too small to have a real station," Coop answered.

He got out of the car.

Alex and I joined him. It felt good to stretch my legs. I couldn't see a hundred feet in the cold fog. It was like standing in the middle of a rain cloud.

Coop pulled a flashlight out of his pocket, something he always carried with him. He flicked it on and started checking out the bus shelter, which consisted of three glass walls, a peaked roof, and a bench.

"What's he doing?" Alex asked.

I shrugged and looked back toward the main part of town, wishing that the grocery store or one of the restaurants was open.

The thick fog lit up with alternating red and blue lights.

A cop car pulled up behind the Taurus. My first impulse was to run. Which is always my first impulse when I see a cop. I don't know why. I'm not wanted for anything. I've never been wanted for anything.

"I'll do the talking," Alex said.

The cop got out of the patrol car. He turned on his flashlight.

Coop turned off his flashlight.

"What's going on here?"

The cop pointed his flashlight at our faces.

The nameplate above his badge read JACKSON.

"My grandson lost his wallet somewhere between Manzanita and Portland," Alex said. "Had some cash in it, but I'm more worried about the credit card. My credit card. I loaned it to him for his trip to the coast."

"It's not here," Coop said. "Sorry, Gramps." He stepped out of the shelter and walked over to us.

Jackson smiled when he shined the light on Coop, which wasn't at all surprising, because this is what almost everyone does when they see Coop for the first time.

I have to say that the missing wallet / grandfather lie was brilliant. It explained why Coop was searching the bus shelter at five thirty in the morning, and it would head off the cop's asking for Coop's ID because it was lost somewhere between Portland and Manzanita.

It wouldn't stop him from asking me for ID, but if he did, he was out of luck. As a kid I wasn't really expected to carry ID, and I didn't have any.

"Any chance anyone turned a wallet in at your station today?" Alex asked.

Jackson shook his head. "This is my second shift in a row. One-man operation today. I'm doing double duty. No wallet turned in." He shined the light on our license plate. "Are you all from Portland?"

"We are now," Alex answered. "Me and the wife moved out from the East Coast so we could be closer to our daughter and the grandsons here."

Jackson stepped closer to the car and shined his light into the Taurus.

"What's your next move?" he asked.

"What do you mean?"

"The wallet."

"Oh," Alex said. "We'll head down to Manzanita and see if he lost it there."

Jackson looked at Coop. "Where were you staying down there?"

"I was camping at the state park."

"Nehalem?"

"Yeah."

"Kind of cold for camping."

Coop grinned. "You aren't kidding. It was freezing. I lasted only two days. I was going to stay the whole week."

Jackson returned the grin. "You live at home with your mom?"

"And my dad, and my grandmother, and grandfather." Coop looked at me. "And my little brother here."

"Well, take it nice and slow," Jackson said. "There are some icy spots south on 101. Don't want you to end up in a ditch."

"We will," Alex said.

"You heading back today?" Jackson asked.

"After it gets light," Alex answered. "Might take a stroll on the beach. Get these boys a serious breakfast."

"There's always a chance that someone found the wallet and hasn't turned it in yet," Jackson said. "Give me your license and I'll punch it into our computer system with a note about the wallet."

"It's a New York license," Alex said.

"No problem. Just give me your current address and phone number along with the license. I'll send you the wallet if it shows up."

I thought Alex had made his first mistake. I seriously doubted that he had a valid driver's license. And even if he did, there was a bigger problem. If the license read Alex Dane, we were dead. On a cold and foggy morning, acting suspiciously, you don't want to have the same last name as the most wanted person in the United States.

Alex pulled a thick wallet out of his back pocket. It took him a while to find his license among all the junk in the ancient leather.

Jackson shined his light on it, looked at Alex, and nodded. "And what's your current address and phone number?"

To my surprise, Coop chimed in reciting Darien's address and phone number as if he had lived there since he was born.

"I'll just put the info into the computer. Back in a minute." He climbed into the front seat of his cruiser. His face glowed pale blue from the dash computer screen.

"We're fine," Alex said under his breath. "I'm not wanted for anything. The ID is solid. I've been using the license since Larry shot me in the leg. The name on it is Jeremy Benson in case the cop asks. He's being very polite about it, but he's definitely checking us out. I think we're okay. We haven't done anything wrong. This is still a relatively free country."

Jackson got out of the cruiser. He handed the license back to Alex. "I hope you find the missing wallet."

"I hope so too." Alex stuffed the license back into his wallet.

"Oh, one more thing," Jackson said. "I noticed your vehicle isn't registered to you."

"I know," Alex said easily, as if he had anticipated the question. "It belongs to Darien Colgate. He rents the lower half of my daughter's house. He's been trying to get me to buy it off him for months. Borrowed it to see how it drives."

"How does it drive?" Jackson asked.

Alex smiled. "Better than it looks. Did well going over the mountains."

"Nice meeting you. You might try eating at the Bunk House Restaurant, just south of Manzanita on the main highway. They have a good breakfast."

"Thanks for the tip," Alex said.

We climbed back into the car. Jackson got into his cruiser and shut off the flashing lights.

Alex started the car. "Told you he was checking us out."

"You might want to concentrate on keeping the car on the road," I said.

"Backseat driver!" Alex snarled.

Coop and I burst out laughing. A second later Alex joined in.

Jackson tailed us all the way up to Highway 101, where he headed north and we headed south. Alex didn't swerve once on the way out of town, although he was going only 20 miles an hour.

About five miles south of Cannon Beach, Coop said, "Kate left us a note." He took a scrap of paper out of his pocket.

"Where did you find it?" I asked.

"In the bus shelter."

FIGURED YOU'D FOLLOW...

If you get this, I'm headed to Manzanita with a girl I met on the bus. She left her car in Cannon Beach and gave me a ride to Manzanita. Her parents own the Ocean Inn, 32 Laneda Ave. She offered to let me stay there for cash under the table. Not sure what room I'll be in, but there are only ten units. It's not far from Nehalem Bay State Park. If I'm not at the inn I'll be at the park.

Kate

"How'd you know she'd leave a note in the bus shelter?"

"When I was in the Deep she told me some things about how the Pod operated when they were above. When they got separated they left notes for each other in what she called logical drops, which I guess are places along their route that make sense. The bus shelter was the logical place."

"If we followed her," I pointed out.

"What else would we have done?" Coop asked.

I thought of a dozen other things we could have done, but I let it go. Coop's logic was not like other people's logic.

We drove into the sleepy little town of Manzanita. It looked to be a quarter the size of Cannon Beach and a lot less commercial.

The Ocean Inn was right on the beach. We pulled into the parking lot next to the only car there, which had to belong to the girl who had driven Kate there.

"How do we find out what room she's in?" I asked. "I doubt the office is open yet."

Coop got out of the car and once again turned on his flashlight. He shined it on the car we were parked next to. I hoped a cop didn't see him. A couple of seconds later he popped his head back into our car.

"Room eight."

I didn't want to ask, but I couldn't help myself. "Okay, how do you know that?"

He held up another piece of paper. "Another note. Stuck under the windshield wiper."

> 11:00 p.m....Decided to bicycle over to the park to see what's going on. It's not far. Don't know how you got down here, but if you're on foot the hotel has free bicycles outside the office. They're locked. The combination is 333. Or you can just wait in #8 for me to come back.
>
> Kate

We found room number eight.

Coop was poised to knock on the door but changed his mind and tried the handle. It wasn't locked.

"Kate?" he whispered.

No answer.

"Kate?"

He fumbled inside the door for a light switch and flipped it on.

The room was empty.

I looked at my watch. 6:17. She had been gone for more than seven hours.

I looked at the bed, wishing I could flop down on it and sleep for three days. The bathroom light was on. Inside was a shower, but I knew I wouldn't be using it, or the bed.

"Let's go," Alex said.

"Maybe we should leave her a note," I suggested.

"She'll know we were here because her note is gone. The trick to disappearing is to stay invisible. Leave no trail. You can't be followed if no one knows you were there."

It took us a while, and several wrong turns, to find the sign for Nehalem Bay State Park. Coop had been there only once, and someone else had been driving because Coop had no idea how to drive a car, and probably never would.

Nobody said a word about how long Kate had been gone, but I knew Coop and Alex were as worried as I was.

A cold rain fell. The windshield wipers were on high. The defrost fan was blowing full blast, barely able to clear the condensation.

Alex pulled to the side of the road just past the park's

unmanned entrance booth. He turned off the headlights but kept the windshield wipers and fan on. It smelled kind of musty inside the car.

Sweat.

Nerves.

Lack of showers.

The windows began to fog despite the fan.

"I think we should go in on foot from here," Alex said. "Can't see without the headlights, and the headlights would give us away."

"Hand me my pack," Coop said.

We pulled out our rain jackets and put them on.

"Do you have flashlights?" Coop asked.

I did. Alex didn't. Coop gave him one. He had plenty to spare.

"Wish I had a tuna sandwich," Coop said, opening his door.

This made me smile. Coop had eaten a tuna sandwich almost every day since he had teeth. He said he had gotten a little sick of tuna when he was in the Deep, but I guess that was over now that he was above.

I wouldn't have minded a tuna sandwich myself.

Outside there was a map of the park behind a Plexiglas-covered board.

We shined our lights on it.

Three hundred seven camping spots.

A horse camp.

"Eighteen yurts," I said.

Alex pointed at the map. "There's an airstrip."

"This place is huge," Coop said. "Maybe we should split up."

"Forget it," Alex said. "We already split up, and look what happened to Kate."

"We don't know if anything happened to Kate," Coop insisted. "She might be perfectly fine. She's probably hunkered down somewhere dry, watching them."

I don't think any of us believed that.

"We don't have a way of communicating with each other if we do find something," Alex said. "If I had known that Kate was going to jump on a bus and follow them out of town, I wouldn't have sent her after them."

"She's a Shadow," Coop said. "She knows what she's doing."

"The Originals also know what they're doing. They trained her. We'll stick together. For the time being anyway." He turned off his flashlight. "It'll be hard to see in the dark, but being blind is better than announcing we're here."

We walked on the right side of the road, ready to dash into the trees and hide if we heard or saw something coming our way.

The first landmark we came across was the airstrip. It was a wide asphalt swath cut into the trees with white lines down the middle. Alex turned on his flashlight, quickly shined it up and down the strip, then clicked it off.

"They fly in from the ocean, then turn around and head out the same way they came in. Didn't see any parked airplanes, but that doesn't mean they didn't use the strip."

"Kate said they were driving motor homes," I said.

"They're probably using everything to get around. Trains, planes, automobiles, trucks, motor homes, trailers, boats . . . Larry didn't pick this park randomly. He thought long and hard about it. For years."

"He knows how to fly a plane?"

"Not that I know of, but I wouldn't put it past him. He, or one of the Originals, has had decades to learn. They didn't spend all their time underground. And they have people working for them above."

We walked on and came to the campsite area. It consisted of two outer oblong roads, one above the other. Inside the oblongs were three smaller circular roads with staggered campsites on both sides of the road.

The first dozen campsites were empty, which wasn't surprising considering the terrible weather, but I imagined the campground was jammed in the summer.

I'd never been camping in my life. In fact, I'd never been to a campground. My parents' idea of camping was five-star hotels, luxury resorts, and fancy cruise ships. Our family would probably die of starvation if we were forced to camp.

"Did you really camp here?" I asked Coop.

"Not really. I was hitchhiking up the coast. One of my rides dropped me here. I made a tuna sandwich and unrolled my sleeping bag. Then I met someone and they gave me a lift to Manzanita, where I stuck my thumb out again and headed north. I don't remember much —"

"Quiet!" Alex hissed. "There's a light ahead."

There were actually several lights ahead on both sides of the road, and we could hear people talking.

Alex led us into an empty campsite.

"We need to check them out," he whispered. "No use in our all going over to eavesdrop."

"What about sticking together?" Coop asked. "I think we should all go."

After a moment's pause, Alex nodded. "But no more talking. If we can hear them, they can hear us."

We quietly cut through empty campsites until we reached the one adjacent to the camp with the closest light.

Two camper trucks.

A big motor home.

A boat on a trailer.

There was a fire burning in the fire pit with a few plastic chairs around it and a plastic tarp spread above to keep the rain out. The motor home door opened. A big, unshaved guy stepped out. He was dressed head to toe in rain gear. He had a frying pan in one hand and a tin coffeepot in the other. He put them on the fire. A second guy stepped out of the motor home wearing a rain poncho. He lit a cigarette and looked up at the gray lightening sky.

"Another beautiful morning in Oregon," he said.

The smell of bacon.

Cold water trickled down the back of my neck.

"On the bright side," the other man said, "we'll have the bay all to ourselves. Nobody in their right mind would go fishing today."

There was activity across the road.

Lights from two other truck campers.

Voices.

Three more rainsuited men crossed the road and joined the first two men.

"Are you kidding?" one of them asked. "Breakfast outside in weather like this?"

"The bet was for breakfast, not where it would be cooked and served."

"You have a perfectly clean and dry motor home."

"And I want to keep it that way. You guys are drenched and stink."

"Coffee ready?"

"Nope."

"Fishermen," Alex whispered. "They aren't from the Pod. We should continue looking."

"I'm going to talk to them," Coop said.

"Why?" Alex protested.

"Because it looks like they've been here awhile. They might know something."

"What? You're going to just walk into their camp and ask them if they've seen Kate?"

"Let him," I said.

Coop walked out into the middle of the road and started walking past their camp.

He didn't look their way.

He didn't speak.

He didn't have to.

"Hey!" one of the men called out.

They were all staring in Coop's direction.

From that distance, in the dim light, they couldn't have

possibly seen what he looked like, whether he was male or female, or young or old.

It didn't matter.

Coop wished them a good morning.

"Kind of wet and cold to be wandering around."

"Come on over and get out of the rain for a bit."

"Coffee's almost brewed."

Coop wandered over and introduced himself as Otto.

One by one, they shook his hand and gave him their names.

"How does he do it?" Alex said.

"He doesn't do anything. He just shows up," I said.

The men started talking over the top of one another telling Coop what they were doing there.

"We're from the Bay Area."

"We come down every year to fish and crab —"

"And drink."

"And shut down our cop brains for a week."

"Same week every year."

"Without the kids and wives."

"They go to a spa."

"Well, not the kids. They're in school."

"We all live within a few blocks of each other. We hire a couple of babysitters to take care of the tribe. Get them to school. Get them fed."

"Except for Martin here, who's retired and divorced, the lucky bum. We let him join us yesterday because he's an ex-cop from LA. The fraternity, you know. The brotherhood."

"And he's the best crab-pot man we've ever seen."

"But terrible at poker."

"We might pay for our vacation if his bad luck holds."

"How about this rain?"

"The weather's usually better than this."

"Remember the weather three years ago?"

"Four years ago."

"Five."

"Anyway, it was worse than this."

"But we stuck it out."

"We always stick it out."

"Otherwise the tradition would be broken and we might not be able to come back."

"The wives might take the perk away . . ."

It went on like this until the coffee was poured, the bacon removed from the pan, and the eggs cracked.

My stomach was grumbling.

It was almost full light out now. Quietly we slipped farther into the trees so we wouldn't be seen, although there wasn't much of a chance of that because the men were completely focused on Coop. They wouldn't have noticed a Sasquatch sauntering down the road.

It wasn't until Coop was seated in one of the chairs eating a pile of bacon and eggs that one of the men asked him what he was doing there.

"Looking for a girl I know." He gave them a description of Kate. "She was riding a bicycle."

The men listened carefully, thought about it for a second, then all shook their heads.

"We would have noticed a gal like that."

"Especially the bike."

"What was she doing here? Camping?"

"Just riding her bike," Coop answered. "I mean she might not have even been to the park. I don't know her very well. We just met, but I wanted to see her again. Thought I'd walk through the campground and see if she was here."

"You have a car?"

"I parked at the entrance. The windows were too fogged to see out."

"Was she alone?"

"As far as I know."

"Then she wouldn't have been with the old folks."

"What old folks?"

"Big group of them on the other side of the campground." One of the men pointed. "They were parked a hundred yards that way."

"Six or seven rigs. Some of the motor homes were pretty nice. Diesel pushers. Humongous things. Must be nice to be retired."

"Were?" Coop asked.

"Yeah. They pulled out last night."

"This morning actually. About two. Made a lot of noise."

"Weird time to hit the road, but old people do strange things."

"Maybe the airplane freaked them out."

"I think it was a helicopter."

"Airplane."

"Whatever it was, it tried to land on the strip a little after midnight. Made several low passes. It might have landed, but it was pretty foggy."

"I thought I heard it take off a little after one."

"Probably one of the senior citizens firing up their rig," the retired cop, Martin, said. "No helicopter could have landed or taken off in this weather. Visibility hasn't been more than fifty feet for twenty-four hours."

"Could have been, but they all left at the same time in a caravan, don't know why you'd start your rig an hour early."

I wondered if they would have investigated further if they'd had their "cop brains" on.

Coop finished the last of his bacon and eggs. "Well, thanks for the information."

"Do you have to go?"

Coop stood. "Yeah. I better be on my way."

"Why don't you go fishing with us. Set some crab pots. Martin will show you how. A lot of fun."

"We have plenty of extra rain gear."

"It sounds like fun," Coop said. "But I don't think I can. I have things I have to do today."

"If you change your mind, we're not leaving until tomorrow morning. If you come back tonight you can share in our fish and crab feed. Freshest seafood you'll ever eat."

"What was the girl's name?" Martin asked.

"Kate."

"If we see her what do we tell her?"

"Just tell her I was looking for her. That I'll see her back in town."

"Will do."

Coop started toward the road, then stopped and turned around. "Out of curiosity, do you know which way the old folks headed?"

"Toward the sun," one of the men answered.

"East?"

"South."

"Old people go south for the winter."

"Only dumb cops go north." They all laughed.

Coop waved and walked down the road in the direction he had been going before breakfast.

I wanted to stick around and listen to what they had to say about their new friend Otto.

Actually, what I really wanted to do was walk straight into their camp and ask them for a plate of bacon and eggs.

Alex had a different plan.

"We'll go counterclockwise, then cut through the woods and figure out where the Pod was parked."

"If it was the Pod."

"It was the Pod all right. Motor homes! Larry's brilliant. No hotels. No train or airplane tickets. Paying for everything with cash. No trace. They must have headed out from the East Coast separately. Met out here."

We cut across the road about a hundred yards upwind of breakfast and began weaving our way through empty campsites. I wondered how we would recognize the Pod's campsites if they had already left.

This turned out not to be a problem.

Coop had beaten us there.

HE WAS LOOKING DOWN AT A BICYCLE

We no longer needed flashlights.

The sun was up.

The bicycle was bright yellow.

The front wheel was twisted.

The derailleur was smashed.

The frame was scratched, but the words were clear.

Property of Ocean Inn Hotel.

And the phone number.

"It looks like it was hit by a car," I said.

"Maybe we should tell the cops," Coop said.

"That's up to you," Alex said quietly. "But I don't think Larry would hurt her. That is, if he has her."

"The bike is pretty clear evidence that he does," Coop said.

Alex was silent.

Coop looked at me. "What do you think we should do?"

I was all for telling the cops, catching the next flight home to McLean, Virginia, and trying to forget that any of this had ever happened.

But it wasn't as simple as that.

Alex finally spoke. "I'll tell you the same thing I told Pat back at the library —"

"I'm going to use the restroom," I interrupted. "Whatever you decide is fine with me."

There was no need for me to hear Alex's reasoning again. I'd thought a lot about what he had said. It had made good sense in the library, but I wasn't sure it would hold up in the woods, standing over Kate's smashed bicycle.

Coop's call.

I crossed the road to the restroom.

When I finished and stepped back outside I could see they were still talking. I didn't want to interfere. I had no idea what we should do. If Alex was right about not being able to stop Lod until we knew what he was planning, then we should follow the sun. If Kate was in danger, then we should tell the camping cops.

If Kate was in danger.

If they even had Kate.

If Kate was still alive.

What if they had hit her bike and she had run off?

What if her showing up had spooked them into taking off in the middle of the night?

She could be hiding.

She could be injured.

She could be limping her way back to the Ocean Inn.

Whatever Coop decided to do we had to make sure she wasn't in the park or back at the hotel.

I pushed open the door to the women's restroom. Another first. Never been to a campground. Never been inside a women's restroom. It was pretty much like the men's restroom, except there were no urinals hanging on the walls. The Pod, or someone else, had been using it because it hadn't been cleaned. Paper towels on the concrete floors. Dirty sinks.

I opened a stall door. I flushed the toilet. I opened the door to the next stall.

Kate had been here.

She had left us another note.

On a paper towel.

> 7 vehicles. 2 cars pulling trailers. 3 motor homes. 1 camper. 1 van. I think. Could be more. Heading south on 101. I'm in a small motor home. They aren't going to hurt me. I'm fine. See you down the road.
>
>   Kate

I ran across the road waving the paper towel.

THEY DISCOVERED ME

before I discovered them. I had just entered the park on the bicycle. I didn't really have a plan except to ride through and see if Bella and Bill's motor home was there. I should have known they would set up sentries at the entrance and Guards throughout the park. That's exactly what I would have done. They must have had a car hidden in the trees. She didn't turn on her headlights. I didn't hear the car. One moment I was pedaling along through the cold fog. The next moment I was flying through the air. I hit a tree, or a rock, and blacked out.

When I opened my eyes I was inside Bella and Bill's motor home looking up at the underside of the dinette table. Bella was bandaging my hand. My other hand was handcuffed to the steel pole beneath the table. Bill was bandaging my leg. There were others in the motor home, but I couldn't see them from under the table. I had a gag in my mouth. I was choking. I couldn't breathe. I started to struggle.

Bella put a knee on my chest and sandwiched my face with her powerful hands.

"Stop!"

I stared up at her, hyperventilating.

"I'll take the gag off, but if you call out I'll kill you where you lie."

I nodded.

Someone passed a butcher knife down to her. She brought the big knife toward my throat.

"I am not kidding, Kate. One sound and I'll cut the noise off with this."

I nodded again.

She cut the gag and pulled it away.

I took several gasping breaths.

"You should have just slit her throat." It was LaNae Fay. "There are a million places to stash a body here. Throw her off a cliff. Let the sharks have her. She was born in the Deep. No record of her ever existing. No problems."

"Shut up, LaNae!" Bella hissed. "We have to find out how she found us. We can't kill Lod's granddaughter without his permission. You're lucky you didn't kill her with the car, or we might be slitting *your* throat right now."

So LaNae had been the one who hit me. Bella was an Original, much higher in the Pod than LaNae, and didn't like her. No one liked LaNae. She was fiercely loyal to my grandfather and was tolerated because she would do anything for him without hesitation, without question. Lod used her to do the jobs no one else wanted to do.

"Listen carefully," Bella said, still holding my face with her hands, making certain that she could see my eyes and that I could see hers. "I'm going to undo the cuffs and get you into a more comfortable position. But you need to promise to cooperate. I don't want to kill you, but if you cross me, I will. You know I will."

I had no doubt.

"You have my word," I said.

"You have got to be kidding me!" LaNae shouted.

A second later I heard a door slam closed.

They picked me up and sat me at the table. I was dizzy and a little sick to my stomach. I closed my eyes, breathing deeply to get both feelings under control. When I opened my eyes again, I saw that there were six Originals crammed into the small motor home. LaNae was not among them. The others looked down at me with cold hatred, not an ounce of sympathy between them.

"Where's Lod?" I asked.

No one spoke. Their expressions didn't change.

"I need to talk to my grandfather."

"He's not here," Bella said.

"I can see that," I said. "But I know he's in touch with you. I need to tell him some things. It's important."

"Tell us," Bella said.

"It's personal."

"There is no *personal* in the Pod."

There was no People of the Deep either, now that everyone had left our underground nest. "I need to speak to Lod," I repeated.

"First you'll answer my questions. Then we will see about you talking to Lod."

It appeared that Bella had not only surfaced, but she had come up in the world. In my grandfather's absence, she looked to be in charge. At least here.

I stared at her in defiant silence.

"If you don't want to answer my questions," she continued, "I can turn you back over to LaNae and let her finish
what she started."

"I am not afraid of LaNae, but I will answer your questions . . ." I hesitated. "As soon as you give me some water."

I wasn't really thirsty, but I needed time to think about
what she was going to ask and how I was going to
answer her.

Bill opened the small refrigerator, pulled out a bottle,
and set it in front of me. I opened it and drained it very
slowly before putting it on the table and asking for another.
Bill gave me a second bottle, which I drank halfway before
setting it next to the empty one.

"How did you find us?" Bella asked.

"I saw you and Bill at the station and followed you."

My answer had the desired effect. Bella and Bill looked
stunned. The other Originals looked at them with a combination of shock and disgust. Bella and Bill had been assigned
to spot and capture me. I wasn't supposed to spot and follow them.

"How?" Bella asked.

I smiled. "I'm a Shadow."

"That's not what I mean. How did you get here? How did
you know we were coming here?"

"I followed you to your motor home from the train station
in Portland. You and Bill talked about where you were going
while you were tying your wheelchair to the back bumper.
Anyone within fifty feet could have overheard you, to say
nothing about hopping out of the wheelchair like an Olympic

pole-vaulter while you were parked in a handicapped-parking zone."

I opened the bottle and took another sip of water.

"Okay," Bella said. "How did you get here from Portland?" She was holding herself together pretty well considering the unhappy stares she was getting from the others.

"I took a bus to Cannon Beach. A girl I met on the bus gave me a lift to Manzanita. Her mother owns a hotel there. They have free bikes for their guests. I rode over here."

"What about the others?"

"What others?"

"You know who I'm talking about. Your boyfriend, Cooper, and his brother, Patrick."

"Cooper was never my boyfriend, and I have no idea where they are. They went their way and I went mine. Haven't seen them since I got above."

"You're lying."

"Think what you want, but I am not lying."

"If he wasn't your boyfriend, then why did you help him escape?"

"Because he and his brother didn't deserve a life sentence in the mush room, or worse. All they did was blunder into the Deep. All they wanted was to be shown the way out. Lod overreacted."

Someone gasped. Bella just raised an eyebrow.

"He's not infallible, Bella. It may not have been the smartest thing I've ever done, but I never intended to hurt the Pod. I did it because I thought Lod was making a mistake

79

by holding Cooper and Patrick captive, and I thought it would hurt us."

"Then why did you run?"

"Because I thought I'd end up in the mush room," I said. "Or worse."

"You were wrong about those boys. They went to the FBI."

"So that's how we were found?" I did my best to look stunned.

"You didn't know?"

"I've been reading the newspaper articles, but they didn't say where the FBI got their information. I swear I didn't know Cooper and Patrick were going to turn us in to the feds. Like I told you, when we got up top, I went my way and they went theirs. You don't actually think I had anything to do with them ratting us out to the FBI?"

"The boys disappeared the same time you did," Bill said. "As you know, we're very good at finding people. Escaping from our net isn't easy. We figured you had to have helped them."

"You figured wrong!" I shouted.

"Would you have helped them up top if you had known they were going to turn us in?" Bella asked.

I paused before answering. "At the time, I was so mad at Lod I might have done something drastic, but that does not include turning in the Pod to the FBI."

"Why were you angry with Lod?"

"That's between him and me. That's why I want to talk to him. That's why I followed you."

"What about Alex Dane?"

How did she know about the Librarian? I had to be very careful here. The best lies are sprinkled with truth. Alex should have killed the Guard, Carl, instead of using a Taser on him. Dead men tell no tales. Carl was probably murdered on Lod's orders for letting us escape, but surely not before he provided a full description of Alex Dane.

"My grandfather's brother," I said. "The uncle I didn't know I had."

"Tell me about him," Bella said.

"Why don't *you* tell me about him!" I made eye contact with everyone standing in the tight space. "You've known him longer than I have. He's one of you. He's one of the Originals."

They all stared back at me without a word. The door opened and in stepped Carl. So he hadn't been killed. Another surprise. Lod was not one to tolerate failure. Carl gave me an icy smile, then spoke to Bella, as if I wasn't there. Bella was definitely in charge.

"The park's clear except for the people who were here. We went back to her hotel. Roused the girl running the place. Searched Kate's room. Nothing there."

"Nothing?" Bella asked.

"A backpack. Just clothes. Nothing else. I have it here."

"Leave it," Bella said. "Keep security in place. We're going to pull out soon."

"What about — ?"

Bella cut him off. "Just keep security in place until I let you know."

Carl nodded, gave me one last hateful smile, and left.

Bella turned her attention back to me. "We were talking about Alex Dane."

"And I was saying that you know more about him than I do."

"Tell us what you know," Bella insisted.

I wasn't about to tell them what I knew, but I had to tell them something. "I knew him as the Librarian, a crazy old man who left me books he thought I would like, books he thought I should read. I didn't know he was Lod's little brother."

"How many years did he leave you these books?"

"Since I was fourteen."

"What kind of books?"

I named some of the titles.

"Banned books," she said.

I shrugged.

"How often did you and he talk?"

"Never. He'd leave a stack of books. When I finished them, I'd return them to the same place. A few days later there would be another stack of books."

"Why didn't you turn him in?"

"I was going to, but first I wanted to figure out how he was getting into the Deep. I tried to follow him a dozen times, but he would simply vanish without a trace. If it weren't for the books, I would have thought he was a figment of my imagination. A ghost."

"When did you find out he was Alex Dane?"

"On the day he took us above."

"Through his secret entrance to the library," Bella said.

Of course they had discovered the exit, but I'm sure it had taken them a while. Enough time for Alex to get out of there. Maybe even enough time for him to get rid of the evidence of his watching them for years. But not all of it. They had discovered something deep in the bowels of the library that had allowed them to hack into his cell phone.

"What did he tell you?" Bella asked.

"That my grandfather had shot him and left him for dead," I answered.

The answer didn't seem to surprise Bella, or anyone else. It was clear that they already knew this. But did they know about my parents? If they did, should I tell them that I knew?

"What else?" Bella asked.

I decided not to bring up my parents. "He said that he had been watching us for years in the Deep."

"Why?"

"He didn't say," I lied.

"When was the last time you saw Alex Dane?"

"The day he led us above."

Bella stared at me. I knew what was coming. Alex had told me about it when I saw him in Portland.

"You texted him from Chicago."

I nodded. "He asked me to check in with him."

"Did you check in with him anytime after Chicago?"

Bella already knew the answer, but I played along.

"No."

"Where did you get the cell phone?"

She knew the answer to this as well.

"Alex gave it to me."

"Cooper and Patrick as well?"

"Yes. He also gave us laptops."

"Why?"

"He said that he wanted to stay in touch with us."

"Did he give you anything else?"

I shook my head. I wasn't about to tell her about the cash that was allowing us to stay off the grid.

"Search the pack."

My stomach lurched. I'd made my first mistake. Bill pulled the contents and spread it out on the kitchen table.

"Where's the laptop? Where's the phone?"

I stared down at the pile of stuff. My mistake wasn't there. The roll of cash was missing. Carl, or someone else, must have taken it when they searched the pack. Thank God for greed.

"I sold the laptop in New York. I needed money for a ticket. I sold the cell phone in Chicago."

"Where's the rest of the money?"

"There isn't any left."

"What were you going to do without money?"

"I had no idea. It was snowing in Portland. I thought I'd reached the end of the line; then I saw you and Bill at the station."

"Why didn't you just come up to us?"

"Because I didn't know what your intentions were. As far as I knew you were there to kill me. What were your intentions?"

84

"It wasn't to kill you," Bella said quietly. "Lod wanted you found."

"What about Alex and the two boys?"

"Our instructions for them were different than they were for you."

A loud roar from outside interrupted the interrogation. Bella took a two-way radio out of her pocket and keyed the microphone. "Are you there?"

"Too foggy to land," my grandfather answered. The sound of his voice gave me a start.

"We have her," Bella said.

This was followed by a long silence. The sound faded, then grew louder again.

"The others?"

"They weren't with her."

"Is she with you now?"

"Yes."

"Step outside."

Bella stepped outside, closing the door behind her. A few moments later she stepped back inside. "We're pulling out," she said. "Right now."

Everyone left the motor home, including Bill, leaving Bella and me alone.

"You'll ride with Bill and me," she said. "It might be best to stay clear of the others for the time being. They're not happy with you."

"I don't blame them," I said. "I screwed up. But it was with the best intentions."

"Don't sugarcoat it," Bella said. "No one trusts you. That

includes me and your grandfather. I'll kill you myself if it turns out that you're lying."

"Can I use the restroom across the way to clean up?"

"Sure, but I'm going with you. And if you're thinking of trying a BJJ move on me, remember who trained you. I can still take you down."

That I doubted, but I had no intention of trying to escape. I was exactly where I needed to be.

THE BUNK HOUSE RESTAURANT

had a good breakfast, just like that cop Jackson had said. I was on my second stack of buttermilk pancakes when Alex excused himself to go to the restroom.

Coop grinned at me from across the table. "Better slow down, Meatloaf. You'll choke yourself."

"Easy for you to say after hogging down that plateful of bacon and eggs."

All Coop had ordered was a large orange juice.

"I have to admit it," he said. "It was delicious."

I swallowed. "So if I hadn't shown up with Kate's note, what would your decision have been?"

"After seeing the smashed bike, I was leaning toward calling the FBI. Knowing that Kate was safe tilted it in the other direction. I'm worried about her, but I think she's okay. For now. I think Lod loves her in his own way."

"I'm sure he loved his son too," I said. "Maybe even his daughter-in-law. Look what happened to them. Then there's Alex. Lod shot him and left him for dead."

"True," Coop admitted. "But I got a chance to listen to Kate and Lod talk to each other. He cut her a lot of slack. More than she cut him. There was definitely a special bond between them. I'm not saying he wouldn't hurt her if she jeopardized his plans, but I think he would keep her around if he thought he could control her."

The waitress stopped by our table . . . again.

"How's the OJ?"

She was in her late fifties, early sixties. This was her fifth visit to the table and the fifth time she'd asked about Coop's OJ, which he'd taken only two sips from. On her third visit I had asked her for another stack of pancakes, which she had brought immediately, setting the plate in front of me and staring at Coop the entire time, asking him how his OJ was again.

"It's great," Coop answered for the fifth time.

For the millionth time, I wondered what it would feel like to be sought after like Coop was. I wasn't resentful, or jealous. Just curious.

"We're going to have to keep an eye on Alex," Coop said, snapping his fingers to get my attention.

"Huh?"

"He's old, in case you haven't noticed. He doesn't have our stamina. I don't like his color. Or how he's moving. I think he's exhausted."

Alex came out of the restroom, making his way to our table, slowly, shuffling his feet as if he didn't have the strength to lift them off the floor. Coop was right about his color. His face was as gray as his suit.

"One of you has to drive," he said. "I'm done. I need to sleep. If you can't drive, we'll have to wait until I can. Sorry."

Our plan, which was not a very good one, was to drive south and try to catch up with the Pod caravan. We'd stop at gas stations, trailer parks, state parks, anywhere that recreational vehicles might stop for fuel and rest. They already had a five-hour head start. If Alex slept several hours more, there was little point in trying to catch up with them. In fact, even if we left right now, our chances were slim.

"I've never driven anything," Coop said, looking at me.

I'd driven a car exactly four times, with my mom giving me instructions. As an ex-astronaut, she was a pretty good instructor, but it was nerve-racking. And the last lesson had been at least six months earlier.

"I don't have a license," I said.

"I don't either," Alex said. "At least a real one."

"What if we get stopped?"

"Do you have a learner's permit?"

"No."

"Then they give us a ticket. Worst-case scenario, they impound the car, and we get another car."

"The worst-case scenario is that I run the car off a cliff, crash into the Pacific Ocean, and we all die," I said.

Alex slid the keys across the table. "One way or the other, I gotta sleep."

Mom's checklist.

Adjust the seat.

Seat belt.

Adjust rearview mirror.

Adjust the side-view mirrors.

Foot on brake.

Start.

Hands on steering wheel. Ten and two.

Release parking brake.

Foot on brake.

Park to Drive.

Foot off brake.

Give it a little gas.

Too much gas!

Step on brake.

Too much brake!

"You'll get the hang of it," Coop said.

"You better hope I do."

"Do a few loops around the parking lot."

Alex said nothing. He was lying down in the backseat.

"Is Alex okay?"

Coop turned his head. "Sleeping like a baby."

"After that?"

"He said he was tired."

I did ten loops around the parking lot, then ventured out onto Highway 101.

There wasn't much traffic, and it had stopped raining. I drove very slowly, pulling off the highway when I could to let the people riding my tail (who knew how to drive) pass me.

Alex was snoring.

Coop's chin was on his chest. He'd always been able to sleep anywhere as long as the sun was up.

I was on my own.

After a while I started to relax and pick up speed, slowing down around the sharp curves, through tunnels, and along cliffs.

Before he'd fallen asleep in the backseat, Alex said we had hours before we had to worry about finding the Pod.

"They're way ahead of us. If I know Larry, he had everyone top their gas tanks off before they got to the park. They might drive straight through to wherever they're going, or they might stop for the night."

"Any idea where they're headed?" Coop had asked.

"None whatsoever."

Alex wanted me to stop at the first place we could get camping supplies and communication gear.

"What kind of communication gear?" I asked.

"They aren't using cell phones. They're too easy to track. That leaves two-way radios and CBs."

"What's a CB?" Coop asked.

"Citizens band radio. Old tech. Not easy to find in the digital age, but we should be able to get what we need somewhere. A truck stop might have them."

I hadn't seen a truck stop. Or a camping gear store. What I was seeing were tiny beach towns, one after another, with hotels, restaurants, small grocery stores, and beach shops selling seashell souvenirs and carvings made out of something called myrtle wood.

The town of Tillamook looked like our best bet. As I got to the outskirts of the town a sign said: WELCOME TO TILLAMOOK. THE HOME OF TILLAMOOK CHEESE. POPULATION 5,000.

Oddly, I was no stranger to Tillamook, or at least their famous cheese. It was my dad's favorite, especially their extra-sharp aged cheddar. The gigantic cheese factory was at the edge of town and open to the public. I pulled into the crowded parking lot and parked.

Coop lifted his head off his chest.

Alex sat up in the backseat.

It took them both a second to orient themselves. Alex had a little more color now. He was the first one to speak.

"Why have you stopped at a cheese factory?"

"Because I have no idea where to buy camping and communication gear in Tillamook. Also because I didn't want to get downtown and have to parallel park. I don't know how to parallel park."

Next up was Coop. "Ha. Tillamook cheese. Dad's favorite. Too bad we can't let him know we're here."

"There are probably parking lots downtown," Alex said. "But for what it's worth, I don't know how to parallel park either. Not anymore."

Coop opened the passenger door. "I'll go in and ask someone where to get the stuff."

"I'll go with you," I said.

"I'll stay here," Alex said. "Hurry."

Coop, of course, never hurried, but he didn't dally either. It was early, but the factory was jammed with tourists and school groups. I had no idea people were that interested in cheese.

"I'll need to talk to a local," Coop said, squeezing through the crowd toward a woman handing out cheese samples.

I wandered over to the glass wall and watched the white-uniformed workers making cheese, which reminded me of the Uncle Milton's Ant Farm that Coop and I had when we were little kids. We spent hours watching the ants dig in the damp sand and move their bloated white larvae from tunnel to tunnel. The ant larvae were the same color and texture as

92

the cheese curds the machines were molding into blocks. Maybe watching the ants all those years ago had inspired Coop to start digging.

Coop came up behind me. He was holding two squares of cheese impaled by toothpicks. "Extra-sharp aged cheddar," he said.

We toasted Dad and popped the cheese into our mouths.

It was delicious.

BELLA AND I TALKED

It wasn't like old times, but it was civil. The farther south we got, the more she seemed to relax and open up.

When we reached the outskirts of Lincoln City she admitted that she hadn't told Lod that she and Bill had led me to them.

"He was in a hurry and didn't ask me how you found us," she said. "He was more concerned about Alex. I assured him that you were alone."

She was clearly relieved that he didn't ask her how I had found them. If she told him the truth, Lod would have been furious.

Bella put her hand on my shoulder and gave me a small smile. "I'd appreciate it if you'd come up with an alternative story. I've talked to the other Originals who were there when I questioned you. We've agreed that the question as to how you found us was never asked. That we were too busy doing countersurveillance to do a proper interrogation."

She was lucky LaNae wasn't there when I told them how I had found them. LaNae would never lie to Lod, which is why I think Lod had kept her around all these years.

"I have your back," I said. "It's the least I can do. You could have turned me over to LaNae. But it will take me a while to come up with a plausible alternative."

"I'll think about it as well." Her relief was obvious. "We have some time. We won't be seeing Lod for a day or two. In the meantime, for old times' sake, how about you and I bake a batch of cookies."

"Absolutely, but do we have everything we need here?"

"Depends on what kind of cookies you want to make."

"Salty oatmeal."

"Your grandmother's favorite. Do you remember the recipe?"

"Not exactly, but if I could write it down on something." They had taken my pocket journal along with everything else in my backpack.

Bella opened a drawer and pulled out a pencil and a small spiral notebook. I was visual. I remembered things I had seen, and I had seen my grandmother's handwritten salty oatmeal cookie recipe a thousand times. As I wrote the ingredients down something came back to me. Something I had completely forgotten.

"Lod's notebooks," I said.

"What are you talking about?"

"The notebook he always carries in his back pocket."

Bella smiled. "Ah, yes, the mysterious notebook. We always wondered what he was jotting down in it."

"Sketches and notes," I said. "And there has been more than one notebook. There have been dozens, maybe even hundreds. When the notebook was full he'd burn it."

"Burn it?" Bella asked.

"On the grill on our balcony. I fished one out of the flames once and he caught me. I thought he was going to hit me. He didn't, of course, but he was furious that I had looked at it."

I had fished out several notebooks over the years, but he had caught me only once. And I didn't stop after he had caught me.

"What was in it?" Bella asked.

"I don't remember," I said. "The point is that he had to have made sketches and notes for this escape plan. When he asks me how I found you I'll tell him that I remember seeing Nehalem Bay State Park in the notebook. When I found myself in Oregon I decided to check it out."

Bella gave me a genuine smile. It was hard to believe that the night before she had threatened to slit my throat.

"That just might work," she said. "If I can just keep the others from telling Lod how you really found us."

"It doesn't matter. If one of them rats you out I'll tell Lod that I made the story up to throw you off-kilter. I'll tell him that I got to the park two days before you got there. Did he track me past Chicago?"

Bella shook her head. "I don't think so. He sent us in every direction, checking out train stations all over the country. Which is another reason everyone is mad at you. It wasn't easy and it slowed us down."

"Sorry," I said, although I wasn't the least bit sorry. "On second thought, if he asks you about how I found you, I think you should tell him that I overheard you and Bill in Portland."

Bella frowned.

"No, I mean it," I said. "One of the others is going to

tell him. You know as well as I do that there are no secrets in the Pod. When I talk to him, I'll tell him about the note-book and getting to the park before you. You'll be off the hook."

The smile returned. She knew I was right about someone telling Lod. The truth always came out.

"Okay, then," she said. "But I do have some bad news."

"What?"

"We have no oats."

We both laughed.

"Do I hear actual laughter back there?" Bill shouted to us from the driver's seat.

"If you want cookies, we need oats."

"Of course I want cookies," Bill said. "We're stopping for fuel up ahead. There's a little grocery store connected to the station. If they don't have oatmeal I'll stop somewhere else. I want cookies."

Bella walked up front to tell Bill about our plan. While they were talking I slipped the notebook and pencil into my pocket. If Bella asked me about it I would tell her I put it there so I wouldn't lose the recipe.

Bella walked back to the kitchen. "I have one more question."

"Go ahead."

"Are you really with us? Has the prodigal granddaughter really returned?"

"That's two questions, but the answer to both of them is yes."

COOP AND I

wheeled two completely full shopping carts out to the car. One filled with groceries. One filled with camping gear.

Alex was attaching an antenna to the roof of the Taurus. He looked at the carts. "Guess we should have bought a truck instead of a car. Where are you going to put all that stuff?"

"It'll fit," Coop assured him.

I wasn't so sure.

I popped open the trunk.

It was empty except for the tire chains and a car battery, which wasn't there when we drove out of Portland.

"That's our power for the CB," Alex explained.

"So you found everything you needed?"

"It will take me a while to get it fired up. I'll work on it in the backseat while we head south."

Which I guess meant that I was still the designated driver.

"They have prepaid cell phones in the store," I said.

"Which will do absolutely no good," Alex snapped. "Who are we going to call? Who's going to call us? And, remember, the Pod somehow hacked into the cell phones I gave you. I don't know how, but they did. If they did it once, they can do it again. I'm not taking that risk. I wish I'd been able to get access to that room where the Originals were always hanging out in the Deep."

Not even Kate had been in that room.

"But you were an Original," Coop pointed out. "You must have been inside."

"Of course, but back then the technology we had was prehistoric. Caveman stuff compared to what they have now. Larry and I were both early computer geeks. Who knows what kind of technology he filched or invented in the years since I was with him. Whatever he's doing has something to do with technology. You can bet on that. He's been recruiting tech wizards the past several years. For what, I don't know. But I've kept up on technology too."

"I can see that," I said, pointing at the antenna.

He grunted, finished installing the antenna, and got into the backseat.

We were on our way.

Coop made a tuna sandwich from the stash of supplies in the cooler at his feet. Three bites into it he fell asleep with the sandwich in his hand.

Alex tinkered in the backseat with his technology.

I drove through the little coastal towns.

Hebo.

Neskowin.

Lincoln City.

Gleneden Beach.

Depoe Bay.

Otter Rock, where Coop woke up and started nibbling on his sandwich again.

Newport . . .

"Ten four! You got that right!"

I nearly slammed into the concrete guardrail on the Newport Bridge. Coop spit a chunk of tuna sandwich onto the windshield.

"CB's working," Alex announced unnecessarily, and turned the volume down.

"We need gas," I said, trying to slow my heart down to normal.

"Good," Alex said. "Might as well start asking people if they've seen a caravan of old people heading south. Don't bother pulling into a station unless it sells diesel. The cops at the park said they were driving diesel pushers. That'll cut out at least half the stations. And the cops said the motor homes were humongous. If the station can't accommodate a big rig, pass it by."

We "passed by" a half dozen small gas stations, listening to Alex fiddle with the CB and two-way radio.

The low fuel light came on.

"I'm stopping at the next gas station regardless of its size, or what kind of fuel it carries," I said.

It turned out the next station was big and it sold diesel. My next challenge was to figure how to get gas. I'd seen my mom and dad fill up hundreds of times, but I'd never done it myself.

Coop got out and headed into the convenience store inside the station.

I got out and headed to the back of the car to try to figure out how to fuel it. I stared at the pump. We had only cash. I started to remove the nozzle.

"What are you doing?" A guy in an attendant uniform shouted.

"Putting gas in my car."

"Not in Oregon," he said. "We don't have self-serve here. I have to pump the gas. It's the law. You must be from out of state."

"Yeah," I said, hoping he didn't notice the Oregon plates.

"How much gas do you want?"

"Fill it up, I guess."

He held out his hand. "I'll need your credit card."

I didn't have a credit card. I didn't think Alex had one either. Too easy to trace.

"Or you can pay cash inside," the attendant added. "I'll fill it up when the pump is charged."

Alex got out of the car. He stretched. I swear I heard his old bones cracking.

"Do you have a credit card?" I asked.

He looked around the station as if he hadn't heard me, but I guess he had. "It'll probably take forty bucks' worth. We'll pay them inside." He looked at the attendant. "New station, huh?"

"Kind of," the attendant said. "About a year old."

"You got a restroom inside?"

"Of course."

"We'll go in and settle up."

I followed Alex inside. Coop was listening to two girls behind the counter who were nearly climbing over each other for a chance to talk to him. On the counter in front of him

101

was a wrapped tuna sandwich he must have gotten out of their cooler. He already had four or five tuna sandwiches in the cooler in the car. Alex went down a short hallway to the restroom in the back of the store.

"I need to pay for some gas," I said.

"Gotta wait your turn," one of the girls said.

Coop didn't turn around. The girls went on and on about what to do in Newport, what to see along the coast, where to eat. They were roommates.

"We live right down the road."

"We get off work in about two hours."

"If you need a place to crash in town you're welcome to stay with us."

They wrote down their number and names on a napkin. When he tried to pay for the tuna sandwich, they said there was no charge and threw in a can of Coke Zero. He thanked them, then turned around and left the store without even glancing at me. I wondered how, and if, Kate would adjust to this if they ever got together as boyfriend and girlfriend. I was used to people being attracted to him; she wasn't.

I put two twenties on the counter.

One of the girls scooped up the money as she stared at the door Coop had just walked through.

"Pump number?"

"Huh?"

"What pump are you parked at?"

"I'm not sure." I turned around and looked. I didn't see any numbers. "It's the one with the green Ford Taurus."

"The one Otto is getting into?"

"You know Otto!"

I nodded. I didn't tell them he was my brother. I just wanted to pay for the gas and get out of there.

"You're lucky."

"Such a great guy."

Aside from his fake name, I bet they didn't know one thing about him.

"Does he have a girlfriend?"

"Yeah."

"Serious relationship?"

"Very," I said.

"Figures," one of the girls said.

"All the good ones are taken," the other girl said wistfully. Good grief.

"Where are you guys going?"

"North," I lied. I'm not sure why, but I guess it had to do with covering our trail.

"Tell him that if he comes back through here he should take us up on our offer."

"What offer?"

"Never mind. He'll know what we mean."

I walked out of the store. Coop was sitting in the front seat washing down his store-bought tuna sandwich with his Coke Zero. I got behind the wheel.

I did not pass the girls' message on to him.

"Where's Alex?" he asked.

"Using the restroom. Did they have any information about the Pod?"

"They said several RVs filled up here a few hours ago. Old people driving them. But that's not unusual. Dozens of motor homes fill up here every day. They thought they were heading south, but that's not unusual either. Almost everyone is heading south this time of year."

The attendant finished pumping our gas and gave me the receipt.

Alex hurried outside and jumped into the backseat. "Let's get out of here quick."

Coop laughed. "You're acting like you just robbed them."

"In a way I did. Take a right. Head north."

"But the Pod is going south," Coop said.

"I want the people in the store to think we're going north."

"I told them we were going north."

"Good," Alex said. "Now we'll prove we're going north. When you get a couple miles up the road do a U-turn and head back south."

I took a right.

"What's going on?" Coop asked.

THIS

Alex handed him a scrap of lined notebook paper.

10:53. South. K

"She was here!" Coop said.

I looked at the clock on the dash. "Two hours ago."

"They are driving slowly," Alex said. "Or else they stopped somewhere along the way before they got to the station."

"Why would they stop?" I asked.

"Doesn't matter why, or even where," Alex answered. "We're close enough to catch them."

"Except we don't know what they're driving," I said.

Alex pointed up ahead. "Turn around up there."

I got into the left lane and cut across traffic into the parking lot of an electronics store. I was going to drive straight through the lot and get back into the southbound lane, but Alex told me to park.

"Why?"

"We need a portable DVD player."

Alex tapped Coop on the shoulder. "Run in and buy one. And no screwing around. Pull one off the shelf, pay for it, and get back out here."

Coop didn't hesitate. He jumped out of the car and headed into the store.

"I better go in with him," I said. "I doubt he knows what a DVD player even looks like."

I caught up with Coop just inside. Five minutes later we were back in the car.

"Drive," Alex said, tearing open the box.

I merged into the southbound traffic, which was relatively light.

"Perfect!" Alex said from the backseat.

I had to keep my eyes on the road. I had no idea what he was so excited about.

We passed the gas station where we had filled up.

"What's going on?" I asked.

"You didn't notice all the surveillance cameras at the gas station?"

Coop and I shook our heads.

"Well, you better start paying attention," Alex said. "There were six of them. Three outside and three inside."

"Do you think the Pod hacked into the cameras?" I asked.

"Not the gas station cameras. It was a closed system. And even if it was open, I doubt the Pod have the time, or the ability, to keep a digital eye on their back trail while they're moving."

"Then what's going on?" Coop asked.

"This," Alex answered, holding up two shiny DVDs.

I was confused. By the look on Coop's face he was too.

Alex rolled his eyes. "I swiped the station's surveillance recordings for the past six hours," he said slowly. "Kate was inside the gas station. She will be on these recordings. The Pod vehicles that stopped there will also be on them. We will be able to find out the make and model of the vehicles. We will also have their license plate numbers. Gas station cameras are usually set up so they can record plates. We might even be able to identify the drivers and passengers."

"Outstanding," Coop said.

"What happens when they find out their DVDs have been stolen?" I asked.

"I doubt they ever will. No one looks at surveillance video unless there's been a problem. I replaced the DVDs with blanks. And even if they did look, there is no way to trace it back to us. Our license plate and time inside the store is on these DVDs. We paid in cash. There is no record that we were ever there. Now can I take a look and see what we have?"

Coop turned around in his seat to watch.

I couldn't watch because I was driving, and I have to say I was getting better at it with every mile I put on the odometer.

"There she is!" Coop said. "Who's that with her?"

"Bella. It looks like she's buying a box of oatmeal and paying for the fuel."

"Oatmeal?" I said. I desperately wanted to pull over and watch. "Is Bella in a wheelchair?"

"She's on her feet," Alex answered. "But even without the chair it would be hard to recognize her from the photos the FBI is circulating. In fact, I'd say pretty much impossible."

"Kate looks like she's laughing at something Bella's saying," Coop said. "She doesn't look like she's there against her will."

"Kate and Bella were pretty tight in the Deep," Alex said. "Kate's smart. We don't know what she told them when they caught her in the park."

Kate was a great liar. I'd heard her tell some whoppers to her grandfather in the Deep, which he seemed to believe, at least at first.

"Kate's going into the restroom," Alex said. "Off-camera. But let's watch Bella and see what she does."

"She looks like she is guarding the hallway that leads to the restroom," Coop said.

"That's exactly what she's doing. See the door at the end of the hallway? That leads to the store's office and storage room. That's where I stole the surveillance tapes. They don't lock it. There's a back door in the office that leads to a small parking area. Bella's making sure that Kate doesn't slip away. They may be laughing, but Bella doesn't trust her one bit."

"Kate's coming out."

"Watch Bella as Kate walks past her," Alex said.

"Kate's smiling," Coop said. "She's saying something to Bella as she walks by."

"Just watch Bella," Alex repeated. "There! Did you see that? Bella glances down the hallway at the restroom and frowns. She wants to go down there and check it out, see if Kate left something behind, but she can't without Kate getting out of her line of sight. Kate's moving quickly. She's already at the front door pushing it open. Bella has to follow. Kate's playing her. And Bella's playing Kate."

Alex started pointing out other Originals, what they were driving and how they had changed their looks. "There's

LaNae Fay. She's a bad one. A Shadow like Kate and an Original wannabe. Except for the shaved head, she doesn't look that much different. She does Larry's dirty work. And there's the Guard who confronted us in the Deep. I think his name is Carl. Not much they can do about his looks . . ."

I tuned out Alex. It was too frustrating to listen to him without seeing the videos. To distract myself I started thinking about Kate.

She didn't know that we were getting her messages. She didn't even know if we were following her. The guy she gave the note and journal to might not have trudged to the library in the snow for twenty bucks. We might not have been there. We might not have acted on it, or been able to act on it without a car and the snow falling.

This got me thinking about faith and hope, two things Kate appeared to have in abundance. Coop had them too. Not in the religious sense. He simply believed in what he was doing. He had a path and was going to follow it wherever it took him, regardless of the consequences. This sense of purpose, or whatever you might call it, had taken him into the Deep, where he had met Kate.

"Did you think all of this would be over when you found Kate in the Deep?" I asked.

"What?" Coop turned back around in his seat.

I repeated the question.

Coop smiled. "Odd out-of-the-blue question. But I guess I did think it was over."

"Were you disappointed that it wasn't?"

"A little. I didn't want to bring you, or Mom and Dad,

into what I was doing. I should have known that you would come after me. And if you hadn't, I would have probably been killed with a lot of other people. Kate could not have gotten me out on her own. You saved me, Lil Bro. You and Kate." He glanced at Alex. "Well, I guess Alex too."

"You got that right," Alex said. I noticed in the rearview mirror that he didn't look up from the DVD. "They're pulling out of the station. Kate is with Bella and Bill in the white Class C."

"What's a Class C?"

"A type of motor home. Cheaper than a Class A. Smaller. Some of the other rigs with them are Class A diesel pushers. At least thirty feet long. Engine in the back."

"No sign of Lod . . . I mean Larry?"

"Nope. Not all of them stopped at this gas station, I'm guessing. And I suspect some of them stayed inside their rigs. Larry could have been in the Class C, but I doubt it. A Class C isn't his style. If he has one weakness, it's living large, even a thousand feet beneath New York."

I had been in the Lord of the Deep's penthouse with Kate. And it was lordly, bigger, and more ostentatious than everyone else's underground apartments.

Alex continued. "If Larry was with them, he would be in the biggest rig, and he'd be in the one with Kate. She looks to be safe."

For now, I thought.

BELLA AND I WERE BAKING

salty oatmeal cookies.

The Oregon coast, which would have been beautiful under other circumstances, streamed past the kitchen window at fifty miles an hour. Bill never drove too fast or too slow. He didn't do anything to attract attention to our little home.

"The smell of those cookies is driving me nuts!" he shouted back to us. "How about bringing a few up here along with a glass of cold milk?"

Bill always did have a sweet tooth, but he'd managed to stay thin and fit in spite of it. Mostly because Bella had kept him in shape over the years with hours of aerobic exercise, weight training, and yoga, just like she had with the rest of us back in the Deep.

Bella took two cookies that had cooled and put them onto a paper towel. She then poured a splash of milk into a glass, took a big bite out of one of Bill's cookies, drank half the milk, winked at me, then carried what remained up to Bill.

"What's this?" he said.

"Cookies and milk."

"You've taken a bite out of one of them, and you drank most of my milk!"

"You're welcome. I'm saving you from diabetes."

"I don't have diabetes."

"And you never will as long as you eat only what I give you."

Bella sat on the armrest of the passenger seat so she could talk to Bill and still keep an eye on me in the back. I was lucky to be with her and Bill and not the others. I doubt I'd be baking cookies. Another batch was ready. I pulled them out of the oven and started sliding them onto the cooling rack. Bella and I had spent hours in the Deep baking cookies. We'd been pretty close. She had been almost like a mother to me. She and Bill had never had children.

I looked down at the remaining dough. There was enough for three more cookies, which made me think of Coop, Pat, and Alex. I wondered where, and if, I'd be able to leave my next note. Were they getting the notes? Had they even followed me?

OTTER ROCK

Population 325.

"No sea otters in Otter Rock," Alex said. "In fact there are no sea otters in Oregon. The last one was killed just north of here in 1907. You'd have to go up to the northern tip of Washington State to find a sea otter, or down to Big Sur or Monterey in California."

I hadn't even been thinking about sea otters. Alex, always the librarian, had been giving us little factoids like this the last several miles. (Or he'd been giving me the factoids because Coop was leaning against the passenger window sound asleep.)

What I was thinking about was the cop car that had been following us two car lengths back for the past three miles.

I'd wanted to pull over and let him pass, but Alex wouldn't let me. He said it would be a dead giveaway.

"There's a viewpoint turnoff up ahead," I said.

"Forget it," Alex answered. "You're not exceeding the speed limit. You're driving right down the center of the lane. You pull over, he'll pull in right behind you, ask you how you're doing, which really means, who are you and what are you doing? Since we can't answer either question with any honesty you're better off just driving on. You need to get used to having cops on your tail. His being behind us doesn't mean he's after us. It could be as simple as he's going in the same direction as us. Cops are always behind somebody when they're driving."

"What if he runs our plates?"

"He probably already has. He found a perfectly legitimate vehicle with current tags, not stolen, and no outstanding arrest warrants. The reason I know this is because the cop up in Cannon Beach definitely ran our plates. If he'd found anything, he would have called us on it. You think the Originals driving the recreational vehicles are nervous about cops?"

"Probably not."

"Absolutely not. They have ironclad fake IDs and friendly believable stories that would fool any cop on earth. Old age is the perfect disguise."

"What's our friendly story? The lost wallet?"

"That story's used up. If we get pulled over, I'll have to think of something else."

The clouds were gone.

Blue sky.

Clear and cold.

Speed limit: 55 mph.

The cop was still two car lengths back.

It was like I was towing him.

Waldport. Population 2,081.

I slowed down to 35 mph.

So did the cop.

"During World War Two, this is where Camp Angel was located."

"Camp Angel?"

"A civilian conservation camp for conscientious objectors. Mostly artists. Painters, poets, actors. They bunched them all together here for three years. Some of them claimed that their three years at Camp Angel were the most creative period of their entire lives."

Alex was old, but not old enough to have been around during World War II. "How do you know all this stuff? Have you been to Oregon before?"

"Nope. First time. Don't know why I didn't come up here. I went to school in California, right next door. As to how I know all this, you forget that I lived in one of the best libraries in the country for nearly twenty years."

"I thought you just worked there."

"I lived and worked there. Of course no one else knew about the living-there part, which saved a lot of money. Once I had the Pod surveillance set up, there was plenty of time to read. That's how I spent most of my time. I didn't think I'd ever get a chance to visit the places I wanted to go to, so I read about them. Doesn't cost a cent, and you don't have to pack. There's a restaurant up ahead. Pull into the lot. I need a restroom and something to eat besides tuna."

"But I thought you told me not to pull —" I glanced in the rearview mirror. The cop car was no longer there.

"He turned off a while back," Alex said. "When you weren't looking. When you weren't paying attention. You need to keep your eyes on everything all the time, just like the Pod. Maybe we should wake Coop."

"Nah, let him sleep." I pulled into the lot. "Noon is his midnight."

"You want anything?"

"I'm good."

"I won't be long." Alex headed into the restaurant.

I walked over to a set of rickety steps leading down to the beach. I'd never been to the Pacific Ocean. Our family vacations had all been on the Atlantic. I wanted to at least touch the Pacific. We were more than halfway down the Oregon coast. The Pod could turn inland anytime. As far as we knew they already had.

I took off my boots and socks and set them on the bottom step.

The tide was out.

The wind was up.

I started across the cold sand.

Halfway to the surf I heard, "Wait up, Meatloaf!"

Coop ran to catch up with me. His pants rolled up to his knees, showing his pale and powerful tap-dancing calves.

"What a difference a day makes! Cold but beautiful. Where's Alex?"

"Getting something to eat in the restaurant."

"I would have given him a tuna sandwich."

"That's what he was afraid of."

"Ha."

Coop hadn't bothered to put on a coat. His phoenix tat was bright in the sunshine, trying to wing its way out of his T-shirt. He ran down to the water and splashed through the foam.

I joined him, but I was less enthusiastic with the splashing because the water was freezing. Well beyond the breakers were several fishing boats. A helicopter flew south, low over the water.

Alex shouted to us from the top of the stairs.

"Race you!" Coop said, and started off before I agreed.

He had done this in every race we had ever had. In spite of his perpetual head starts, he had never beaten me. Coop could tap, but I could run. I reached the stairs twenty feet ahead of him.

Alex ignored us. He was watching the helicopter flying over the water. I put on my socks and boots.

"I'll drive," Alex said. "You should try to get some sleep."

COOP WAS ASLEEP

in the front seat before Alex swerved back out into traffic. I closed my eyes, but sleep wouldn't come. It wasn't due to Alex's erratic driving, which had improved a little. It wasn't because I wasn't tired. I was exhausted. Every muscle in my body ached from driving tension. It wasn't the constant clicks, buzzes, and crackling voices from the CB and two-way, although the sounds were annoying. Something else was keeping me awake. Something I couldn't put my finger on.

Yachats.

Florence.

Dunes City.

Reedsport.

Winchester Bay.

Lakeside.

North Bend.

I'm sure Alex had interesting things to say about all these towns, but he hadn't spoken a word since we had left Waldport. I thought he was concentrating on his driving, but that wasn't it. He was listening to the chatter on the radios.

Coos Bay. Population 16,000.

"Turn it up!" Alex shouted.

At first I didn't know what he was talking about.

"The CB! The two-way! The volume! The volume! Turn them up!"

Coop snapped awake. "What's going on?"

I was fumbling with the knobs, trying to find the volume. Alex pulled the car to the curb and slammed on the brakes.

"Can someone tell me what —" Coop asked.

"I heard Larry's voice," Alex explained, trying to unclick his seat belt. "I couldn't tell if it was on the CB or the two-way."

I finally found the volume buttons on both units, but it did little good because no one was talking at the moment. Although someone had been talking when Alex came unglued. A man, but he sounded like every other man jabbering over the radio for the past hundred miles. Where to eat. Traffic. Speed traps. I had tuned out the conversations because they were giving me a headache.

"Are you sure it was Larry?" Coop asked.

"I've been listening to him talk on the two-way for decades. It was Larry."

"What did he say?" I asked.

"Something about picking him up. I didn't catch much of it."

We stared at the now-silent radio equipment. Alex reached over and turned the volume down on the CB, then picked up the two-way and adjusted its volume.

"What do you want to do?" Coop asked.

"If we heard Larry on the radio, he has to be close by. And if he's close, the others aren't far away."

The two-way came back to life.

"I'm going to head up and down for a bit, just to make sure. A few hours. Beautiful day out."

"That's Larry," Alex said.

"Roger that. I'll send someone to pick you up when you're ready. Just let me know."

"That's Bella."

"Out."

"I don't know Bella's voice," Coop said. "But that's Lod all right. What do you think they're up to?"

"Get the road atlas out."

Coop opened it and found Coos Bay.

"How many state parks are there?"

"Four. The closest to us are Sunset Bay and Shore Acres. The other two are farther away. Bullards Beach and Cape Blanco."

"They could be at any of them, or all of them. Larry isn't fond of putting all his eggs in one basket if he can help it. He's clearly not with them. At least not yet."

"How do we know they've parked?" Coop asked. "They could be talking to each other as they drive down the road."

"The transmissions are too clear," Alex said. "No fading in or out. No distortion. Why would Larry need them to pick him up?"

I was staring down at the map in Coop's lap when I saw it.

"Because he's not driving," I said, pointing at the map. "He's flying." There was an airport just north of Sunset Bay State Park.

"The helicopter that tried to land at Nehalem Bay last night," Coop said.

"Maybe the same helicopter we saw at the beach," I said.

"Maybe the same one I spotted several times this afternoon after the weather cleared."

This is what had been bugging me in the backseat when I should have been sleeping. I'd forgotten all about the helicopter trying to land at Nehalem Bay.

"He's running countersurveillance," Alex said. "Making sure no one is following them. I suspect he also has a couple of cars moving south with the caravan."

"Do you think he's seen us?" Coop asked.

"No doubt about it. But does he suspect us? That's the question."

A SHOWER

hot and long with soap and shampoo. It wasn't a great hotel, but all that mattered to me was *the shower*, which I stayed under until the water went cold.

I walked out of the bathroom wrapped in a towel. Coop was lying on top of one of the two queen-size beds in his underwear.

It was still light outside.

Coop's eyes were closed.

The phoenix was completely exposed. It was bigger than I had thought, running from his neck almost down to his waist.

The CB, one two-way, and the car battery were on the floor. Alex had taken the antenna off the car. It was now hanging out the window. He had also taken most of our cash. He needed it to buy a different car in case Lod was suspicious of the car we'd been driving. He'd been gone for a couple of hours. We were supposed to call him on the two-way if we heard from Lod. There was a lot of chatter on the CB, but none of the people talking sounded like Lod. Coop was supposed to have been listening while I was in the shower, but it didn't look like that had worked out.

"I'm not asleep," Coop said with his eyes still closed. "Did you leave me any hot water?"

"No."

"Some things never change."

"I did leave you a dry towel."

He grinned, eyes still closed. "It's a miracle. No word from Lod or Bella. The others could be talking on the radio, but I wouldn't recognize their voices. It sounds like a mundane evening on the southern Oregon coast. People looking for dinner and hotel recommendations. Truckers telling other truckers where they're going to park for the night. Before cell phones, I bet there was a lot more radio traffic. The CBs were abuzz."

He opened his eyes and sat up. "I guess I'll go take a cold shower."

I got dressed in relatively clean clothes, then paced the room knowing that if I sat or lay down I would fall asleep within seconds.

"Half an hour."

I stopped in midstep. It sounded like Lod.

"Sorry. I didn't copy that."

Bella?

"Half an hour. All clear."

"Copy. We'll be there. Out."

I picked up the two-way, dialed in the agreed frequency, keyed the talk button, then let it go. What was I going to say? *Hey, Alex. Pat here. Coop's little brother. Just heard Lod tell Bella he'll be landing in half an hour. Thought you'd want to know.*

If we were monitoring radio transmissions, *they* were probably monitoring radio transmissions.

Coop came out of the bathroom shivering.

"That was invigorating, Lil Bro. Thanks." He noticed I was just standing there with the two-way in my hand. "What?"

I explained the problem.

"That is a conundrum." He held his hand out for the two-way. Reluctantly I gave it to him. "Now how do you talk on this thing?"

Coop the tech whiz.

"Maybe we should just wait until Alex gets back," I said.

Coop keyed the talk button.

"Jerry. Otto here."

"Yeah, what do you want?"

"Did you get the beer?"

"I got it."

"How about my kite? Axel says that it finally came down."

There was a hesitation.

"Okay. I'll swing by and see if I can find it. Talk to you later. Out."

Coop tossed the two-way on the bed and gave me his trademark grin. "What did you think?"

"It sounded pretty much like all the other stupid conversations we heard today. Jerry?"

"Short for Jeremy, which he uses on his driver's license."

"Do you think he understood?"

"We'll find out."

We did not find out for nearly two more hours. Even Coop, who never appeared to be concerned about anything, was showing signs of worry by the time Alex finally showed up.

He walked in carrying several bags, which he set down on a bed.

"I didn't bring you beer," he said. "Nor did I find your kite. But that was pretty good. You guys might become Pod members yet. You're beginning to show a real aptitude for paranoia, a primary ingredient for joining the gang."

"Did you see Lod?" Coop asked.

"I wish you would both just call him Larry. The Lord of the Deep, or Lod, makes him sound like the former archangel Lucifer. He's as smart as a devil, but he's just a man named Larry."

"Sorry," Coop said. "Larry. Did you see him?"

"From a distance. Through binoculars. I bought two pairs. He was in a Bell Helicopter with a pilot and another guy. I suspect the other guy is a pilot too, and maybe a spotter as well. Larry doesn't believe in leaving anything to chance. If the pilot keels over dead, there's another person on board who can fly the helicopter. Larry always has an exit plan."

"Were they Originals, or from the Deep?" I asked.

"Nope. Never saw either guy before, which isn't surprising. They were both young. Thirty or so. Fit. The Originals are all old like me. Of course they're going to use youngsters to help them with the things they can no longer do, or things they don't know how to do, like flying a helicopter. The two guys moved like ex-military. Foreign if I had to guess. Hired help. But I'm speculating. I was a quarter mile away and couldn't hear them talking."

"Did you find out where they went?" Coop asked.

"First, let's talk about how they went. Three small SUVs. Not old. Not new. Nondescript. We've seen hundreds of them on the road. So many of them they're nearly invisible. Larry got into the middle one along with the pilots. They left the airport at three-minute intervals. Lead car, Larry's car, then a chase car. They're definitely watching their front and back trail. I'm certain we passed the SUVs, or they passed us driving south. We're lucky to have been so far behind the caravan. If we had been closer they would have checked us out and might have made us."

"Did they travel like this all across the country?" I asked.

"Some version of it. They probably weren't together all the time. And they may not be all together now. I doubt that the whole group was with Bella and Bill at the train station in Portland. I think Larry is sending people out on side trips as needed. Maybe even stopping the big group from time to time to let the others catch up with it. They had to have stopped someplace earlier today or we wouldn't have caught up with them. This is a very orchestrated migration."

"The question is, where are they migrating to?" Coop asked.

"We'll know when we get there. Right now they're at Sunset Bay State Park."

"You followed them there?" I asked. "You just said that we were lucky they hadn't —"

"Simmer down. I was behind the chase car and I was perfectly disguised." He walked over to the window and opened the curtains.

In the parking lot just outside our room was a truck with a camper on the back. Behind it was a small trailer with a boat.

"Now you get to learn how to drive a truck," Alex said.

Lucky me.

"What about the boat?"

"Came with the camper. We'll ditch it in a day or two, which will change our profile from the air. Look at the plates."

They were California plates.

"We're just one of many happy campers heading home after the holidays. Shouldn't raise too much suspicion, even if they spot us on different days. And there's a bonus: The camper is equipped with a CB unit in the cab."

"Did you follow them right into the park?" Coop asked. "Did you see Kate?"

Alex shook his head. "Turned around before I got to the gate. There was only one entrance. What we'll do tonight is get in front of them, wait for them to pass us. Hopscotch with them down south. While you guys load the camper, I'll take a quick shower. We'll head south when I'm finished. I hope you left me some hot water."

"Brace yourself," Coop said. "Pat hogged all the heat."

I shook my head. "Coop was the last one in the shower."

LOD

is on his way," Bella said.

She had been very secretive the past few hours. She had closed the curtains and told me not to look outside. When we pulled into our campsite, I asked if I could go out and stretch my legs.

"No. The others are still angry with you. I'm not certain what they would do if they caught you away from my protection."

This was ridiculous. None of the Originals would dare lay a hand on me without Lod's express permission. The fact that I was still alive meant that I was under Lod's protection, not hers.

We had been parked at the campsite for more than two hours. During that time, Bella had stepped outside the motor home several times with her two-way, leaving Bill to keep an eye on me. The last time she had stepped out she'd been gone for nearly a half hour. When she finally came back inside she was clearly uptight about something, but when I asked her about it, she said that everything was fine, she was just hungry. We made sandwiches out of cold cuts and were halfway through our simple meal when I heard the cars drive by.

"Let's go talk to Lod," I said, starting to get up from the table.

Bella put her hand on my arm and shook her head. "We need to wait until he asks for us."

I was going to protest but thought better of it, and sat back down. Bella and I had been getting along pretty well. There was no point in antagonizing her, or Bill. Right now, they were the only allies I had.

We finished our sandwiches.

Another half hour passed. Then an hour. Bella and Bill said nothing, not even to each other. Bill got up and started pacing back and forth in the tiny motor home. Four steps to the front, four steps to the back. I think Bella would have been pacing too if there had been room.

Bella's two-way came to life.

"Bring her," Lod said. *"Bill too. And her backpack."*

Bella looked at me and said, "Are we clear about how you found us?"

"Crystal clear," I said. "I have your back."

We stepped out of the motor home into the dark. There were twelve recreational vehicles parked nearby that I could see: trailers, truck campers, and motor homes. The lights were on inside them. Curtains pulled. I didn't see anyone outside, but I knew they were there. Lod always had people out running security for him. I had been one of those people when we lived in the Deep.

Bill switched on a flashlight and we walked down the road, past several empty campsites.

"Where are we going?" I asked casually, feeling anything but. I was nervous. Why were we walking away from where the others were parked?

"Lod's motor home," Bella answered. "He doesn't park with us. Security."

It was more than security. Lod always kept himself apart from the others. In the Deep we lived in the highest and biggest apartment. He rarely invited anyone over. All the cookies Bella and I had made over the years had been baked in her kitchen, not Lod's.

I was certain we were being watched, and probably listened to as well, but I didn't spot any Shadows lurking in the empty campsites we passed.

I was relieved when I finally saw lights in the distance. They weren't taking me out into the dark to shoot me in the head. The sound of breaking waves got louder with every step we took. Finally Lod's motor home came into full view. Not surprisingly it was bigger than the others, not flashy, but certainly more luxurious. The curtains were pulled down. Two SUVs were parked nearby. I could see the silhouettes of people sitting in the front seats.

We walked up to the door. Bella tapped on it twice, paused, then gave the door another double tap. A muffled voice said something from inside. Bella opened the door and we entered, single file, Bella in front, Bill behind me. The motor home smelled of fresh-brewed coffee, which brought back memories. Our apartment in the Deep always smelled like this.

Lod was alone inside, seated on a white leather sofa with a steaming mug of coffee in front of him. If I hadn't known who he was, I'm not certain I would have recognized him. He'd lost ten or fifteen pounds. He was clean-shaven. His eyes were now blue. His hair had been cut short and dyed white. The changes were subtle by themselves, but grouped together he no longer looked anything like Lawrence Oliver Dane.

He fixed his blue eyes on Bella and Bill without even glancing at me. "Explain yourselves."

There was no disguising the voice. It was as cold and menacing as it had been in the Deep.

"What do you mean?" Bella asked.

"How did you manage to let Kate spot you before you spotted her, then follow you all the way from Portland to Nehalem Bay?"

"Because your granddaughter is the best Shadow we ever had."

"I do not have a granddaughter," Lod said icily, without a glance at me. "And that still doesn't explain how stupid you were to let her overhear you and Bill talking about your destination on a public street."

Busted. I wasn't surprised. He'd had plenty of time to talk to the other Originals before he called for us. One, or all of them, had caved.

I had to be careful about when I stepped in to save Bella and Bill. If I did it too quickly Lod would know that we had conspired against him. If I waited too long he would think that I had concocted the notebook story while I was standing there because I felt sorry for Bella and Bill. He had always said my greatest weakness was empathy, sticking up for people. I was going to use this to my advantage if he didn't march me out to the ocean and drown me first.

Bill stepped forward and spoke up for the first time. "I don't remember having had a conversation on the street that anyone could have overheard."

"Then not only did you make a disastrous mistake, you're compounding it by lying to me."

"He's not lying," I said. "I was lying."

Lod slowly, almost reluctantly, looked my way. I met his gaze. The blue eyes were somehow more icy and unforgiving than his brown eyes had been, but I did not look away.

"I was at Nehalem Bay two days before Bella and Bill and the others got there."

"How did you know they were going to Nehalem Bay?"

"I guessed."

His eyes narrowed. "Really?"

I nodded.

"And how did you guess?"

"I'm not sure you really want to know."

"Tell me."

I shrugged. "I saw the name in one of your little notebooks."

His hand reflexively touched the notebook in his shirt pocket.

"When?"

"The day I took your notebook out of the fire."

I could see him trying to calculate if the name could have possibly been in the half-burned notebook I had rescued.

"Why did you lie to them when they asked you how you had found them?"

"Because I was angry. LaNae hit me with her car. She wanted to kill me. I wanted to throw them off, put the blame of my finding them on their incompetence. I thought it might save me."

"The only person who can save you is me," he said.

"I didn't know if you'd be around to save me."

I looked at Bella and Bill. They looked angry and surprised, which is exactly how they should have looked if what I was saying was true. "I'm sorry," I said.

They said nothing.

"You two can go," Lod said. "I'll call you when I'm ready for you to take Kate."

They filed out without a word.

Lod took a sip of his coffee and said, "Give me your pack and sit down."

I gave him the pack and sat down in the chair across from him. He emptied the contents of the pack onto the floor, carefully examining everything before stuffing it back into the compartment it had come from.

After he had zipped and buckled everything back up he said, "Tell me about the notebook."

"It was the one I took off the grill. It was pretty far gone, but I remembered Nehalem Bay."

"What else do you remember?"

I shook my head. "Nothing. Like I said. There wasn't much left. Then you came out onto the balcony freaking out and took it away from me."

"But you saw the words *Nehalem Bay*."

He'd either written it down in a notebook, or he hadn't. If he hadn't I was dead. So were Bella and Bill.

"I don't remember writing that down in any of my notebooks."

I shrugged. "How else would I have seen it?"

Another sip of coffee. I noticed the coffee was black. Lod always drank his gallon of coffee with a lot of cream. Cutting out the fat might account for some of his weight loss.

"So you saw the words *Nehalem Bay*?"

I nodded, relieved that he had either written *Nehalem Bay* in one of his little notebooks, or he couldn't remember. But you never know with my grandfather. He might have been certain he didn't write it down and was just waiting for me to deepen the lie.

"How did you know we would be at Nehalem Bay?"

"I didn't. I was shocked when I found the Pod there. It was the only place name I had."

"You were looking for us?"

"Why else would I go there?"

"You ran away. You helped those boys escape."

"And if you'd been smart, and had just let them go, they might not have turned you in."

His face tightened in anger, which is exactly what I had intended. I wanted to make him angry. The only thing my grandfather truly respected was fearlessness. People tiptoed around him. They were terrified of making him angry. I had to show him that I was not afraid.

He got up, dumped the remains of his coffee into the sink, refilled his mug, then sat back down.

"What happened from the moment you were confronted in the Deep by Carl and his dog?"

I repeated the same story I had told Bella and Bill, which I was certain he had already heard from the other Originals.

When I finished, he stared at me for a few seconds, then said, "Kind of a long shot."

"I don't understand."

"Remembering Nehalem Bay, then coming out here and actually finding us."

"More like a miracle," I said. "My only plan when I left New York was to get as far away from you as I could."

"Why?"

"Oh, please. You know as well as I do that you were going to punish me for what I did. Maybe even kill me."

Lod shook his head. "I wouldn't have killed you, Kate, but you're right about the punishment. I would have done something. Probably isolated you until you came to your senses."

By isolated, I assume he meant that he would have sent me to the mush room.

"I came to my senses outside Chicago," I said. "I decided to go back to the Deep. I was in a station in Iowa trying to figure out how to cash in my ticket for a return ticket to New York when I saw the first newspaper article. It said that you had left the Deep. My only choice was Nehalem Bay. It was the only hint I had. A long shot, but I guess I hit the target."

"And you haven't heard from the O'Toole brothers?"

"I have no way to get in touch with them, and even if I did, I have no desire to talk to them. Bella told me they were the ones who went to the FBI. They must be in police custody."

Lod shook his head. "No, they are not. I would know if they were. We've had our eyes on their parents and everyone they know since we left the Deep. We also have contacts in the FBI. No sign of those boys. They're at large."

"Well, I'm sure they aren't pursuing you. You're the last person on earth they would want to run into."

"We'll see," he said noncommittally.

If he was watching their parents, he had a lot more people working for him above than I had ever imagined. I wanted to ask him a thousand questions, but I couldn't. My only goal was to survive this interrogation.

"Tell me about Alex," he said.

"I don't know much about him. He left me books to read. We never really talked until the day we left the Deep."

"What did he say?"

"He said he was your brother. He said that you shot him in the leg."

"Did he say why I shot him?"

If I admitted to Lod that I knew he had shot my parents, he would have me killed. He might even do it himself. Even if he didn't kill me, he would never trust me again. How could he?

"He said you had a disagreement about something. He wouldn't say what it was. He said that you had left him in an alley for dead."

Lod thought about this for a few moments, sipping his coffee.

"Is that all?"

"Yes, other than the fact that he had been keeping an eye on the Pod."

"Why did he save you from Carl?"

"I have no idea. He never said. He led us up top through the library and told us we needed to disappear."

"Why did he give you the laptops and cell phones?"

I wanted to know how he knew this, but of course I couldn't ask.

"He said he wanted us to keep in touch with him. He gave us backpacks with some clothes as well."

"As far as I can tell Coop and his brother haven't used their phones."

I shrugged as if I couldn't care less about them. "Maybe they sold them like I did. I didn't have any cash. Maybe they didn't either. Like I told you, they went their way, I went mine."

Lod gave me a small smile, his first since I had stepped into his motor home. "Kate, I have always been honest with you, and, until recently, you have been honest with me . . ."

He had lied to me my entire life. It was all I could do not to blurt out: YOU MURDERED MY PARENTS! He may have been an expert at external disguise, but I was an expert at internal disguise. I'd been masking my emotions and feelings since I was a little girl.

Lod continued, "I sent Bella and Bill and the others out looking for you at great risk to our goals, even our lives. I wanted to talk to you. I wanted to hear your explanation for what you had done."

"Now you know," I said quietly, looking down, as if I was ashamed. "I wanted a chance to talk to you too. I didn't mean to cause you all this trouble. I know there is nothing I can do to undo the damage I've caused, but I am sorry."

"I'm not ready to accept your apology. You did cause a great deal of damage. What I need is more information about Alex."

"He looks a little like you, but frailer. He has gray —"

"I know what he looks like." Lod raised his voice. "I need to know what he's doing."

I shook my head. "All I know is that he was watching us in the Deep."

"Why?"

"I have no idea."

"And you didn't ask?"

"No. I was afraid of what you were going to do if you caught me. All I wanted to do was get away."

"And those two boys?"

"I can see why you're worried about Alex, but I wouldn't waste another thought about them. They are long gone. I should have let you put them in the mush room."

"I'm not sure what I'm going to do with you, Kate. For the time being you'll be in the custody of Bella and Bill. If you run, we will find you." He patted the sofa next to where he was sitting. "Put your foot up here."

"Why?"

"Do it."

I put my foot up.

He opened a drawer and pulled out a black rubber bracelet with a little box on it. "This is a tether, or a security ankle bracelet. Law enforcement uses them to keep criminals in the confines of their homes. Since you're going to be moving, this one is set up a little differently. There's a proximity sensor. If you get more than two hundred feet from Bella, try to take it off, or tamper with it in any way, an alarm will go off. I will know you violated your probation. One strike and you're out. No questions. No excuses. I will have you taken care of."

I didn't have to ask him what he meant by this. If I strayed too far from Bella, he would have me killed.

He put the bracelet around my ankle and began securing it with a special tool.

"How long will I be on probation?"

"As long as I say you are. It might be for the rest of your life. You really messed us up. I had planned to leave the Deep at some point, but not at this time of year, and not with the feds in pursuit. There." He set the tool on the table.

I put my foot down. "I hope I'll be able to prove to you how sorry I am one day. I know I could be useful."

"I hoped you had learned something *useful* about Alex, but since you didn't, you are pretty much *useless* to me. If I were you, I'd spend some time thinking about everything he said, everything he did, and everything you saw when you were with him. I know more about Alex than you do, and I was only in that rat hole he lived in for ten minutes." He picked up his radio and said, "I'm ready."

"On my way," Bella said.

"Both of you."

"Copy."

He clipped the radio to his belt. "I'll be coming in and out as we travel. We'll be talking again."

"I'll try to remember whatever I can about Alex."

"Do that. He's the one thing I didn't expect." He pulled his little notebook out of his pocket. "And you are certain you saw only one of my notebooks?"

"Only one."

I wasn't going to admit that I had actually pulled burned bits and pieces of at least a dozen notebooks out of the grill over the years. I'd even sneaked into his bedroom for a quick peek a couple of times while he was sleeping. At the time it was a lark, something exciting to do while I was cooped up in our apartment day after day. Lod was a pretty good artist. I enjoyed the sketches. I wished I had paid closer attention to what I had seen and read.

"I'm curious," he said. "What has it been like for you being above?"

This time I answered honestly. "Terrifying. I'm sure this contributed to my wanting to go back into the Deep. There are so many options above, too many choices, too many routes, too many people."

"How did you cope?"

"By simplifying. Staying focused on one thing at a time."

"Nehalem Bay?"

"That's right. I had absolutely no plan beyond getting

there. If I hadn't stumbled onto the Pod I don't know what I would have done."

"I'm sure you would have figured something out. In fact, think about that. Next time I see you let me know what you think you would have done. I'm always fine-tuning the plan. I thought I would eventually find you, but I didn't think that you would find me."

He sounded more like the old Lod, the private Lod, the grandfather who sometimes showed himself when it was just him and me.

"Why were you looking for me?"

"Because you are my granddaughter, my flesh and blood. And that's the only reason you're still alive. We are about to save the world from itself. I so wanted you to be a part of this, but you let me down. You —"

There was a tap on the door. Lod gave the door an irritable frown. "Come in!"

Bella stepped inside.

Lod looked back at me. The grandfatherly tone was gone. "Take your pack and wait outside."

I quickly stuffed my meager belongings into the pack and stepped out into the night. Bill was waiting for me. I started to explain what had happened inside, but he grabbed my arm and whispered in my ear, "Don't talk. Watchers."

I spotted four of them. Two in the front seats of cars, two concealed behind trees. There could have been more. The Pod had to be traveling with a lot of people working different shifts.

Bella came out of the motor home. We walked down the road to our campsite. When we got into their coach, I pulled up my pant leg and showed them my ankle bracelet.

"You're not alone," Bella said. She lifted her pant leg, revealing an identical bracelet. "We're tethered. Joined at the hip, or ankle, I guess. I hope you can earn Lod's trust soon so I can get this thing off. It itches."

WE ALL DIE

Alex said.

We were sitting in the back of our used camper at Bullards Beach State Park, twenty miles south of Coos Bay.

Alex was drinking a mug of green tea and eating one of Coop's tuna sandwiches.

I didn't have the stomach to eat or drink anything.

I was trying to settle down after driving the camper on the twisting road, pulling a boat with thirty-mile-an-hour winds blowing us all over the place, Alex yelling at me to stay on the road, and Coop laughing as if we were on an amusement park ride.

"From the womb to the tomb," Alex continued.

After we had gotten the camper set up — electricity, water, toilet — which took a long time because none of us knew what we were doing, Alex decided it would be a good time to tell us more about his brother so we would have a better idea of what we were up against.

"Larry believes that a few years, or a few decades, makes little difference in another person's life. It all ends the same way. He feels completely justified in killing anyone who gets in the way of his grand plan. To him, extinguishing a life before its time is nothing more than speeding up an inevitable result."

"No guilt?" Coop asked.

"None," Alex continued. "He has much more empathy for wildlife than he does for human life. At heart Larry is a frustrated militant environmentalist. People and their governments are the enemy. The only life that matters to Larry is his own life. And the reason it's so important is because he's carrying the grand plan in his head."

"He seemed pretty fond of Kate," Coop pointed out. "Even when she was defying him."

Alex nodded. "I think Kate might have been his fail-safe. If he had gotten sick before he could launch his plan I think he would have passed the plan off to her to carry out, which brings me to my next subject —"

The teakettle whistled, nearly launching me from my seat. Coop laughed.

Alex got up and turned it off.

"Little jumpy, Lil Bro," Coop said.

"I'm still driving the truck in my head," I said.

"You did fine. We're alive."

Alex sat back down. "Larry has lived a lonely life. He was smarter than almost everyone he knew. That would be like living in a country where you understood the language but no one there could understand *you*. He got impatient and bored with nearly everyone because he was so far ahead of them. He told me once that when he talked with people it was like they were speaking in slow motion. It took him years to stop finishing sentences for people after the third word was out of their mouth. He had to train himself to act like he was listening to people so they didn't get angry with him. He learned to feign interest in what people were saying when his mind was off on something entirely different. In the early days with the Originals he would sit in our meeting room, nodding, smiling, frowning, looking thoughtful and concerned, understanding everything that was said, without an iota of genuine interest in what anyone was saying."

"What about you?" I asked. "Did he listen to you?"

Alex shook his head. "No. I was his little brother. He valued my opinion even less than the other Originals. He always underestimated me, but with luck, that will change soon. The reason I'm telling you all this is so you have an idea of Larry's mind-set. The Originals are getting old. The road ahead of them is a lot shorter than the road behind them. Your arrival, and Kate's betrayal, woke them up, got them moving, but you aren't the reason they moved. They aren't running. They are relocating."

I was getting hot sitting in the back of the cramped camper . . .

"Larry's escape is brilliant!" Alex continued. "The FBI and other law enforcement agencies have become so dependent on technology, they've lost their edge tracking people who are off the grid. In the old days when we were on the run — before cells, electronic transactions, the Internet — they were pretty good at tracking people down. Nowadays if someone on the run doesn't leave an electronic footprint, the FBI doesn't know where to start."

"Do you think they're planning some kind of nuclear attack?" Coop asked.

Alex laughed. "If I thought that, I would have gone to the

FBI myself by now. I have no doubt that given the right components Larry could build a nuclear bomb, but those materials are hard, if not impossible, to come by. One of the reasons we went into the Deep is because we thought there was going to be a nuclear disaster. Larry isn't interested in destroying the earth. He would much rather take down the people in charge of running the earth."

"What are we going to do about it?" I asked.

"I need to get inside to wherever they're going — either personally or through Kate — see what they're up to, and stop them before they implement their plan. Larry has been recruiting computer whizzes for the past several years, so whatever they're doing must have something to do with computers. I think I have something that can stop them. It might be our only chance."

"What do you have?" I asked.

"I can't give you the specifics, but it will put an end to all of this."

Alex yawned, then looked at his watch.

I guess the session was over.

Coop stood. He was wide-awake. It was after midnight.

"I'm going out for a walk," he said.

"I'll go with you," I said quickly, eager to get out of the camper.

"If you talk, whisper," Alex said. "There are other campers here, and some of them might be Pod members. The closer we get to them, the more dangerous they become."

CLAUSTROPHOBIA

Coop said.

I sucked in a deep breath of cool night air. "Nah."

"Then why were you sweating inside the camper with the heat off? Midfifties inside. Low forties out here."

"If you're cold, I can go back in and grab your jacket," I said.

"Very funny, Meatloaf. You know I'm right. Let's go for a nocturnal talk."

I had to smile at this. It had been more than a year since he and I had gone for a nocturnal talk, something we had done almost every night of our lives when we were kids.

"I'm not claustrophobic," I said. "Kate took care of that in the Deep."

"Not entirely. But you are a lot better. If this was a couple of years ago you would have kicked a window out of the camper and tried to squeeze through the opening."

Coop was right, of course. My claustrophobia hadn't been cured. I hadn't recognized it because it had come on so slowly.

We were parked in an area called the Devil's Kitchen.

We passed a big motor home, two campers, a trailer, and a tent. All of them were spaced two or three campsites apart. All of them were dark. The Pod? If they were, the ghosts were sleeping.

The wind had died down.

A damp salty haze hung in the air.

I could hear the ocean.

"Have you been to this part of the coast before?"

"I'm sure I have, but I don't remember it. I spent only a couple of nights sleeping outside."

"How did you get by?"

"Pocket change. I relied on the kindness of strangers. I stayed in people's houses if they were locals. If I got picked up by a tourist, they usually let me crash in their hotel room."

"Did you work?"

"A little. I mowed a couple of lawns. Washed some restaurant dishes. My longest period of employment was teaching a kid to tap-dance in Los Angeles. He was trying out for a part in a movie. Couldn't tap a lick when we started, but he wasn't bad after a couple of weeks. He got the part. His parents were grateful."

"How old was he?"

"Seven. His mom caught me tapping under an overpass in Hollywood. She and her husband were both in the film business. I'm still not sure what they did. But they had a lot of friends. Parties every weekend at their house. I was staying with them. That's where I met the makeup guy who gave me the overhaul before I got to Portland."

We came to a weatherworn sign that read BEACH.

The tide was out.

The breakers glowed in the distance with bioluminescence.

We stepped onto the beach and walked toward the white rolling waves, keeping our shoes on as a barrier against the cold.

"Do you trust Alex?" Coop asked.

"Sure. Don't you?"

"Not really."

This stopped me dead in the sand. I always thought Coop's universal trust was one of the reasons everyone was attracted to him. He was completely nonjudgmental. He had walked a million miles in other people's shoes, and all those shoes fit him perfectly.

"What do you mean? You trust everybody."

Coop shook his head. "Just because I listen to people doesn't mean that I trust them. Alex Dane is not telling us the truth, at least not the whole truth. He's not quite right in the head."

"That's something you should be used to by now. Nobody from the Deep is right in the head. Alex is an old man who has lived by himself underneath a library for years. Of course he's not right in the head."

"It's more than that," Coop said. "He's lying to us about something."

"Then he's a pretty good liar."

"Of course he is. He's from the Deep, an Original. We need to keep that in mind. He's one of them, or was for years, until he and Lod had their falling-out."

"Over Kate's parents being murdered in that alley and thrown into a Dumpster."

"We'll see," Coop said quietly.

"Do you know something that I don't know?"

"No, Meatloaf. Cross my heart. It's just a feeling I have. I'm not hiding anything from you."

"Do you think we should take off?"

Coop shook his head. "He's our only chance of catching up with Kate."

"We can always call Tia Ryan at the FBI."

"That's the one thing I think Alex is telling the truth about. Whatever Lod has in mind is already in the works. If the FBI swoops in and picks everyone up, his master plan will continue. If Alex is right about no one knowing what the plan is they won't be able to tell the FBI anything."

"But Lod knows the plan. If they caught him I'm sure —"

"You think Lawrence Oliver Dane is going to tell them anything after waiting so long to make his move?"

"I'm sure they have ways of making people talk."

"Lod knows that. Remember? He has a plan for every contingency. The only thing he doesn't have a plan for is us, because he doesn't know we're here."

I didn't even want to think about what Lod would do if he discovered that we were following him.

"We'll just keep heading south," Coop said. "We'll stick with Alex for the time being." He picked up a perfect sand dollar and turned his flashlight on to look at it. "One more thing, and I know you aren't going to like it. But I have to give you the option."

"What?"

"You don't have to stick around for any of this. I'm sure between us we have enough money to get you back to McLean or anywhere else you want to go."

"You're kidding, right?"

"I am not kidding." He sailed the sand dollar back into

the ocean. "I'm worried this is not going to end well. I don't want you to get hurt."

"This is all about the tunnel, isn't it?"

A few years earlier, I had helped Coop dig a tunnel through our neighborhood back home. The tunnel had exploded and collapsed. That's where I'd gotten my claustrophobia. Coop had saved my life.

"A little," Coop admitted. "I still feel bad about it."

"You can forget the tunnel. And you can forget about me not sticking this thing out. I'm here until the very end, no matter what. And if I leave, who's going to drive? How do you think Alex would do behind the wheel of that truck?"

"You're sure?"

"I am sure," I said. "And I'm exhausted. I need to get some sleep so I can drive tomorrow. Let's head back."

"I'm wide-awake," Coop said. "I think I'll wander around for a while."

"Big surprise. I'll see you later."

When I got back to our campsite I didn't have the desire . . . well, the courage . . . to go back inside the cramped camper. Coop was right about the claustrophobia. He was probably right about Alex too. I got a sleeping bag and pad out from behind the front seat. I was going to roll them out on the ground, but then I saw the boat attached to the back of the camper and thought that might be a better option. I lay down between the two bench seats. It smelled like dead fish, but I didn't care. I closed my eyes and thought about Kate. As strange and dangerous as our situation was, her situation had to be worse and even more dangerous.

THEY WERE SNORING . . .

both of them.

When we had gotten back to Bella and Bill's motor home, we'd talked quietly for a few minutes about Lod. We were relieved that we might have pulled it off, but we all knew Lod well enough to know that he might just be letting us think that we had pulled it off. I had seen him watch people lie to him for weeks; then, when they least expected it, he'd call them on every lie they had told him, then send them to the mush room, never to be seen again.

Bella and Bill were in the small bed above the cab. I was lying on the sofa next to the little kitchen. The ankle brace-let itched. The snoring was *loud*. I didn't need the tether. If they kept me up all night with their snoring, I'd barely be able to keep my eyes open tomorrow, much less run away.

I got up, quietly opened the door, and stepped outside into a fog so thick I couldn't see ten feet in front of me. I sat down on top of a picnic table with my feet on the bench. There was a camp restroom across the road. I was certain it was less than two hundred feet away. I thought about wandering over and leaving a note, then berated myself for being stupid.

The notes had been an impossible long shot. If by some miracle Alex, Coop, and Pat had found any of them and managed to track us, Lod would have caught them by now.

He would not have tethered them. He would have killed them. And it would have been my fault.

I should have guessed how tight his security would be. Leaving the notes had been an unnecessary risk. If Bella or Bill had discovered even one of them I'd be at the bottom of the ocean, or buried at the base of a Douglas fir.

I shook my head in disgust. I was a Shadow. I needed to harden myself. I needed to get my head back in the game. But what was the game now? Why was I here? Why had Alex sent me after Bella and Bill? The train station had obviously been their last stop. If I hadn't pursued them, I could have joined Coop and Pat at the library and disappeared. Forever.

I tried to think back to what Alex had said to me outside the station. His exact words. I closed my eyes and concentrated.

He had appeared out of nowhere, just like he had in the Deep. One moment the snowy sidewalk ahead of me was empty, the next moment he was standing in front of me, blocking my way.

"Where are Coop and Pat?"

"I'm meeting them at a place called Voodoo Doughnuts. Bella and Bill are in the —"

"I know," he interrupted. "They're still inside the station. We've been compromised. Larry hacked us in Chicago. Give me your phone and computer."

I had pulled them out of my pack and handed them over without question.

"What are you doing here? How did you find —"

"No time. Coop was on the last train. The snow has stopped all the other trains. Bella and Bill will be coming out any second. I want you to follow them. Find out where they go. I'll take Coop and Pat to the Multnomah County Library. Main branch. It's on Southwest Tenth, between Yamhill and Taylor. Got that?"

"Yes."

"Here they come."

I turned around. Bill was wheeling Bella out of the station, having a difficult time negotiating the snow. When I turned back around, Alex was gone. Poof! Just like he'd always disappeared in the Deep. Bill pushed Bella to a small parking lot across from the station. I hurried over, squatted behind a car, and heard everything they said as they put the wheelchair into the back of the motor home.

I didn't think Alex had meant for me to follow them all the way to the coast. That was all my doing. If the bus station across the street hadn't had a bus leaving for the coast right then . . . If there hadn't been a kid willing to sell me his ticket. If I hadn't met the girl from Manzanita. If her hotel hadn't had bicycles. If, if, if. But the biggest if was me. If I hadn't wanted to follow them, I'd be in Portland with Coop . . .

I was no different than the tracker dogs I had trained in the Deep. I had picked up Bella and Bill's scent, and I wasn't going to give up until I found out where they were going and what they planned to do.

My fault.

My training.

And maybe something else. Maybe I wanted to find my grandfather. Maybe I wanted to find out why he had killed my parents. Maybe I wanted to kill him.

"What are you doing here?"

A giant appeared out of the fog. If he hadn't spoken, I might have thought it was a bear standing on two feet.

"That's none of your business," I said. "And keep your voice down. People are sleeping."

"I can hear them." He stepped closer. It was Carl. "Bella and Bill always sleep away from everyone else so they don't wake people." He gave a small laugh, which sounded more like he was choking.

He had cut his bushy beard and trimmed his hair. There was nothing he could do about his height. He had to be six six. He sat down on the bench near my feet and was still taller than I was sitting on the table.

"What are you doing here?" he repeated.

"Couldn't sleep. Getting some fresh air."

"I meant, why did you come after us?"

I looked at his profile. The lack of facial hair hadn't improved his appearance.

"That's none of your business. But, just to clarify, I am part of the *us* you're referring to."

"You always did have a smart mouth."

He was right about that, but I had no idea how he knew this. I had seen him only a dozen times in my life and had spoken to him maybe twice.

"What are you doing out here?" I asked.

"Doing what I do. Watching."

"Fabulous. Why don't you go off and watch. I don't need watching. And I don't want company."

"You shot my dog."

"I did not shoot your dog. The old man shot your dog after you threatened to have your dog tear us apart."

He coughed out another laugh. "The old man. Alex Dane. I didn't even know Lod had a brother."

I didn't know it either at the time, but I wasn't about to share that with Carl.

"The dog wouldn't have hurt you," he continued. "I sent him after the boys. What are those boys to you anyway?"

I was tired, a little cold, but alert enough to realize that Carl had not just been wandering by when I stepped out of the coach. He'd been waiting for me, hoping I would step outside so he could have a little chat with me. A friendly chat, or his version of friendly. The question was, had Lod sent him, or was he here on his own and for his own reasons?

"Those boys are nothing to me," I said. "Not anymore. I was just trying to get them up top. Sorry about the dog."

I was sorry about his dog, but there had been no choice.

"I miss that dog," he said.

"I bet." I missed my dogs too. I planned on getting another one as soon as I could, which brought up another question I hadn't thought about. Many people in the Deep had a dog. Dogs and dog training had been an important part of our Community lives. People's cleverness was often judged by the cleverness of their dogs.

"I haven't seen any dogs here," I said.

"No dogs allowed. Lod thought they would attract too much attention. We'd have to stop and let them out to do their business. He's right about that. You have a dog, people come up to you."

"Smart," I said. And it was smart. Lod thought of everything, every detail.

"Your grandfather's smart all right. How did your meeting go with him?"

Finally — the real reason for this chance encounter. Carl had dropped by to pump me for information. But on whose behalf? His own, or Lod's?

"I'm alive," I said. "So it went as well as could be expected. I don't blame any of you for being suspicious of me. If I were in your place, I'd be suspicious too."

"Heard he put you on a tether."

"Two hundred feet."

"Did he mention anything about your backpack?"

"What do you mean?"

"You know, what you were carrying in the backpack you had with you."

This was the reason for his visit.

He had taken the cash.

He wanted to know if Lod knew.

I shrugged. "He searched it."

"Was anything missing?"

I looked at him for a moment trying to decide how I was going to handle this.

"My money," I said. "It wasn't there, but I knew it wouldn't be. It wasn't there when Bella searched the pack earlier."

"How much money?" Carl asked, almost in a whisper.

"I think you know, Carl. It was a lot of money."

He stared at me. I tensed my legs, readying myself to jump off the table if he made a grab for me. He was a powerful man, but he didn't look quick. All I had to do was get two hundred feet away from him and my tether alarm would sound. I lifted my pant leg and showed him my ankle bracelet.

"If you're thinking about doing something, I'd think again. You can't haul me very far away with this thing on my leg."

"I don't know what you're talking about."

"You took the money, Carl. And I don't care. If I was concerned about it, I would have told Bella when I first discovered it was missing. I didn't say anything to Lod either because I don't want him to know about it. I'm in enough trouble with him as it is."

"You didn't tell him?"

I shook my head. "And I'd appreciate it if you didn't tell him either. If you tell him, we'll both be in trouble."

Carl visibly relaxed. "I took it because —"

"Because you thought I'd be killed. Understandable. They would have buried the backpack with me, or tossed it into the ocean. Why throw away perfectly good cash? I would have done the same thing."

This last part wasn't true. I'd never thought about money before coming up top with Coop and Pat. In the Deep we didn't really use money. We didn't need it. If we wanted something, all we had to do was ask for it, and within a few days it would magically appear. There were restrictions, of course. Nothing electronic. No newspapers, magazines, banned books, alcohol, drugs, and a few other corrupting things. We did carry cash when we were up top in case we got stranded someplace and had to catch a cab, or jump on the subway. *Dead presidents*, as Lod called cash, were only to be used in case of emergency. He kept close track of what people spent, or had in their pockets. The rest of the cash was kept in the dead-presidents vault in his bedroom.

"Where did you get all that money?" Carl asked suspiciously.

"I've been collecting bills from Lod's safe since I was a kid. Just something to do. Never thought I'd need it. I don't need it now. I'm happy to be back, and I'd appreciate if you'd keep the dead presidents to yourself. You actually did me a favor when you swiped them."

Carl scrutinized me carefully, looking for a lie. There were plenty of lies there, but he didn't push me further.

"Okay, then," Carl finally said. "We're square." He put his giant hand out for me to shake.

I shook it.

"Again, I'm sorry about your dog. You and your dog were just doing your job. I wish Alex hadn't shot him. He didn't deserve it."

Carl got up from the table. "Forget it. Collateral damage. I better get back to my watch."

Bella, Bill, and now Carl. They owed me. I'd get information from them if I didn't push too hard. Simple questions.

"So, do you sleep during the day?" I asked.

He turned back to me. "When I work graveyard, yeah."

"Where do you sleep?"

"In one of the rigs. Lod tells me where I'm going to bunk. There's a bunch of us running security. Day and night shifts."

"You prefer nights?"

"Doesn't matter to me, but nights are quieter because we're parked. During the day Lod runs the show from a helicopter. A lot of driving, running ahead, hanging behind, countersurveillance. You know the drill."

I did know the drill — it was the same thing we had done in New York when we had business above, although we did it on foot. I had suspected Lod was watching from a helicopter, or an airplane, but this confirmed it.

He must have all the vehicles marked. Probably a number on the roof, or perhaps a color, or . . .

Suddenly I remembered something from one of his notebooks. A sketch. I didn't know what it was at the time. It was a series of rectangles, one in front of the other, between two parallel lines. The rectangles had numbers in the lower right-hand corners.

"What are you smiling about?" Carl asked.

I hadn't realized that I was smiling. "I was just thinking about some of the runs we made above."

"Good times," Carl said, and disappeared back into the fog.

THE BOAT WAS ROCKING

"Time to wake up, Meatloaf."

I opened my eyes.

Coop was sitting on the bench seat looking down at me.

"How'd you sleep?"

I barely remembered climbing into the boat. "Good. I think."

I sat up.

It was foggy out.

The sun was up.

I looked at my watch. 7:22.

"Alex wants to get on the road. There was a Pod member camped here. Small Airstream trailer being pulled by a red truck. We walked past it last night."

I didn't remember seeing it. My brain was as foggy as the campground.

"Alex heard them on the radio. They just pulled out. He wants to get in front of them."

I quickly rolled up my sleeping bag and pad and stuffed them behind the front seat of the truck before getting behind the wheel.

Alex slid open the window between the camper and the cab. He had on a pair of headphones. He must have picked them up the night before when he was out getting the camper.

He pulled the headphones down around his neck. "They're

on the move. A lot of chatter. Larry must be in the air already. You okay to drive?"

"I think so."

"I'll hang back here. See if I can't ID a few more of their vehicles."

"I'll ride up front with Pat," Coop said.

"First you need to help me back the boat out of here." I looked at Alex hopefully. "Unless you want to dump the boat here?"

"Not yet. If I think Larry is paying attention to a camper pulling a boat, we'll get rid of it. From what I've been able to overhear, he's having his countersurveillance team check out vehicles he has suspicions about. You guys will need to put on your disguises, such as they are. If a car drives up alongside you to get a closer look, try not to look back at them and be cool. You're just a couple of guys in a camper heading home after a fishing trip."

What we were was a couple of guys who didn't have the first idea how to back up a trailer. It took me a half a dozen tries, scraped paint, and a severely dented trailer bumper, which we had to pull away from the tire. I finally figured out that Coop was worthless at giving directions, and that the best way to back up a trailer was to go slow, use the side mirrors, and follow the trailer.

Finally we were back on the highway, heading south.

It was a much quieter ride with Alex back in the camper, listening on headphones, than it had been the day before. As usual, Coop was fast asleep before we hit the highway.

SIXTEEN

I climbed down from the ladder leading to the roof of the motor home. Sixteen had been painted onto the bottom right-hand corner of the roof just like the sketch in Lod's notebook. Our motor home was number sixteen. So there were at least sixteen vehicles heading south.

Bella was over at the camp restroom taking a shower. She hated the small shower in the motor home. Bill was checking the engine oil. I had watched Lod pull out of the park at dawn. At least I thought it was him. Three cars. Two people in each car. Half an hour later other coaches began rolling out of the park at ten- or fifteen-minute intervals. Lod's big motor home had pulled out while I was on the ladder checking the roof. LaNae was behind the wheel. I saw that she had cut her hair very short. She didn't even look my way as she rolled past.

Bella walked across the street drying her hair with a towel.

"Ten minutes," she said to Bill. "Looks like we're driving middle of the order today."

We climbed inside. I sat in the back. Bella and Bill sat up front.

"*Okay, sixteen,*" Lod said over the radio.

We pulled out of the campsite.

BANDON

Langlois.

Sixes.

Town after little town.

Either I was getting better at driving, or the camper was easier to drive than the car, which didn't seem likely. I was feeling so confident behind the wheel that I managed to pass a car and merge back into my lane without smashing him with the boat.

Alex poked his head through the window. "Nicely done," he said.

"No big deal."

"I think they're going to blow by you up ahead on that straight stretch."

"How do you know that?" I looked at the car in the side mirror. It was still a long way back, puttering along.

"Watch."

Sure enough the car started to pick up speed as we approached the straightaway.

"Keep it at fifty-five," Alex said, like he was reading my mind. "It's not a race. Eyes on the road."

The car passed us going at least seventy-five and disappeared behind a rise in front of us.

"Okay," I said. "How did you know that slowpoke was going to pass us?"

"Spotter car. Countersurveillance. He was told to check us out, saw nothing, and moved on. The FBI don't tail people in campers pulling boats, although they should give it a try. It's good cover."

"So we're safe," I said. "They won't be checking us out again."

Alex laughed. "On the contrary. I figured out some of the code they're using. Larry is up in the air managing this run like an orchestra conductor. I think we've somehow ended up in the middle of the pack, rigs to the south, rigs to the north, the spotters moving ahead, hanging back, all under Larry's direction. There's a viewpoint in about three miles. Pull into it. We need to do some touristy things on the way so Larry doesn't get suspicious."

We were on a stretch of highway hugging the Pacific. Blue sky with a few cottony clouds above the horizon. I pulled into the viewpoint. Another car and a motor home were already parked there, windshields toward the ocean. From the back Alex asked about the vehicles. He couldn't see them from where we were parked. I described them.

"Do you recognize the car?"

"Not really. It isn't the car that passed us. Looks like there's a man and a woman sitting in the front. Maybe some kids in the back."

"What about the motor home?"

"White. Class C."

"Plates?"

"I can't see them clearly. I think they're California plates."

"We need to start a database of some of the plates we see. Cross off the ones we know aren't Pod."

"Want me to jump out and get the number?"

"Sure, but don't act like you're getting the number. Act like you're checking the boat or taking in the view. Take the binoculars to make it look good. If you have a hood on your jacket use it."

I put up my hood and grabbed the binoculars. I glanced at Coop. He was sound asleep, dead to the world. I closed the door quietly, not that slamming it would have disturbed him.

I was glad I had my hood up. It was colder than it looked.

PAT

At least it looked like Pat.

How do you look at someone without appearing like you're looking at them?

Bella was lying on the narrow floor next to the sofa, trying to do yoga. Bill was squeezed into the tiny bathroom loudly brushing his teeth. He'd always been fastidious about his teeth.

I was sitting on the sofa staring out the window. A few minutes earlier Lod had radioed in, telling everyone to stop. Bella said he did this every once in a while and that there was no cause for alarm. He'd observe the stationary caravan for potential threats, then have everyone start out again.

I couldn't see Pat's face clearly under his hoodie, but I knew it was him by the way he moved, the hunch of his shoulders, the splay of his feet as he walked.

Where did they get a camper?

He had a pair of binoculars around his neck. He walked around the back to the boat they were towing.

Where did they get a boat? Why did they have a boat? Had they gotten my notes? Did Pat know he was parked right next to me? Where did he learn to drive? Where were Coop and Alex?

My head whirled with shock, joy, and fear.

Get your game face on! I told myself. *Don't blow this.*

I needed to let him know I was here without drawing attention to him. It had to be handled with finesse.

I turned away from the window and looked down at Bella. "Awkward place to do yoga," I said.

"You're not kidding. I'd ask you to join me, but there's barely enough room for the mat. I can't manage a tenth of my poses."

I had done yoga with Bella since I could walk. Daily yoga practice and jujitsu were required discipline for all Shadows. I hadn't done either since I escaped from the Deep. I missed them. Another thing to add to my list. Dogs. Yoga. Brazilian jujitsu.

"How'd you and Bill end up with the small motor home?"

Bella laughed. She was in a half-tortoise pose with her forehead on the floor and her arms stretched out above her head. "You think this is cramped? You need to see some of the other rigs. LaNae is driving Lod's rig today, but she's usually driving a clunker of a car, pulling a tent trailer. As you can imagine she hasn't been too happy about that. Her car broke down yesterday. Lod had her leave it where it was. I think she sabotaged it."

Like everyone else in the Pod, Bella was not a big fan of LaNae Fay.

"Wouldn't put it past her," I said, stretching my arms above my head.

Bella came out of her tortoise pose in slow motion with complete control, showing off her strength. I wanted to burst through the door and run outside, but I couldn't help but be amazed at her fitness. I didn't know how old she was, but she had to be in her midsixties.

"Lod assigned the rigs," she continued. "Not sure what the formula was, but you know him, there's a reason for everything he does. Probably took him months to figure it out in that little notebook of his. But it seems to be working well. We have twenty-two vehicles on this route. Not one of us has been pulled over by the cops. He doesn't let us drive at night, so we're alert during the day. Also, there's more traffic during the day."

"The best place to hide is in a crowd," I said. One of the many Shadow mantras. I stretched out my legs like they were stiff and sore. All this was taking too long. If I didn't get outside soon, Pat might be gone.

"I forgot to ask," Bella said. "How'd you sleep last night?"

"It got a little stuffy in here. I got up and went outside for some fresh air. Other than that I slept fine."

A lie. I hadn't slept at all. I'd spent most of the night thinking about Lod's little notebooks.

"I didn't hear you get up." Bella went into the cow pose. "Bill and I sleep like the dead."

The noisy dead.

"How long do you think we'll be stopped here?" I asked.

"Hard to say. If you want to go out and stretch your legs, go ahead."

Finally. The trick was to get them to suggest something, rather than having to ask.

KATE

I couldn't believe my eyes. I caught myself a millisecond before calling out to her. I had been scanning the ocean with the binoculars when she stepped out of the motor home. We were less than fifty feet away from each other. She didn't even glance in my direction, but I knew that she recognized me. She picked up a stick and wandered over to the far side of the viewpoint and sat down on a bench. If Coop opened his eyes and saw her now, I wasn't sure what he would do. I started back to the camper, moving slowly, which is one of the hardest things I've ever done. I wanted to sprint. When I got to the door, I opened it casually, got into the driver's seat, and closed the door quietly.

Coop was still asleep.

Alex had his binoculars out, zeroed in on Kate through the windshield.

"Don't worry," he said without removing the binoculars. "They can't see me back here through the dark cab. You handled her appearance perfectly."

"Did you know she —"

"No," Alex interrupted. "But we were bound to run into a Pod member face-to-face eventually. In fact, we probably already have and didn't know it. I just didn't think we'd bump into Kate."

"I should have stayed out there. I thought she recognized me, but maybe she didn't."

"She recognized you all right. She must have seen you from inside the camper. See where she's sitting? It's a blind spot. They can't see her from the camper. I doubt they saw you either. Once a Shadow always a Shadow."

"What about Shadows?" Coop asked, suddenly wide-awake.

Alex reached through the little opening and grasped Coop's shoulder.

"Don't freak out," I said, pointing through the windshield.

"Kate!" Coop sat straight up and reached for the door handle, but Alex held him firmly in place. "Does she know we're here?"

He didn't take his eyes off her as I told him about my close encounter.

"No one is watching her," Coop said. "Let me see your binoculars."

"Not a good idea," Alex said. "They can't see me sitting back here, but they might catch you through the windshield."

"What should we do?" Coop whispered. I'd never seen him so anxious before.

"Nothing," Alex answered. "We're going to sit tight until they leave. Kate appears to be doing just fine. She obviously has some freedom." Alex laughed. "I wonder what she told them to explain her sudden appearance at Nehalem Bay. It had to have been a very convincing whopper, or she wouldn't be wandering around on her own."

The door to the motor home opened. Bella stepped out. She said something we couldn't hear. Kate got up from the bench and headed back toward the motor home. Bella smiled and said something. Kate returned the smile and held the door open. Bella stepped inside and Kate followed, but just before she shut the door behind her . . .

KATE WAVED

We watched them pull out of the viewpoint and head south.

"Did you get the plate number?" Alex asked.

After I spotted Kate, I had completely forgotten why I had gotten out in the first place. "Sorry, I —"

"Just kidding," Alex said. "I caught it when they pulled out."

"We better get going before they get too far ahead," Coop said.

"No hurry. We'll be able to catch them easily. And we don't want to follow too close. Is anyone else parked here?"

I looked. The car that had been there was gone. "Just us."

"Coop, why don't you wander over to that bench she was sitting on and see if she left us anything."

Coop opened the door.

"Slowly," Alex warned. "Larry has eyes everywhere. Put your hood up. Sit there for a couple of minutes before coming back."

A few minutes later Coop got back into the cab.

"Well?"

"She left us another note, but I didn't read it. I didn't want to take a chance of someone seeing me." He fished the note out of his pocket.

We are #16. Numbers on top of rigs. I
think we have 22 vehicles in this group

now. There might be another group. Lod is flying in a helicopter, watching and directing. Security very tight. They use two-ways and CBs to talk in code. You need to be careful. I'll leave notes when I can. We stop every night to rest and travel during the day. I don't know where we're going ... yet. They don't trust me ... yet. But I am safe for now. I have spoken to Lod. He thinks you are all a long way from here. Do not approach us. You will be caught. Hello to Coop. I want a dog. Love, Kate.

"A dog?" I asked.

"Kate loves dogs," Coop answered.

"We'll just keep doing what we're doing," Alex said. "Providing they stay on the coast road, I should be able to figure out where they're going to spend the night. We'll have to be very careful. They'll probably have people everywhere keeping an eye on vehicles flowing south with them."

"Guess we should dump the boat," I said.

Alex shook his head. "Not sure about that yet. There's a chance that Larry has ID'd our camper, boat or no boat. If he has, and he sees we've gotten rid of the boat, he'll want to know where and why. He'll send in spotters to find out. If they get a close look at us, we're dead. If he had been flying

174

over when Pat bumped into Kate we'd already have a spotter on us taking a closer look. We're behind enemy lines now."

"Almost forgot," Coop said. "There was something else with the note."

He pulled a paper towel out of his pocket.

Wrapped inside were three cookies.

OREGON THANKS YOU
COME BACK SOON

the sign read as we crossed the border into California.

Bella came back to replenish Bill's coffee cup.

"Short run today," she said.

"What do you mean?"

"We're staying in the redwoods tonight. It's only a little way south of here."

The redwoods. Lod's favorite place on earth. When I was a little girl, he read picture books about the redwoods to me. When I got older, he showed me photographs of the giant trees. His favorite quote about them was: "The redwoods are the last sentinels of our past, reminding us of what was and what should be again."

Our destination wasn't coincidental. If someone were to ask me, what's the one place your grandfather would most want to see again before he died, I'd say the redwoods.

Bella was acting like this was just another stop, but I knew it was more. There were a lot more direct routes from the East Coast to California than the one Lod had mapped out. He had come this way for a specific reason.

"Lod is very fond of the redwoods," I said.

"I know, just like he loves all nature. As we all do."

"I think it's more than that. The redwoods are his special place."

176

"Really," Bella said vaguely.

She was playing with me. She knew a lot more about this stop than she was letting on. It was time to get down to it.

"How long have you known Lod?" I asked.

"You know that as well as I do. We met at the university. I was twenty years old. I'm an Original. I've known him for nearly fifty years."

"And he never mentioned the redwoods?"

"In passing, maybe. Why?"

"He talked to me about the redwoods a lot when I was little. Showed me photos. Read to me about them."

"Lod reading to you. That's hard to imagine."

I shrugged. "What about Alex Dane?"

Her eyes narrowed in suspicion. "What does he have to do with the redwoods?"

"Nothing. I've just been thinking about him. Actually, Lod asked me to think about him. I'm trying to remember everything he said to me in the Deep. He was an Original. You must have known him for a long time too."

"Longer than I've known Lod, or as we called him back then, Lawrence. And it was never Alex, it was Alexander. If you called him Alex, he wouldn't acknowledge you were even there. Alexander introduced me to Lod. He was in the Weather Underground before Lod. I think he introduced Lod to most of us. We'd all been Weathermen a couple years before Lod came along."

"What happened between them?"

Bella shrugged. "They were always bumping heads. Alexander thought he was a lot smarter than Lod, and he was smart, but not nearly as smart as his older brother. There was a nasty rivalry between them. Eventually Alexander went up top. It was the best thing that ever happened to us. After he left, everything settled down."

"Did you ever wonder what happened to him?"

"Not really. He wasn't the most popular guy in the Deep. I figured he just went his own way."

"You must have been surprised when you found out he had been watching you all those years."

"Shocked would be more accurate. Along with those two boys showing up, and you taking off. But Lod had planned for all of it, almost as if he knew it was going to happen. You know how he is."

"Actually I don't know how he is." This was out of my mouth before I knew it.

"What do you mean?"

"Nothing, really."

"Tell me."

Bella wasn't about to let this go. Suddenly my tenuous status was in jeopardy. I wished I'd kept my mouth shut. Bella's intense eyes were locked on me.

"Tell me what you meant."

Lod was above reproach. Untouchable. No one ever questioned him, although I had gotten away with it a few times. I could have gone defiant with Bella at this point, but that would have undone everything I had gained with her the past couple of days. I needed Bella and Bill to find out what was really going on.

"While I was heading west, I came across some newspaper articles," I said.

"So?"

"They said that Lod had sarin gas ready to be released above, on innocent people, and explosives set to destroy the Deep and those left behind."

I didn't know how she would react to this, but I didn't expect the reaction I got. She laughed.

Long and hard.

Bill looked in the rearview mirror. "What's so funny?"

Bella told him, and he started laughing with her.

When Bella had recovered enough to speak, she said, "And you believed it?"

I nodded.

"You are very naïve," she said. "I guess that's Lod's fault in a way. He should have made you an Original like we agreed. If he had, none of this might have happened."

"What are you talking about?" I'd never been more confused in my life.

"Bombs. Sarin gas. That's not what we are about. Well, maybe in the old days it was. But we've evolved. Lod would have never hurt his own people. We couldn't take everyone with us, but he had no intention of killing those left behind. They were left on their own with enough food and water to live for decades in the Deep."

"What about the sarin gas?"

"We never had an ounce of it. Killing thousands of innocent New Yorkers would not have accomplished anything.

Even in the old days we made sure that the government buildings we blew up were empty."

"But the newspaper articles."

"Lies," Bella said. "The FBI planted that story to outrage the public, and to scare those left behind into telling them what they knew. Ridiculous, because the people we left back there have no idea what we're doing. The story is a diversion to take the public's eye off the embarrassing fact that we operated right under the FBI's noses for decades without them knowing it."

I didn't believe what she was saying, but I was certain she believed it. She and Bill didn't know about the explosives and gas. Lod hadn't told them. Just like he hadn't told them about Alex and my parents.

"You said something about me being made an Original," I said.

Bella nodded. "I voted you in. So did Bill and everyone else. But Lod wanted to wait. He said you were close but not quite ready. It turned out that he was right, as he usually is."

Even if he had made me an Original I doubt I would have acted differently after learning that he murdered my parents. "Not much chance of becoming an Original now," I said.

"You never know. It's a new world. A lot of changes coming our way."

"Like what?"

"Not even I know everything."

"If you don't know, you can't tell," I said. Yet another Pod mantra.

"Ha! And you don't need a weatherman to know which way the wind blows."

This wasn't quite true. They did need a weatherman.

Lod was the only person who knew which way the wind was blowing.

THEY'VE STOPPED

Alex poked his head into the cab. "From what I've been able to hear, I think they're in the redwoods along with several other rigs. Maybe all of them, for all I know."

"Kind of early for them to stop," I said. "It's only three o'clock. Kate said they were traveling during the day and stopping at night."

Coop had Kate's note out. Again. He must have taken it out of his pocket fifty times since he had found it. He had to have memorized the hundred words by now.

"Something's changed," Alex said. "Something's up. Have you seen the helicopter?"

I hadn't, and there wasn't a cloud in the sky. It was a perfect day for flying.

"Not that easy to spot a helicopter from the cab of a truck," Coop pointed out.

"What do you want to do?" I asked.

"We'll go to Arcata," Alex said. "It's just south of where they are. There's an airport eight miles north of the city."

"That's pretty specific," Coop said. "Sounds like you know the area."

I thought Alex was going to say it was one of the places he had traveled to through books, but he didn't.

"I know it well," he said. "I went to Humboldt State University. I got accepted at Stanford like Larry, but my parents didn't have enough money for both of us go to Stanford at the same time. In our family, it was always about Larry. I got stuck in Arcata. I transferred to Berkeley for my postgraduate work."

"What did you major in?" Coop asked.

"Computer science."

"Like Larry?"

"Yeah, like Larry. But he got the computer science bug from me. Computer science was one of his later degrees, and he wasn't very good at it."

"I guess that changed when he got into the Deep," Coop said.

"A chimpanzee could use the systems they have today," Alex said.

"You set up a pretty decent surveillance system to keep track of the Pod," I said.

"Child's play," Alex scoffed. "I got most of the hardware I used in the library out of Dumpsters. Obsolete junk that nobody wanted. If I'd been able to get inside the Originals' room and hack their system I'd be able to tell if Larry had brushed his teeth this morning. It's all about the software, but you have to have access to the hardware to run it."

"So did Larry ever drive up from Stanford to visit you?" Coop asked.

"Almost every weekend. My parents bought him a brand-new Volkswagen van, but he rarely stayed with me at my flophouse. He had this big thing for the redwoods. He'd go out among the giant trees to commune with them, usually with a girl to keep him company. Even then he needed an adoring audience to preach to. What are you getting at?"

"So he knows this area pretty well," Coop said.

"I guess. I never went into the redwoods with him. I was busy in the computer lab working, and the few times I offered to go with him he turned me down, claiming three's a crowd."

"Don't you think it's interesting that after thousands of miles of driving and flying he's ended up in what is obviously one of his favorite places on earth?"

Alex stared at Coop for a long time, then shook his head. "The redwoods can't be his final destination. It's one of the least populated areas on the west coast of California. Whatever he has in mind has to do with hurting people. Politicians and businesspeople in particular. The redwoods are state and federally owned. This isn't the tourist season. Nobody's here. And he'd never do anything to jeopardize his beloved trees."

I HAD FALLEN ASLEEP

I felt someone shaking my shoulder, gently, saying my name. I thought it was Bill. I opened my eyes. It was Lod.

I sat up.

Lod was sitting on the edge of the sofa.

There was light coming through the windows. I looked out onto hundreds of giant trees.

"Redwoods," Lod said quietly.

Bella and Bill weren't there. This surprised me almost as much as Lod's unexpected appearance. I couldn't believe I had slept right through our arrival, which was usually a noisy process, with backup alarms, hydraulic leveling feet being deployed, and Bill and Bella shouting parking suggestions at each other.

"How long was I asleep?"

"I have no idea." Lod looked at his watch. "It's a little after three."

"Where are Bella and Bill?"

"Bill's helping some of the others set up their rigs. Bella is out checking on security. Want to go for a walk?"

Lod seemed a lot more relaxed than he had been the night before. He was almost cheerful, which made me a little suspicious, but my only choice was to agree.

"Sure," I said.

"Let me see your ankle."

I put my foot on the sofa. He took the small tool out of his pocket and removed the bracelet, which was a huge relief.

"I took Bella's off too. I'll put them back on when we get back."

"That's not necessary. I'm not going anywhere."

"I will decide what's necessary. You're lucky you're still alive."

I was hit by a bolt of anger, but I held it back.

"I know," I said quietly, with as much meekness as I could manage.

When I stepped outside, my anger was whisked away by the sight of the giant redwoods. The photos I had seen, and Lod's descriptions of them, hadn't prepared me for the real thing. I was awestruck. Speechless. I'd seen a lot of new things since I'd left the Deep. In fact, almost everything had been new. Beautiful rivers, the Great Plains, the Rocky Mountains, the Pacific Ocean . . . but none had moved me as much as these giant, prehistoric trees. It was as if we had entered a different dimension, another world, where we were insignificant, the smallest beings on a newly discovered planet.

"Magnificent, aren't they?" Lod said.

Unwillingly, I looked away from the trees. Lod was smiling, a rare expression for him, even in the Deep. It made him look ten years younger.

"They are unbelievable," I said, and I meant it.

Lod laughed. Another shock. I hadn't heard him laugh in

months. "You look pretty much like I must have looked when I first saw these trees fifty years ago."

I glanced around the campgrounds. Several people were outside their rigs setting up camp chairs and starting fires in the fire pits like real campers. It seemed that Lod wasn't the only one in a good mood.

"There's a trail at the end of the road."

We started to walk. People watched us as we passed their campsites. Even with their disguises they were recognizable. I'd known them my entire life.

"Have you been here before?" I asked.

"Dozens of times."

"Did you ever think you'd get back here?"

"I certainly planned to get back, but of course you never know. Did you think more about Alex last night?"

"I was up most of the night thinking about him, racking my brain, trying to remember if there was anything he said, or did, that I forgot."

"And?"

I shook my head. "Nothing."

Lod frowned.

"But I'll keep thinking about it."

"Do that."

We reached the trailhead.

"There's a tree down the trail that I was particularly fond of. I've always wanted to show it to you."

I caught a movement to my left and saw LaNae just before she disappeared behind a tree. She had always been a lousy Shadow. I looked to my right. Carl was fifty feet away, paralleling our route, not even bothering to hide himself. Guards rarely tried to hide themselves. Their job was to intimidate. To do that, they had to be seen. I guess he was off the graveyard shift. He and LaNae were working security. Lod rarely went anywhere without someone watching his back, although I was surprised he needed it for a walk in the woods with his granddaughter, even if she was an alleged traitor. LaNae flitted to the next tree clumsily in clear view.

"She's not very subtle, but she has her uses," Lod said.

"I have no idea why you made her a Shadow. She should have been a Guard."

"I made her a Shadow because she wanted to be a Shadow. LaNae's best attribute is her loyalty, which I value above all else."

This, of course, was a personal dig at me, but I let it go. This was not the time. Actually, it was never the time to get into it with Lod. I'd never been on a walk with him. All the times we had been above in New York didn't count because I had been in front of him or behind him, acting as his Shadow.

It was cool out. Shafts of misty sunlight shot down from the tops of the trees to the ground. The trail was soft from the recent rain, blanketed with sweet-smelling needles.

"*Sequoia sempervirens*," Lod said.

The Latin name for the redwood. Lod had taught me the name when I was little.

"Forever living," I said.

"You remembered," he said. "Some of the redwoods here are a thousand years old. That's not forever, but it's a very long time. Much longer than I have."

Lod was close to seventy now, but he was still pretty fit. As far as I knew he didn't have any life-threatening diseases. The Deep was a healthy place to live. We sometimes caught colds, and when I was little the flu went through the group, but other than that it was a disease-free zone. We had a physician and a dentist in the Deep. I hadn't seen them above, but I was sure they were in one of the rigs. Lod wouldn't have left them behind.

"Are you okay?" I asked.

"You mean my health?"

"Yes."

"As far as I know, it's fine. I'm old. So are most of the Originals. We're not redwoods. We don't have that many years left. You pushed my plans up by a few months, which made little difference to me personally because everything was already in place. But you did do great harm to yourself."

I didn't say anything.

"You don't know what I'm talking about, do you?" he said.

I didn't want to repeat my lies about my intentions being good, and not knowing that Coop and Pat were going to report the Pod to the FBI. My intention was to bring Lod down. I helped Coop and Pat put together the Beneath report, which had saved a lot of lives.

"I guess I don't," I finally answered.

"By helping those boys, by not reporting Alex, you ruined your future. I was on the verge of making you an Original. I wanted you to take my place one day. The reason I was so hard on you in the Deep was to toughen you up for the job."

I stopped walking. I knew about the Original promotion from Bella, but I couldn't let Lod know this, or she would get in trouble for speaking out of turn. I still needed Bella on my side. I didn't think she knew about Lod's long-range plan of having me take his place. She was a good ten years younger than Lod. I suspect she, and several other Originals, saw themselves inheriting Lod's crown.

"It would have been nice to know this before I met those two boys," I said.

"Would it have made any difference?"

"Yes," I lied.

It wouldn't have made the slightest difference.

"I'm not planning on dying anytime soon," Lod said. "It will take a long time, but there might be a chance for you to redeem yourself, to gain back the Pod's trust, perhaps even take my place. It all depends on how you conduct yourself from this moment on."

"I doubt I'd ever be able to take your place," I said. "But I would like to gain the Pod's trust again."

"Good." Lod put his head back and looked at the tops of the tall redwoods. When he looked back down he was smiling again. "I think you've gained Bella's trust, and Bill's, and surprisingly, maybe Carl's. He said he talked to you the other night and that you felt remorse over the death of his dog."

I doubted Carl used the word *remorse*. I doubted Carl knew what the word *remorse* meant.

"I did," I said.

I guessed now was the time to spill my guts to Lod, which I suppose is what prodigal granddaughters did in these circumstances. He had obviously been grilling everyone about everything I had said to them. I needed to repeat some of these things so he didn't think I was talking behind his back.

"I asked Bella about the explosives and gas left in the Deep."

"What did she say?"

"She said that the FBI lied about the explosives."

"Of course they did. They always try to make the people they are after worse than they are, so that when they catch them the FBI looks more heroic."

"You did blow up buildings in the old days."

"Buildings. But not people. There was some collateral damage, but it was unintentional. We don't target innocent people. We never have and we never will."

What about my parents? I thought. *What about Alex? What about Coop and Pat?*

"I know what you're thinking," he said.

I hoped that wasn't the case.

"You're wondering about all those people I sent to the mush room. The people who tried to leave the Deep, the people who tried to defy me over the years and threatened to destroy us. I'll be honest, some of those people did die. I ordered their deaths. If I hadn't, we would have lost everything. I'd be rotting in a jail cell instead of walking in the redwoods. You would have been put into the foster care system with complete strangers raising you. Do you think you could order someone's death? Or kill someone yourself?"

I'd already demonstrated that I couldn't, or wouldn't, do this in the Deep. I had told him that I had pushed Coop into the River Styx, which he later learned was a lie.

"I'm not sure," I said.

"Well, if you ever take my place, those are the kind of decisions you're going to have to make. There are always power struggles within a group. For the good of the group, the perpetrators need to be put in their places. Sometimes there is only one way to do this. If you don't do it the group will be destroyed. You do what is necessary and move forward without looking back, without regret. I want to shake things up. I want to change things, but it won't be by setting off bombs, or poisoning people I don't know. If people die, it will be by their own hands."

"What do you mean?"

"I mean all of us are living on borrowed time. There are too many people on earth. We are like locusts. We are devouring the earth, depleting it faster than she can regenerate herself. If we don't stop what we're doing, the planet will be nothing but a dried-up empty husk floating in space, uninhabitable, a dead planet." He gestured wildly at the treetops. I'd never seen him speak so passionately before. "These trees will be gone. Everything, and everybody, will be gone. When we first settled into the Deep, I thought the world as we knew it would end in a series of nuclear explosions. I was wrong. We're going to kill the earth by eating it up until there is nothing left. The governments around the world lack the moral courage to do anything about it. All anyone cares about anymore is making themselves comfortable. Life is brutal. Hard decisions have to be made. We haven't surfaced to kill people. We've come up top to save what we have left and level the playing field."

I'd heard this before, from Lod and the other Originals, but not with such fervency. We rounded a corner in the trail. Up ahead about two hundred feet was a bench made out of a downed redwood. Three people were sitting on the bench. They had their hoods pulled over their heads against the cold. When we reached them, they pulled their hoods off and smiled at me.

Bob Jonas. Susan Stronach. Carol Higgins.

All of them had been sent to the mush room in the past ten years at different times for various infractions. Susan and Carol had been promoted to Originals. Three months after their promotion Lod had sent them to the mush room for undermining his authority and trying to take his place. Bob Jonas was a computer expert recruited from up top after a two-year evaluation. Everyone in the Deep loved him. He hadn't been promoted to the Originals, but he'd been well on his way when he violated security protocols with the computers inside the Originals' private room, then tried to run.

I couldn't believe they were still alive. I couldn't believe they were sitting among the redwoods smiling at me.

"Long time no see, Kate," Bob said.

I looked at Lod. "You took the people from the mush room with you?"

Bob, Susan, and Carol all laughed.

"The mush room is a myth," Lod said. "A fabrication. It never existed outside of the minds of those who were afraid of going there. We invented it to explain where people went when they left the Deep."

"My parents?" I asked. I couldn't help myself. If Bob and Susan and Carol were alive, perhaps . . .

Lod's expression tightened and he shook his head. "No. They starved while making their way to the top. They took a wrong turn. It was lucky they hadn't taken you with them. You know this."

I nodded, trying not to show my disappointment and my anger over what I really knew about their deaths.

Lod quickly changed the subject, as he always did when my parents' death came up, which was seldom. People knew not to ask him about it.

"I can't remember who came up with the idea of the mush room," he said. "It might have been Bella. But it has served us well over the years. Without it, we would not have been able to explain people's long absences without giving away their missions. We invented grave infractions for them, sent them to the mythical room, and no one ever asked about them again. Not only was the terrible room a great cover, it also reinforced discipline in the Deep."

"What missions?" I asked.

"The vehicles we used to get out here for one. We've been gathering them for years from all over the US. They were stored in a warehouse in New Jersey. We had to have people to buy them, drive them to New Jersey, keep the registrations current, and maintain them. This took three people working full time. All of them were former members of the Pod supposedly gone bad."

I looked at Bob, Susan, and Carol.

"Not me," Bob said. "I'm no mechanic."

"I'm a terrible driver," Carol added.

"That's not to say that everyone that we sent to the mythical mush room was on a mission," Lod said. "We talked about that. Hard decisions had to be made."

Meaning that those not sent out on missions were murdered.

"What about the helicopter? Did you send Pod members up top to learn how to fly?"

Lod shook his head. "Hired help. Paid them off. We won't be needing air cover anymore."

"Why?"

"Because we're almost there."

"Where?"

Lod smiled. "An upgrade." He looked at Bob.

"The Deep Two Point Zero," Bob said.

NOT A PEEP OUT OF 'EM

Alex said.

We were a few miles north of Crescent City, California.

"The sound of silence," Alex continued. "Radio silence that is. They're up to something. I can feel it."

I pointed at a sign for the Jedediah Smith Redwood State Park campground.

"Want me to take it?"

"No," Alex said. "Drive on. There's a chance that they all sped ahead. We might be out of radio range. We can always come back if we don't pick up a signal south of the redwoods. And there are other state parks up ahead with plenty of redwoods in them."

Coop had fallen back asleep, Kate's note still clutched in his hand. It was starting to get dark, which meant that he would be waking up soon. He had taken only one bite out of his cookie. It was sitting on the dashboard. I was tempted to grab it. We passed the turnoff for the Jedediah Smith campground.

"Did you see that?" Alex asked.

"The exit?"

"No, the camper parked on the side of the road next to the exit for the park, and the SUV parked next to it."

"I didn't notice."

"I've seen the SUV before."

I'd seen fifty just like it before.

"I couldn't see inside the camper cab clearly," he continued. "But I think there are two guys sitting in the front seat. One guy in the SUV."

"So?"

"So the SUV is one of the vehicles that picked Larry up from the airport in Newport."

"You're sure?"

"Positive. The nearest airport is in Crescent City. I don't think they'd be there unless Larry was already here."

"You mean in the park?"

"Not necessarily. But he's around here somewhere. They might be parked there watching his back trail. See who's driving south."

"What do you want me to do?"

"Keep going. We'll go to the Crescent City airport. See if his helicopter is there."

"Isn't that a little risky?"

"Of course it's risky. There's the exit."

I took the exit for the Del Norte County Regional Airport. Alex had me drive right past it and park at the Point Saint George beach trails on the west side of the airport.

"I'll get out and see if I can spot Larry's helicopter parked on the tarmac," Alex said. "Let me know if you hear anything on the radio."

I watched him jump a guardrail and limp east across grass-covered sand dunes at a pretty good pace, which surprised me. Until that moment, he had moved like the old man he was.

Coop awoke. Head up. Eyes alert. Like always. He was never groggy. He was either awake or asleep. No in-between. The first thing he did was grab the cookie on the dashboard and take another tiny bite out of it.

I was disappointed.

He asked me what was going on.

I pointed at Alex, who was still moving rapidly across the grassy sand dunes, getting smaller and smaller with every step.

"Who's that?" Coop asked.

"Alex."

"You're kidding." He rolled his window down for a better look.

I told him what Alex was up to.

"He's moving so fast!"

"I know."

Alex disappeared behind a dune.

"What's the rush?"

"The fact that he hasn't heard a word out of them in over an hour. I think."

Coop finished his cookie, slowly, as he watched the dunes.

"What?" I asked.

"Alex," Coop answered.

I'd thought a lot about our conversation about Alex on the beach the night before. Alex was a little strange, but I trusted him. The only thing that bothered me about him was that something about him bothered Coop.

"We can still contact the FBI," I said.

"I already did," Coop said.

"What?" I shouted. "When?"

"This morning when you were asleep in the boat."

"What did they say?"

"Nothing. It was a one-way conversation. I sent Agent Ryan a postcard."

"A postcard," I said, stunned. "Why didn't you just call her?"

"I didn't see a phone booth, but I wasn't really looking. They're kind of hard to find these days."

Alex appeared from behind the dune, moving toward us, a little slower than when he had left, but steadily.

"What did you say on the postcard? 'Dear Tia, we're on the Oregon coast having a blast. Wish you were here.'"

Coop laughed.

Alex was two hundred yards away.

"I told her what was going on as best I could in the little space postcards have. The guy at the postal store said he thought it would get to her tomorrow morning if I put the postcard in an express envelope."

Only Coop would think to put a fifty-cent postcard into a twenty-dollar express envelope. But he had a reason. He always had a reason for the weird things he did.

"Why?" I asked.

Alex was one hundred and fifty yards away.

"I didn't want to tell her too fast," Coop said. "But not too slow either. I don't think we're in any immediate danger. Kate seems to be doing okay. She's baking cookies."

I didn't necessarily agree, but I didn't interrupt him. I was trying to listen to Coop like he listened to other people. *Listen is an anagram of silent.*

"I contacted Agent Ryan with the postcard because I don't think we need her yet," he continued. "I told her that we were with Alex, and that Kate was with the Pod. I said that it was probably too late to stop whatever Lod was up to. I listed all the towns and parks we had been to. I told her that the Pod were driving motor homes and that Lod was watching the caravan from a small helicopter."

Only Coop could have gotten all this onto a small postcard. When he wrote something down, which was rare, he printed his letters and words with microscopic precision.

"Once she gets the postcard she'll catch up to us pretty quickly," Coop continued. "If we get into a jam before she shows up we can always call her. Pay phones are probably out, but the next time we stop at a store you might want to pick up one of those prepaid cell phones. Just make sure Alex doesn't find out about it."

Alex stopped a hundred yards away from our camper, hands on his knees, catching his breath.

"Okay," Coop said. "Now for the weird part . . ."

As if what he had just told me wasn't weird enough. I braced myself.

"Remember how I told you I feel I've been heading into the Deep my entire life, but I didn't know it until I finally got there . . . ?"

I knew this but didn't understand it. At all.

"Well, I think I got my first glimpse of it right here."

I had to break my silence. I couldn't help myself. "You've been at the Point Saint George beach trails?"

"No. But it was near here. Somewhere near the redwoods. I was hitchhiking north. Pouring down rain. One o'clock in the morning. Standing on the shoulder wearing a rain poncho. A car was coming toward me. It slowed down as it passed. I thought it was going to stop, but it didn't. As soon as the headlights shined in my eyes, it sped up, wheels screeching on the wet asphalt. I watched the red taillights until they disappeared into the night. You know how it is with me. When people see me they stop. They approach me. Hitchhiking for me has always been faster than me driving a car. Not that I know how to drive."

"I wish you did know how to drive."

"No chance of that, Meatloaf. But back to the car that sped away. Sometimes I'd have two or three cars stop at the same time to give me a lift. But not this car. It was like it wanted to get away from me. I knew at that moment that something bad was going on in the area, something that needed my attention, something I should stick around for, something I should look into."

"But you didn't," I said.

Alex was fifty yards away.

"No. Within a minute another car came by and picked me up. In my relief at getting out of the rain and cold, I forgot all about the car that sped by. I didn't remember it until we passed through Brookings, which is where the guy who picked me up dropped me off."

Alex was twenty-five yards away.

"You were asleep when we passed through Brookings," I said.

"I was dozing in that dreamlike state between sleeping and waking."

He took the keys out of the ignition.

"You need to get Alex to drive," he said hurriedly. "Tell him you're too tired to go another mile."

"Why?"

"His backpack. It weighs a ton. There's a lot more in it than clothes. We need to know what he's hauling around. One of us needs to get into the back and check it out. Act like you're out of it, Meatloaf, which shouldn't be too hard to do."

I didn't have time to laugh. Alex was at Coop's window.

"His helicopter wasn't there," Alex said. "At least that I could see. We'll head down to the Arcata airport and see if it's parked there."

"You'll have to drive. Pat's out of it."

I tried to look out of it.

"It's not very far," Alex said.

"I can't," I said. "It wouldn't be safe. I just need a little sleep. An hour or so."

"I'll stay in the front seat and keep you company," Coop said.

Alex took the keys. "Fine. Let's go."

BARBECUE SMOKE

was everywhere, so pungent it masked the sweet smell of the damp redwoods. There were more campers than there had been before our little walk. Every campsite on both sides of the road was occupied, and everyone was outside manning a grill, cooking bratwurst, burgers, corn on the cob, skewered shrimp, and vegetables. The fine mist and the cool air didn't seem to bother any of them in the least.

Originals and their children, their grandchildren, and in some cases, their great-grandchildren. What did the kids think of this? Especially the young kids who knew nothing but the Deep because they had never been above? What did they think of the long trip west? The cities, the broad rivers, the mountains, the Pacific Ocean, and now the giant redwoods. I had been stunned by all of these sights. But I knew beforehand they existed. I had read about them in the books Alex had given to me over the years.

All the men were wearing these little vests and baseball caps adorned with dozens of buttons.

"What is all this?"

"An annual reunion of a group of Vietnam vets," Lod answered. "This many rigs showing up here in the dead of winter would be very suspicious without a cover story. We even have a website. Nobody bothers vets, especially old vets."

Typical Lod. Everything covered. Nothing left to chance.

People glanced at us as we walked by, but no one talked to us as we strolled down the center of the road past them, which I was sure was exactly what they had been instructed to do.

LaNae was still awkwardly weaving through the redwoods to our right, and Carl was walking on our left like a Sasquatch.

"Where did they learn to barbecue?" I asked. As far as I knew, Lod was the only Pod member who had owned a grill. I remember the day he had gotten it. I was around ten years old at the time. He was very proud of it. He would "grill out," as he called it, a couple of times a week.

"Each rig was equipped with a grill and a grilling manual," he answered. "Required reading. And they were happy to do it. When I got that old grill of mine in the Deep everybody wanted one. We couldn't allow it. Too much smoke for us to vent. It would have set off every fire alarm we had."

I stopped walking.

"What?" Lod asked.

"You got the grill because you knew that one day you would be here grilling with everybody from the Deep."

"So?"

"That was ten years ago."

"Our plans have been in place longer than ten years, but yes, that's why I got the grill." He smiled. "Which I recall you complaining about cleaning every time I asked you to do it."

I had complained, and I returned the smile, but my mind was on the fact that all this, from the buttons on the vests to the brats sizzling on the grills, had been planned out years ago, maybe even before I was born.

I started walking again. So many questions, but to ask Lod anything more would create suspicion and show doubt. He expected blind obedience and that's what I was going to give him.

Like all the others, Bella and Bill were outside their camper. Bill was manning the grill. Bella had spread a red checkered tablecloth on a picnic table and was setting it with utensils. In the center of the tablecloth was a pitcher of lemonade. Like all the other men, Bill had on a button-covered war veteran's vest and cap. A couple Originals had served in the Vietnam War, but not Bill. He had been an antiwar leader, back in the day, and had served jail time for protesting.

"Are you going to stay for dinner?" Bella asked Lod.

"Sorry. I have things to do." He took a piece of paper out of his pocket. "Here are your directions. We'll do it in order. Radio silence. After you memorize it, burn it. No trail." He nodded at the motor home parked in the campsite next to us. "When fifteen takes off, wait fifteen minutes, then go. The roads are marked. The tail car will pick up all the marks after everyone passes through."

"What's the mark?" Bella asked.

Lod smiled. "A rain cloud with lightning bolts."

He pulled the little tool out of his pocket. Bella and I put our feet up on the bench.

"Forget it," he said, putting the tool back in his pocket. "Just stay in your campsite. No wandering around. We'll call it a test."

It wasn't much of a test. There were Guards everywhere. I was sure he had passed the word to keep an eye on me. I wasn't going anywhere.

Before leaving he checked the burgers on the grill.

"These are overdone," he said.

IT WAS A LITTLE CLAUSTROPHOBIC

in the back of the camper, which didn't make sense. The cab was a lot more confined. Maybe the three windows in the cab had tricked my claustrophobia.

"Unplug the headphones so I can hear the radio traffic," Alex shouted from the front seat.

"Done."

The radio was silent.

The ride in back was not nearly as comfortable as it was up front. It was like a rattling earthquake. I sat on the bench at the tiny dinette table. Alex had bungee-corded the radio equipment to it so it wouldn't fall off. The sink was filled with dirty dishes and empty cans. A bad smell was coming out of the tiny toilet room.

I couldn't see Alex's backpack from where I was sitting, and I could see everything except . . .

I looked up.

Above me, to my right, was the slot for the bed over the cab. I wasn't looking forward to crawling into it, but it was the only place Alex's pack could be, and it was the best place to rifle through his pack because he couldn't look through the rearview mirror and see what I was doing.

"Ten minutes to Arcata?" Coop asked, loud enough for me to hear.

"Less to the airport," Alex answered. "It's north of town, right next to Clam Beach."

I needed to slip into the dark clamshell above the cab.

Now.

I boosted myself into the slit, trying not to think about it. As soon as I got up there I turned on my flashlight. Light always helped. It smelled like Alex. Old and musty, with a tinge of stale pipe tobacco. He had one of the sleeping bags we had bought rolled out. His backpack was at the open end of the bag. He must have been using it as a pillow, which couldn't have been too comfortable.

I started to sweat.

Five or six minutes to the Arcata airport. I knew I wouldn't last three minutes up there.

Alex hit a bump in the road. My entire body flew up into the air like I was on a trampoline. The back of my head slammed against the roof. There wasn't time to take the pack below, search it, and put it back. And I didn't want to climb back up there. Coop should have volunteered for this duty. He loved places like this.

I put the flashlight in my mouth and unzipped the pack. In the main compartment were clothes, toiletries, and a laptop computer.

Alex made us toss our computers but had kept a laptop for himself?

His laptop wasn't sleek and minimal like ours had been. It was heavy-duty PC that would break your foot if you dropped it. It looked like it was brand-new, and had to weigh at least fifteen pounds. On the side of the laptop was a small antenna that flipped up. I opened the cover. The screen came to life instantly, asking for a security code. I wasn't about to try it. There wasn't time and I didn't want Alex to know that I had tampered with it. What I wanted to know was what the antenna did. It wasn't hard to figure out. In the upper-right corner of the screen was a blank Wi-Fi icon.

I closed the screen and looked at the opposite side from the antenna. It had a DVD drive. We didn't need to stop and get a portable DVD player. He had a DVD drive in his pack. He didn't want us to know that he had the laptop.

Why?

I unzipped an outside pocket. Inside was a cell phone, or at least what looked like a cell phone. It was a little bigger than a normal cell phone, clunky-looking, with a thick antenna sticking out of the top. At first I thought maybe he had picked it out of a Dumpster. He said that he had put together his surveillance system in the Deep with discarded junk. But this phone wasn't junk. There wasn't a scratch on it. It looked as new as the laptop in the pack. The peel-off screen protector was still in place. I turned it over and shined the light on the tiny words on the back.

It wasn't a cell phone. It was a satellite phone.

I put the laptop back where I had found it. Coop was right. Alex was keeping things from us. I wanted to keep something from him, and we might need a phone. I shoved the phone into my pocket.

I felt the camper slow and veer to the right. We were leaving the highway.

Quickly I unzipped another pocket.

More surprises.

A revolver. Where had he picked this up?

I fumbled the cylinder open. It was fully loaded. I dumped the bullets out and put them in my other pocket, next to my digital recorder. If Alex wanted to shoot someone, he was going to have to ask me for the ammo.

The last pocket looked like it was empty, but I checked it anyway just to make sure. At the very bottom was a small aluminum container the size of a pack of gum. It took me a second to figure out how to open it. Inside, wrapped in foam to cushion it, was something that looked like a USB flash drive. It was obviously important or he wouldn't have packaged it so carefully and put it by itself.

The camper slowed to a crawl.

I put the aluminum box into the pocket with the six bullets and the recorder.

Alex was obviously going to figure out that things were missing. I would return his stuff as soon as he told us how he was going to use it.

The camper came to a stop. ·

I backed out of the tight space and lowered myself down, relieved to be out of there, and pleased with how I had handled it. I might still have my claustrophobia, but it had gotten better.

I looked through the opening to the front seat. Alex was behind the wheel peering through a pair of binoculars.

"I told you that you wouldn't get much sleep," he said.

I nodded at Coop. He nodded back.

"Aren't you going to get out and look?" I was eager to tell Coop what I had found.

"No point," Alex answered, still looking through the binoculars. "The private airplanes and helicopters are tied down right here, and I don't see Larry's. He's either still up in the air, or he's landed somewhere else. We'll head into Arcata."

"What's in Arcata?" Coop asked.

"Humboldt State University. I need to check something out."

"I can drive," I said.

"I got it," Alex said, and put the camper into gear.

THE BURGERS *WERE* OVERDONE

I'd taken only a couple bites out of mine. It tasted like a rawhide bone. Not that I've ever eaten one. Although I did taste one once because my favorite dog in the Deep, Enji, absolutely loved them. No amount of ketchup and mustard could soften it. Bill had a lot to learn about grilling. I wondered if the other "vets" had botched their meals.

The sun had gone down, and with it the clouds and mist had disappeared.

A gas lantern hissed on the table, lighting our mostly uneaten feast. Bella and Bill had both memorized the directions and burned the slip of paper to ashes on the grill. We'd barely spoken since Lod had brought me back. The reason for this was that LaNae and Carl had lingered within hearing distance for at least an hour after Lod had left. They were clearly no longer running clumsy security for Lod. They were watching me.

"I think they've gone," Bella whispered.

"Ten minutes ago," I said. "I think I can still hear them crashing through the woods."

Bill laughed.

"What happened on your walk?" Bella asked.

Bella was just like every other Original. When Lod wasn't around, they constantly pumped people who might know something they didn't know. I had been pumped for information since I could talk. I had learned long ago what to say and what to hold back. When I was little, I think Lod sometimes leaked information to me that he thought I would pass on.

"I saw Bob, Susan, and Carol," I said.

If this was a surprise to them, they didn't show it.

"How were they?" Bill asked.

"They looked pretty good, considering I thought they were dead."

"That was one of our better-kept secrets," Bella said. "Did Lod explain?"

"He did. And it made sense. But I was still shocked to see them."

"What did they say?" Bill asked.

"Not much. I think Lod took me there to see them, not to talk to them. Bob said something about an upgrade. The Deep Two Point Zero."

"So that's what they are calling it," Bill said. "Bob was always a funny guy."

"Are you saying you didn't know about this?" I asked. "I thought you were *they*."

"We are," Bella said. "But we don't know everything."

"Like the location," Bill said. "No one here knew where it was until Lod gave us the directions. It was a precaution. If someone got picked up or decided to defect, they wouldn't be able to tell the feds anything."

"I doubt anyone here would defect," I said.

"You never know," Bella said. "We thought you defected."

"Lod still thinks I defected."

"Time will heal that," Bill said.

"What else did Lod say on your walk?" Bella prodded.

I told them, skipping the part about me, perhaps, taking his place someday. When I finished, I could tell by their expressions I hadn't told them anything they didn't already know.

"It's getting cold," Bill said. "I guess we should start packing up."

"How about starting a fire instead," Bella said. "I haven't sat next to a campfire since I was a little girl. We're number sixteen. We have several hours before we leave."

I helped Bella put wood into the fire pit while Bill cleared the picnic table. It might have been decades since Bella had built a campfire, but she hadn't forgotten how to do it. After she had the paper, kindling, and logs stacked it took only one match to ignite it.

Bill brought out folding chairs and blankets. We sat with our feet toward the crackling flames, blankets on our laps, watching cinders dance up into the redwoods. I wanted to know what they knew about the place we were going to, but of course I couldn't ask them directly. I needed to get them to talk about it.

"I hope they have dogs wherever we're going," I said. "I miss my dogs."

"Everyone misses their dogs," Bella said. "Of all the things we left behind, that's the one regret people talk about the most."

"We won't need dogs where we're going," Bill said. "No

complicated labyrinth to find our way through, no homeless people living next to us, no city above, no reason to go up top. It's a closed system."

Maybe it was because they were sitting in the redwoods next to a warm fire. Maybe it was because we were almost at our final destination. But Bella and Bill were at ease, as relaxed as I'd ever seen them. I felt I could ask them some direct questions.

"You mean once we go down we're not coming back up?" I asked.

"Not necessarily," Bella said. "It means that we don't *have* to come up unless we want to, or need to. It's been operating perfectly for nearly three years now without a glitch."

"Have you seen it?"

"Bits and pieces of it on streaming video," said Bill, "which is not like seeing it in person, but I've seen enough to give me an idea what it will be like. It's similar to the Deep in New York. The government got a lot right in the fifties when they built that secret nuclear shelter, but they didn't have the technologies we have today. We had to retrofit technology as it became available, which was hard to do in a concrete underground structure. We made crude fixes, and they worked after a fashion, but this facility is different. It was built from scratch with everything we learned when we lived under the city."

"All the vulnerabilities of our old space, and there were many, have been engineered out of the new facility," Bella said.

"It's like a spaceship that isn't going anywhere, but nobody can get to it," Bill added.

"We're the core group, but there are already a lot of people there," Bella said. "We've been recruiting and placing people in the new facility for years."

"But who ran it?" I asked. "Who was in charge?"

"Lod," Bill said. "And of course some Originals. Lod used video conferencing and emails, just like he ran Cloud's Mushrooms for all those years."

"We thought about coming out west with the first wave," Bella said. "But decided that we'd be more useful in New York."

"Not sure that was the right call," Bill said. "But someone had to stay in the old place while the new place was being built."

A motor home started up. We listened as it pulled out of its campsite.

"What are we going to do in the new place?" I asked.

Bella glanced at Bill, and that's all it took to shut the conversation down.

"What we always do," Bella said. "Live our lives, bide our time, wait."

"Providing you live," Lod said from behind us.

I nearly fell out of my chair. We all stood and faced him.

Carl was standing on his right, LaNae on his left. She was smiling, but not in a friendly way.

"Didn't hear you walk up," Bill said nervously.

"I know," Lod said. "But I heard you spilling your guts to Kate."

"I didn't tell her anything she didn't already know."

Lod laughed. "Yes, you did. And Kate knows more than she's saying. Isn't that right, Kate?"

I eyed the shadowy redwoods for a potential escape route. Carl wouldn't be able to catch me, but I wasn't certain about LaNae. She was clumsy but fast. And where would I go?

"I don't know what you're talking about," I said.

"Beneath," Lod said.

"What do you mean?"

He took a large envelope out from behind his back. "All of you sit back down."

We sat.

He stepped closer to the fire and faced us. He pulled a sheath of paper out of the envelope.

"This," he said.

"What is it?" I asked.

"You know exactly what it is. You and those two boys gave it to the FBI. This is a copy of the original dossier. It's called 'Beneath.'"

I shook my head. "I don't —"

"Stop, Kate. It's over. I read every word. It arrived from one of my couriers while we were out for our little walk. We don't use the mail, or the Internet, or cells. So it took a while to get to me, but it came just in time."

He flung the dossier at me. It bounced off my chest and landed at my feet. I picked it up with shaking hands.

CLASSIFIED

BENEATH BY PAT AND COOP O'TOOLE

THE LIBRARY

isn't far from here," Alex said.

He pulled the camper into a parking lot across from Humboldt State University, taking up three parking spots with the boat and rig.

I was happy to get out of the back and eager to tell Coop about my find.

But it wasn't to be. Not yet anyway.

Coop and Alex climbed out of the cab.

I heard a familiar tapping sound.

"You had tap shoes in your pack?"

"Behind the seat," Coop said. "I've wanted to put them on all day. My feet hurt after my long walk on the beach last night. This is an old pair that I left in LA. Broken in. They feel great."

He danced a couple of steps.

"Coop and I can wait here for you," I said.

"Let's stick together," Alex said. "We're getting close to them. Safer if we're in a group."

"What do we need in the library?" Coop asked, still tapping, getting happier with each click on the asphalt.

"We need to look up something on their computers."

I pointed to the coffee shop across the street from the parking lot. "I bet they have free Wi-Fi."

"I'm sure they do," Alex said. "But it won't do us any good without a computer."

How about we fire up the massive laptop in your pack? I thought.

"I could use a walk," Coop said, giving us another little tap.

"Even if we had a computer," Alex continued. "Library computers are safer, more anonymous."

He started walking. Coop and I followed, but not far enough behind to have a private conversation.

It was cold but clear. The moon was full and bright. Students carrying small backpacks walked the paths with their earbuds in, tapping on their smartphones. None of them glanced up to look at us. Coop was right. No one was paying attention to where they were going or who they were with. They had eyes and ears only for their phones. Coop picked up his pace and we caught up with Alex.

Tap . . . tap . . . tap . . .

"Brings back memories," Alex said.

"I thought you didn't like it here," Coop said.

"I didn't say that. I said that my parents sent me here because they couldn't afford to send me to Stanford."

"Because they spent their money on Larry," Coop said.

Alex frowned. "That's right."

It almost seemed like Coop was trying to get under Alex's skin, but he didn't have time to push him any further because we had arrived at the library.

"We can wait out front," I said.

"Let's go in," Coop said, completely missing the point that I needed to talk to him alone.

Tap . . . tap . . . tap . . .

Up the stairs to the library.

Alex hurried through the door and made a beeline for the computer room as if he knew exactly where he was going. I doubted they had a computer room when he was going to school here, or even computers for that matter.

The computer room was about the size of a broom closet. Three computers sat on three tiny desks. No one was there. And why *would* anyone be there? Everyone carried a laptop, a tablet, a smartphone, or all three with them at all times. No point going into a closet.

Alex sat down and started typing. Within seconds the reservation site for state park campgrounds came on the screen. He clicked a link, scrolled through the screen, shook his head, closed it, then opened the next one.

"I doubt the reservation is going to be under the Pod, or Lawrence Oliver Dane," I said.

"The site doesn't list names," Alex said, still typing. "Ah, here it is!"

He was on the Humboldt Redwoods State Park reservation site.

"That's where they are?" Coop asked.

"Absolutely. Fifty miles southeast of here, just outside of Eureka, which I'm sure has some kind of ironic significance for Larry."

"What do you mean?" I asked.

"Word games. Larry loves them. Take the name Cloud's Mushrooms. He was wild about the irony. Although I thought of that name, not Larry. *Eureka* means 'I have found it.' The phrase was coined by the ancient Greek mathematician Archimedes in a bathtub. It would be just like Larry to have his final destination near a town called Eureka."

"But how do you know they're at the park in Humboldt?" Coop asked. "There are a half dozen state parks around here."

"Because there are fifty-three campsites reserved right next to one another in the dead of winter. Hardly any other people at the other parks." Alex pointed at the screen. "It's them. All together at the same spot. Some of them must have taken different routes across the states. That's why Larry was slowing down the group we were following. He wanted them to arrive at roughly the same time. I think their final destination has to be in this vicinity."

"But you said his final destination would be somewhere more populated," I said.

Alex shrugged. "The sudden radio silence convinced me that Larry's old stomping ground was the place." He slumped in his chair. "I need to tell you boys something."

THE TRUTH

Coop asked.

Alex gave him a slight grin. "I'll admit that I've left some things out, but it wasn't to deceive you. One of them is between Kate and me, and has nothing to do with you. I didn't have time to tell her in New York or Portland. But now that we're so close to catching up with them, I should tell someone. In case I don't get a chance later. In case something happens to me." He let out a resigned breath. "I'm Kate's great-uncle . . . and her grandfather."

Apparently I was a little slow in the genealogy department because I didn't understand what he was saying. Coop got it right away.

"Larry's son married your daughter."

"The Deep's version of marriage, yes."

"You mean your daughter married her first cousin?" I asked.

Alex nodded. "Not the normal thing to do, but in a closed society with a limited population it isn't uncommon. My wife died a few years after we went into the Deep. Lung cancer. We had a girl named Rebecca. She and Larry's son, Tom, grew up together. They were inseparable. No one was surprised when they committed to each other."

Committed must have been the Deep's version of marriage.

"So what really happened to them?" Coop asked.

"Rebecca and Tom were both Shadows. A few weeks after they had Kate they decided that they didn't want to raise her in the Deep. They came to Larry and me and said they wanted out. Of course, no one gets out of the Deep. We told them no. They took our refusal pretty well — too well, because their intention was to leave regardless of what we said. Three days after we met, they left. Larry took two Guards and went after them.

"I caught up with Larry and the Guards a couple of hours after they got above. Larry was in a rage. He could not believe that his son would leave the Pod. He blamed Rebecca, and to a lesser extent me, saying that if I had raised her better Tom would not have been poisoned against him. Rebecca had never been a big fan of Larry. She had told me many times that she thought we should leave the Deep and expose the Pod, which I'm sure Larry was aware of. Rebecca was a lot like Kate. She wasn't good at keeping her opinions to herself. It was well known in the Pod that she wasn't happy living in the Deep. These bad feelings only intensified after Kate was born.

"Anyway, the Guards cornered them in the alley. Larry demanded that they come back with him. They, of course, refused . . ."

Tears formed in Alex's eyes. He wiped them away.

"The alley was dark that night. There was a total lunar eclipse. A blood moon. Larry took a gun from one of the Guards. I tried to stop him, but he shot me in the leg, then tried to finish me off with a head shot." He parted his gray hair and showed a scar. "The second shot grazed my skull and knocked me out. I don't know what happened after that. The next thing I knew was that the moon was back and Terry Trueman was tending to my wounds. He got me to a private doctor. You know the rest."

"We don't know the rest," Coop said. "Why did you wait so long to contact Kate?"

"Because as soon as I recovered, I got out of town. The newspapers didn't mention me being found with Tom and Rebecca. Larry was looking for me, and it wasn't to invite me back into the Deep."

"The articles didn't mention finding a baby either," I said.

"I know. But that didn't mean that Larry had taken her back into the Deep. The only way for me to find out was to return to the Pod, which would have been a death sentence. The Originals are loyal to Larry."

"Even if they learned he murdered his son and daughter-in-law?"

"Probably. Larry has a lot of power over them."

"What about the Guards?" Coop asked. "They witnessed the murders."

Alex nodded. "I'm sure he swore them to secrecy. I'm also sure that he eventually murdered both of them. When I finally hacked into the Deep's cameras, I never saw them again."

I was confused. "Are you saying that the Originals didn't know what happened in the alley that night?"

"I doubt it. I don't know what Larry told them. For all I know, he pinned Rebecca and Tom's murder on me."

"What did he say about Kate?" Coop asked.

"Probably that her parents left her behind in the Deep because they knew their escape plan was so dangerous. That would tie in perfectly with the ridiculous cover story about Tom and Rebecca getting lost on their way above. As Shadows, they would have never gotten lost, but spreading that rumor would have had its advantages. If a trained Shadow got lost and died Beneath, there was no hope of a regular Pod member escaping. That's how we controlled people. The mush room being the best example."

"There's no mush room?" I asked.

Alex shook his head. "No. People who caused problems were quietly killed, dumped into the underground river, and washed out to sea."

I remembered the bullets in my pocket. "Did you ever kill anyone in the Deep?"

"I did not. That was Larry and the Guards' deal. But I'm just as guilty, because I never asked about those who disappeared. None of us did."

I hadn't spent much time thinking about what it must have been like for Kate and the others living in the Deep with Lod and the Originals deciding what people could read, what they could say, where they could go, who would live, and who would die.

Coop broke the silence. "Where did you go?"

"Tallahassee, Florida."

"Why?"

"No particular reason. It was just a place to go. A place to get away. I established a new identity there. I got a job waiting tables. Good tips. Cash. No trail. In my spare time, I hacked into a few university computer systems and came up with fake transcripts. I couldn't use my own credentials. I enrolled at the University of Florida and got my master's in library science. After living in the Deep so long, I wasn't very good at being social. Waiting tables almost drove me insane. I wanted to get a quiet job, and I figured working as a research librarian would keep my interaction with people to a minimum."

"Wasn't it risky coming back to New York?"

"It was a risk, but when I came back I had no intention of staying. My idea of the perfect research librarian job was somewhere in the Midwest. Chicago, or maybe even Kansas City. I came back to New York to check on Kate. To see if she was still alive. There wasn't much hope, but I had to give it a shot — I owed Rebecca that at least. I couldn't go back into the Deep, but I knew some of the places Larry and the other Originals visited when they went above. I staked them out, disguised as a homeless person. I kept waiting for the one or two Originals I might be able to approach without them freaking out or telling Larry I was back in town. They never showed. I was about to give up and head west when I saw Kate, or at least a little girl who I thought might be her.

"It was late at night. I was watching an apartment building where we had a couple of people who helped us above from time to time. First the Shadows came down the street, then a couple of Guards. I knew Larry would be next. And he was, but he wasn't alone. A little girl was with him, or near him. She was fifteen feet ahead, dressed in black, moving like a wraith down the empty street. She was the right age, and I thought she looked a little like Rebecca when she was that age. When they reached the apartment building, Larry gave her a pat on the shoulder and had her sit down on the stoop. It was all I could do not to run across the street and take her in my arms. Maybe even take her away. But there was a lot of security lurking around. I wouldn't have gotten half a block. And then there was Kate. She sat on that stoop scanning everything in sight, including me. I was slumped against a wall in filthy clothes with a bottle of cheap wine in my lap, acting like I had passed out. Kate was well on her way to becoming a Shadow. If I'd grabbed her, even at that age, she might have gouged my eyes out. Ten minutes later Larry stepped out of the apartment building. He never spent much time above, and the group floated back down the dark street, disappearing as if they had never been there.

"The next day I went to the New York Public Library and asked if they had any volunteer positions. I made myself indispensable. Eventually they hired me. I set up shop in one of the subbasements and started watching the Pod, but mostly I watched Kate."

Alex got to his feet, bones creaking as he stretched.

"So what do you think Larry is up to?" I asked. "Why is he stopping here?"

"I've been thinking about that. I have a pretty good idea of why he's here." He looked at his watch. "I'll tell you about it as soon as I get back from the restroom. Wait here."

And with that, he hurried out of the computer room.

WHOA

Coop said. "I might have misjudged him."

"You were right about him holding things back."

"But he filled in the gaps."

"Not entirely."

I took out the satellite phone, the six bullets, the box with the flash drive, and my digital recorder.

"Backpack?"

"Yeah, except for the recorder."

"I assume there's a pistol for those bullets."

"I left it in the pack. He's out of ammo."

"And he had a cell phone all along?"

"It's not a cell phone. It works off satellite signals. Doesn't need a cell tower. He also had an industrial-grade laptop with a built-in DVD drive."

"So he made us buy the DVD thing so we wouldn't know about his computer."

"That's what I figure. The laptop is huge. That's why his pack is so heavy."

"So we didn't have to come to the library."

"No. Although there's a possibility he thinks the Pod has somehow hacked into his computer and he's afraid to use it. But that doesn't explain making a special stop to get a DVD player when he had one in his pack. You don't need to turn on the Internet to play a DVD. Your computer can't be hacked unless it's connected to a network."

"How'd you learn this stuff?"

"You're the only person on earth who doesn't know this stuff, Coop."

He smiled, picked up the little aluminum box, and opened it.

"What kind of flash drive is this? Looks fancy."

"I don't know. The question is, what kind of information does Alex have on it? It was in a pocket all by itself in that box."

Coop looked at the computer. "Could we —"

"Maybe," I said. "That depends on how long Alex will be gone."

Coop went to the door and looked out. "I don't see him. Library's empty. I'll let you know when he's coming."

He tossed the flash drive to me. I almost stuck it into the USB port of the computer Alex had been using, but thought better of it. All we needed was for him to walk in and see his data splashed all over the screen. I chose the third computer down instead. I looked over at the door. Coop gave me a thumbs-up sign.

"Let me know as soon as you see him. I'll need time to yank the drive and blank the screen."

"Will do."

I put the flash drive into the slot. The screen went immediately dark. I waited for something to happen. Nothing. I was staring at a black hole.

"Well?" Coop asked.

"Hang on. Keep looking for Alex."

I checked the power cord, thinking maybe I had kicked it loose when I sat down. It was plugged in and the surge protector light was on. I hit the restart button on the computer. Nothing happened. I unplugged the computer, plugged it into another socket, and hit the restart button again. Nothing.

I looked over at Coop.

"Coast is clear. They're starting to turn lights off. I think the library is about to close."

"Keep watching," I said.

I pulled out the flash drive and repeated every combination. Nothing worked. The computer was as dead as a doornail.

"They're definitely closing up, Pat. No sign of Alex. He's been gone a long time."

I went over to the other computer and put the flash drive into the slot.

The computer went dead.

"A security guy is coming this way," Coop said. "But I don't see Alex. I wonder what's keeping him."

I pulled out the flash drive, scooped up the bullets, grabbed the phone, the recorder, and jammed everything into my pockets.

"Hey, guys," the guard said. "We closed up ten minutes ago. The doors are locked. I'll have to let you out."

"Sorry," Coop said. "Guess we lost track of time."

The guard gave him an eager, forgiving smile. "No problem. It happens."

"We're with our grandfather. He said he had to find a restroom."

"Dressed in gray?"

"That's the guy."

"He left twenty minutes ago. Seemed to be in a hurry."

"He gets forgetful sometimes." Coop smiled like this was no big deal. But of course it was a huge deal. Alex had apparently ditched us.

The guard unlocked the front door and we stepped outside.

Coop stopped on the top of the steps. "What did that flash thing do?"

"I don't think it's a flash drive. Forget it! What about Alex?"

"Tell me about the —" Coop persisted.

"It killed the computers."

"What does that mean?"

"It means that as soon as I inserted it, the computers went blank. Gone. Poof! Dead."

"Why?"

"How do I know? I'm not a computer expert."

"But Alex is. At least that's what he studied in school before he became a librarian. He's probably going to want that flash thing back."

"Yeah, and his ammo. We need to catch up with him."

I hurried down the stairs, thinking Coop was right behind me. I should have known better. I turned to check and saw he was in the exact same spot, looking out onto the campus as if he didn't have a care in the world.

He can be so irritating. I wanted to scream.

"It's too late for that," he said. "He's long gone."

"You don't know that!" I shouted.

But I knew he was probably right. Alex had had his own agenda the whole time, and we had been scratched off it.

Coop walked down the stairs, *tap, tap, tap,* ignoring my outburst.

"Let's go, Lil Bro."

We walked across the campus toward the parking lot. Students were still wandering around. Night classes, I guessed. We came to a large group of students setting up equipment in the campus events field.

"I need to check this out," Coop said.

Of course he needed to check it out. At this rate, we'd be getting to the parking lot around sunrise. I followed him into the center of the field and saw they were setting up tripods, cameras, and telescopes.

"What's going on?" Coop asked.

Everyone immediately stopped what they were doing and smiled at him. It looked like some of the girls might faint. I revised the parking lot ETA to tomorrow afternoon.

"Astronomy class," one of the girls said, then they all started talking at once.

"Some of us made our own telescopes."

"We even ground the glass for the lenses."

"Hope they work."

"Newspaper is coming to do an article."

"We're lucky it cleared up."

"Would have had to scrap the entire show."

"What show?" Coop asked.

Everyone stopped talking and stared at him.

"The lunar eclipse," a boy answered.

Coop's eyes went as wide as the moon.

Mine too, I suppose.

Coop was born twenty years ago on Christmas Eve during a lunar eclipse in a traffic jam on the 495 Beltway in Virginia. Kate's parents were murdered during that same lunar eclipse in New York City and thrown into a Dumpster.

"We have to go," Coop said.

"If you get a chance, come on back."

"The eclipse won't start for a few hours."

"We're going to have food."

"What's your name?"

"Where are you . . ."

Tap, tap, tap, tap, tap, tap, tap . . .

I almost had to jog to keep up with Coop. He didn't slow down until we were around a corner.

"What are you thinking?" I asked.

"Maybe it's nothing. Maybe it's just a coincidence. Maybe it's everything. I don't know. But it kind of freaked me out."

"I can see that."

By the time we left the campus, he looked less freaked-out. We crossed the street to the parking lot.

The camper was gone, but Alex had left us the boat.

"It's going to be interesting for whoever runs the lot to find a boat without a truck tomorrow morning," Coop said.

We walked over to it.

I hoped Alex had thought to throw our packs into the boat before he took off. He hadn't, but he had left my sleeping bag. It was rolled out between the benches. It was covering something. Something the size of a human being.

We stared down at it.

"Is that your sleeping bag?" Coop asked.

"Yeah," I said, my mouth suddenly very dry. "It was rolled up behind the front seat."

Coop turned on a flashlight and slowly reached his other hand over the gunwale. He took ahold of the top of the bag and quickly flipped it back.

I was sure it was going to be Alex. That someone killed him and had taken the camper.

It was a woman. Her gray hair was shaven within a quarter inch of her scalp. She looked to be in her fifties, maybe her early sixties. Her brown eyes were opened in surprise. Blood from the back of her head was still leaking onto the bottom of the boat.

"It just happened," I said.

Coop felt the artery in her neck.

"No pulse, but she's still warm."

I'd never seen a dead person. I couldn't take my eyes off her. My stomach lurched, but I continued to stare. I had no idea who she was, but there was something familiar about her. Something . . .

"I think she's a Pod member," I said. "I recognize her from the newspaper sketches. Her hair was longer, but she's one of them. I'm sure of it."

"Her name is LaNae Fay," Coop said. "I saw her on the video from the gas station. But how did she end up dead in our boat?"

"Alex?"

"Probably." Coop covered her face.

"I guess we should call the police," I said. I took the phone out of my pocket.

"That would be the logical thing to do, but not necessarily the right thing to do. If we call the police, and stick around, they're going to haul us in. When we tell them our story, they're not going to believe it . . . at first. We'll have to get them to call Agent Ryan. She's going to tell the police to hold us. I doubt that Arcata has an FBI office. There are only seventeen thousand people here. This means that agents would have to fly or drive in from somewhere else. By the time they get here and get organized, it will be too late. The Pod will have already done whatever they're going to do."

"We could call Agent Ryan, quickly tell her what's going on, then get out of here."

Coop thought about it for a moment. "Okay."

He gave me the number. I punched it in and was about to hit the talk button when he stopped me.

"What?"

"Wait a second."

I looked up at the full moon, giving him a chance to think about it.

"None of this has to do with the lunar eclipse," Coop said. "The eclipse is something personal to me because I was born during an eclipse, and may be personal to Kate because her parents were murdered during the same eclipse."

"I was looking up at the moon because I don't want to look down at the dead woman in our boat," I said.

I hadn't thought about the lunar eclipse, or anything else, since we found her.

"Oh," Coop said.

"But the lunar eclipse thing is interesting, and pretty weird."

"I doubt the Pod even knows there's a lunar eclipse tonight. I guess I should have sent the postcard to Agent Ryan a couple of days earlier."

"All I have to do is hit Talk."

Coop shook his head. "Same results. We wouldn't make it out of town. Every cop within a hundred miles would be looking for us."

"We're leaving town?"

"We need to get to the park, or at least I do."

"If you mention us splitting up one more time, I'm going to split your lip."

Coop grinned. "Sorry."

"I mean it."

Coop looked back into the boat. "We need a head start. Maybe we can leave a note with Agent Ryan's phone number and a rough outline of what we're doing. By the time someone discovers the body, we'll be long gone."

"Hitchhike?"

Coop nodded.

I reached into my pocket and realized my writing stuff

was in my pack, but I did find my digital recorder. I held it out for Coop.

He shook his head. "Go ahead. You're better at it than I am. But make it quick."

When I finished I hit Play.

"That sums it up pretty well," Coop said. "But maybe you should add something about what we're going to do."

"Okay."

I hit the record button.

"We're going to hitchhike to the state park. Maybe catch up with Alex Dane. Maybe find Kate. Maybe figure out where the Pod is going. Someone has to stick with the Pod and find out where they're going and what their plan is.

"I guess that someone is Coop and me.

"There isn't anyone else."

PERFECT

Coop said.

He held out his hand for the recorder.

I gave it to him. "Where are you going to put it?"

"Somewhere where it won't get lost. Somewhere where they won't miss it. He flipped the sleeping bag off LaNae, this time revealing her entire body. Lying next to her right hand was a knife. Coop shined his light on the blade. There was fresh blood on it.

Alex did not get away unscathed.

"You think he's okay?" I asked.

"I'm not sure that Alex was ever okay," Coop answered, flashing his light around the rest of the boat. "There."

One of the oars was drenched in blood. "Guess we know how he . . ."

"I guess so," I said, wishing he'd get this over with.

He put the digital recorder in LaNae's hand, wrapped her fingers around it for several seconds until he thought it would hold, then covered her up again.

"Let's go."

He put his hood up and started walking with his head down as fast as I had ever seen him walk.

Tap, tap, tap.

We passed several people on the sidewalk. None of them

even glanced at us. I realized that Coop's hood-up-head-down-fast-walk was a disguise. He didn't want to be stopped. He didn't want to listen to anyone. He wanted to get to where he was going, wherever that ended up being.

"When are we going to start hitchhiking?" There were plenty of cars driving by.

"This is all local traffic," Coop answered. "Getting in and riding a few blocks isn't worth it. We'll walk to the edge of town and catch someone heading south to Eureka."

We walked.

And walked.

Traffic started to thin, then almost disappeared altogether. We left the lights of Arcata behind and started walking on the shoulder of 101, which was called the Redwood Highway through this stretch.

Four lanes.

Two north.

Two south.

Coop finally stopped.

He pulled his hood down and looked up at the sky hanging above Arcata Bay and the Pacific.

"The eclipse is starting. The blood moon."

A reddish brown was spreading across the full moon.

"How long does it take?"

"Two or three hours from start to finish."

I couldn't help but think about the woman's blood in the bottom of the boat.

We watched for a while, so intent on the slowly changing

moon that neither of us heard the truck until the door slammed closed. A camper was parked on the shoulder thirty feet in front of us. A man walked toward us.

"Alex?" I whispered.

Coop shook his head. "Our camper is a different color."

It was difficult to see what color the camper was, lit only by taillights, but it did appear to be darker than the camper we'd been driving.

"We weren't even hitchhiking," I said.

"Otto?" the man asked.

"Yeah," Coop replied.

"I thought that was you," the man said, putting his hand out. He was at least six feet tall, dressed in overalls, and looked like he hadn't shaved in days.

"Martin, right?" Coop shook his hand.

It was the retired cop from Nehalem Bay, the one the other cops had been poking fun at.

"Did you find that girl?"

"No," Coop said.

Martin looked at me. "Who's this?"

"My brother, Axel."

"Ha! Your parents must have been Jules Verne fans. *Journey to the Center of the Earth*, right?"

A well-read ex-cop.

"Martin Holds." He put his huge hand out to me. I shook it.

"Where are the other guys?" Coop asked.

"Back with their families by now. I decided to spend a couple of extra days fishing."

"How'd you recognize me? It's kind of dark along this stretch of road."

"Once a cop, I guess . . . I didn't know it was you for certain, but you were the same height and same build as the kid we met at Nehalem. You being with another guy kind of threw me off — I thought you were traveling alone. But what the heck. Worth checking it out. Enjoyed talking to you up north. We were all hoping you'd come back and go fishing with us."

"I got a little hung up," Coop said.

"Where are you headed?"

"Humboldt Redwoods State Park."

Martin looked us over. "You're traveling kind of light to go camping."

That's because a guy who just bashed a woman's head in took our backpacks, I thought.

"We're meeting some other people there," Coop said. "They have our gear."

"I'll give you a lift. I'm going right by there. I'm fishing my way back to LA. I like driving at night. Less traffic. You'll both have to ride up front with me. The camper is a toxic-waste dump."

We walked up to the truck and opened the passenger door. It was hard to believe that the camper could be worse than the front seat.

"Just sweep that trash off the seat."

We pushed the empty cans, bottles, candy wrappers, burger boxes, and chip bags onto the already garbage-compacted floorboards. Coop took the middle, which I appreciated. It meant I was able to crack open the window and breathe.

Martin talked about fishing, LA, his girlfriend, his apartment, his days as a cop, all the way through Eureka to the little town of Fortuna, where something happened to him. He stopped talking in the middle of a sentence.

I waited for him to continue, but the only sound was the old truck camper rattling down highway 101. A minute passed, then two minutes, then Coop finally said something.

"You okay, Martin?"

It took him ten more seconds to answer. "Yeah, I'm fine. I'm just kind of curious about you and your brother. You know a lot about me, but I don't know anything about you. You're kind of tight-lipped."

The reason Coop had been tight-lipped was that Martin had been loose-lipped, like everyone else who had ever talked to Coop, never giving him a chance to speak.

"What do you want to know?" Coop asked.

"Let's start with your real names. I don't believe the *Journey to the Center of the Earth* thing."

Uh-oh, I thought.

"Axel and Otto aren't your real names. I need to know who you are."

The simple-cop-on-a-fishing-holiday thing was over. In an instant, he had transformed into a smart, suspicious, nononsense cop.

"My name is Cooper O'Toole, but I prefer to be called Coop."

Martin looked over at me. "And you?"

I glanced at Coop. He gave me a resigned shrug.

"My name is Patrick O'Toole, but I prefer to be called Pat."

"Younger brother?"

"By five years."

He turned his attention back to Coop. "So what are you really doing out here?"

"It's a long story," Coop said.

Martin looked at his watch. "If I drive slow, we have about a half hour before we get to the park. If you don't finish your story by the time we get there, I'm going to drive by without stopping."

"For what it's worth," Coop said, "I was going to tell you the truth before we got there, or have you drop us off before we got to the park so you didn't get caught up in any of this."

Martin looked at his watch again. "Now you have twenty-nine minutes."

Coop started talking. He summarized almost everything that had happened from the moment he got to New York until Martin picked us up, leaving out a few key things, like the flash drive, the satellite phone, and the dead woman in the boat. Coop had probably forgotten about the flash drive, but he hadn't forgotten about LaNae. Probably best not to share this little detail with a cop, even an ex-cop. If Coop had told him, Martin might have thought we were accessories to murder. Why else would we have rushed out of town?

"What kind of gun did the old guy have?" Martin asked.

"I don't know," I said. "It had six bullets. I have them in my pocket."

"Any other ammo in the pack?"

"No."

"Did you check the camper for ammo?"

"No."

"And you say he flew in to Portland?"

"That's what he told us."

"Then he probably bought it off somebody out here to avoid the waiting period," Martin said. "The gun probably didn't come with extra ammo."

I wasn't sure why he was spending so much time on the empty gun.

He pulled the camper off to the shoulder.

"What are you doing?" Coop asked.

"Wrapping my mind around everything you just told me."

"We need to get to the park."

"I understand. The entrance is a mile ahead. If what you say is true, providing they are still at the park, they'll have sentries posted. We won't get very far if they figure out who we are. We need to take a few minutes to think about this. So, that girl Kate was snatched up at Nehalem?"

Coop nodded.

Martin laughed. "I got those SF cops' phone numbers before I left. Wait till I tell them we were parked less than a hundred feet from the Pod, fishing. It's going to kill them. Every cop in the universe is looking for those wackos. They're going to regret taking off so fast to get back to their families."

"This isn't your problem," Coop said.

"It's more my problem than it is yours. Once a cop, always a cop. You don't have cell phones?"

Coop shook his head. I followed his lead.

"Unfortunately, neither do I. Mine is on the bottom of Nehalem Bay. The smart play would be to drive ahead, find a phone, and call in the cavalry. The question is how fast can they get here, and what kind of cavalry are they?" He drummed the steering wheel with his fingers for a moment. "I think we should just pull into the front entrance."

"They'll see us," Coop said.

"Of course they'll see us. That's the point. From what you said they'll see us even if we try to sneak in a back way. It's a campground. We're in a camper. Weary travelers looking for a place to sleep in the middle of the night. Nothing suspicious about that. And I suspect that your friend Alex went into the park the same way. They aren't blocking the roads, checking each vehicle with flashlights. If they tried to do that the park staff would be all over them."

"They'll recognize us," Coop said.

"Not in the dark they won't. And even if they're using night-vision gear they won't pick up any details. All they'll know is that there are three people in the cab."

"Maybe we should climb into the camper," I said, although it was the last thing I wanted to do, and not just because I imagined it was even filthier than the cab.

Martin shook his head. "Better to go in like we have nothing to hide. They're going to be watching our camper after we park. Don't want to give them any surprises like two extra bodies jumping out of the back. Our best defense is to get them to drop their defenses. When we get out of the cab, we'll use flashlights. That will screw up any night-vision gear they might be using. If we convince them that we're just three tired campers they'll back off, and maybe we'll have a chance to look around and see what they're up to. Maybe even figure out where they're headed."

It all made perfect sense to me. In fact, Martin made it sound simple. Maybe too simple. Like he wasn't taking the Pod seriously enough.

"Do you have a gun?" I asked.

"Of course. And mine has bullets in it. When I leave my apartment, I grab my keys, my wallet, and my gun."

Martin put the truck into gear and pulled out onto the highway.

TEN, ELEVEN, TWELVE

More?

I'd lost track of how many campers, motor homes, and trailers had rumbled by.

But Bill was paying attention.

He was sitting in the open doorway on the little pull-down steps watching the Pod drive past, one by one.

I was sitting at the kitchen table handcuffed to the pole holding up the table. I had a strip of duct tape across my mouth. My legs and arms were manacled and stretched out about as far as they could reach. They hurt. But I guess that was the point. They wanted me to hurt. They wanted to tire me out so I couldn't resist, so I couldn't fight.

Bella was sitting across from me reading the FBI document, turning the pages one by one with her right hand. In her left hand, she was holding a butcher knife. When she cuffed me to the table I'd told her the tape wasn't necessary. I wasn't going to call out for help. She smiled and slapped me across the face. Hard.

"I don't care if you scream or not," she said. "No one here is going to help you. I gagged you so I don't have to listen to any more of your lies. I told Lod the truth about how you got to Nehalem Bay, but he had already figured it out, because he knows exactly what he wrote in his notebook and what he didn't. Carl also confessed to Lod about the money he took from your pack. You have no friends here. Bill offered to kill you himself, so did Carl, and so did I. Lod said he would think about who would get that honor and let us know. He didn't want to leave any corpses above for the cops to find."

Since then Bella hadn't uttered a word.

I could still feel the sting from her slap. If I had hadn't been cuffed I would have . . .

I took a deep breath, trying to quell my anger, then realized that I no longer had to hide my true feelings. As soon as Bella finished she would know everything, and she would pass it on to everyone else. Her slap had taken away my last shred of sympathy for Lod, or anyone else in the Pod.

For as long as I was alive, which I predicted was not going to be much longer, they were going to get the real Kate.

MARTIN

pulled into the entrance of the park just as another motor home was exiting.

"Odd time to be leaving," he said. "Is that your girl's rig?"

"Hers is smaller," Coop said.

"A Class C," I added.

"And the old guy who ditched you?"

"He's in a camper like yours," I answered. "It's white."

"Keep your eyes peeled for it. If he's smart he parked away from the swarm."

"The Pod," I said.

"Whatever, keep an eye out for your friend. It would be good to catch up to him and find out what he knows before we start poking around."

We drove by several campers, motor homes, and trailers. All of them had their lights on.

"I guess there's something to your story," Martin said. "All these lights on at this time of night is pretty weird."

"You mean you didn't believe us?" Coop asked.

Martin laughed. "You have to admit that it was a little far-fetched, but I believe you now."

Coop pointed out the window. "I think that's Kate's motor home!"

In the dark I couldn't really tell, but it was the right size.

Someone was sitting on the steps. He, or she, watched us as we drove by.

"Best not to be pointing at people," Martin said. "We're supposed to be road-weary travelers looking for a quiet spot to sleep."

"Sorry," Coop said.

I was relieved Martin had seen us on the highway. He seemed to know what he was doing, which is more than I could say for Coop and me. If we'd been here on our own, Coop might have walked up to Kate's motor home and knocked on the door.

We passed several more campsites, all lit up. A couple of people were outside their rigs watching us as we drove by, but we didn't give them more than a cursory glance. No one had pulled out since we had entered the park, so maybe the motor home we saw leaving wasn't connected to the Pod. If they were leaving, they were taking their time about it.

We passed a large motor home, lit up like the rest, then nothing for about a quarter of a mile.

"There!" Coop said, pointing.

I don't know how he spotted it. His night vision must have been better than mine or Martin's — all that time Beneath, I guess. Backed into a campsite as far as it could go was Alex's camper.

No light on inside.

It looked like it had been parked there for years.

"Are you sure?" Martin asked.

"Yes!" Coop and I said in unison.

Martin pulled his truck off to the side of the road and turned off the engine.

"Anything else I should know about Alex besides the fact that he's toting what we hope is an empty revolver?"

I looked at Coop and could see by the look on his face that he was trying to decide whether he should tell Martin about LaNae Fay.

"One more thing," Coop said resignedly. "We found a dead Pod member in the boat we were hauling. We're pretty sure her name is, or was, LaNae Fay."

"Are you kidding me?" Martin said. "That's a pretty big thing to leave out. Did you call the police?"

"No. We thought if we called the police, they'd detain us."

"You got that right. What did you find exactly?"

Coop explained.

"So Alex is wounded," Martin said after he finished.

"We don't know."

"Fresh blood on the knife? I doubt this LaNae woman stabbed herself. So, you didn't tell anyone about what you found?"

"Not exactly," I said. "We left a digital recording, which we hope the police pass on to the FBI when they find her."

"What was on the recording?"

I told him.

"All right, let's go," he said. "Here's how we'll do this. We'll circle around to the back of his camper, quietly. You're going to knock on his door and announce yourselves. Again,

251

quietly. We don't want to arouse any suspicion. I'll hide in the trees behind you so he doesn't get spooked. I'll also make sure he's not being watched by the Pod. As soon as you explain to him that I'm a good guy, I'll step out from the trees and introduce myself."

KNOCK, KNOCK

"It's us," Coop whispered. "Coop and Pat. Are you in there? Are you okay? Open up."

All we could hear was the light wind blowing through the tall redwoods.

Coop tried the door. It was locked.

He knocked again.

"Alex? It's Coop . . ."

I was standing to the side of Alex's camper with a clear view of the road and the back of Martin's moonlit camper. I saw movement. The door to Martin's camper opened.

". . . and Pat. Open up."

Knock, knock, knock.

"Coop?"

"What?"

"Someone is getting out of the back of Martin's camper."

"Martin is in the woods watching our backs."

"It isn't Martin. It's —"

Click.

The door opened.

"You shouldn't have followed me," Alex said.

He was holding a bloody towel to his shoulder with his left hand. In his right hand he held his revolver.

I hoped he had figured out his pistol was empty, and I hoped I was mistaken about his having spare bullets —

because he was going to need them. The man who had gotten out of the back of Martin's camper was now close enough to recognize. He had shaved his beard and trimmed his hair, but there was no mistaking the giant Guard who had sent his vicious dog after us. Carl. The last time I'd seen him, he had been twitching on the ground, grimacing.

Now he was smiling.

And carrying a shotgun.

He pumped a shell into the shotgun.

Now was the time for Martin to burst from the trees and slay the giant.

But that wasn't going to happen.

Because Martin had known that the giant was inside his camper the whole time. They were working together.

Martin stepped out of the trees, his gun pointed at Alex and Coop.

Four other people joined him, all of them armed.

Alex pointed his revolver at them and pulled the trigger.

Click. Click. Click.

Martin laughed.

"Kid took your bullets."

Alex grabbed the handle of the camper door.

"Hold on there," Martin said. "If you're thinking about shutting yourself back inside, you should reconsider. If you close that door I'll shoot Coop and Pat, then set fire to your rig with you inside while they're bleeding out."

Alex let go of the door and raised his arms in surrender.

CHANGE OF PLANS

Lod said, not even glancing in my direction.

"What's going on?" Bella asked.

"No questions. Move her to my rig."

Bella quickly unlocked the cuffs, then remanacled my wrists like a veteran prison guard.

"Carl will be riding with you and Bill in my motor home. There's an SUV outside for transport. As soon as you get there, fire up the rig. Be ready to go. We're speeding up our exodus. When Carl joins you I want you to take off. We're still in radio silence, but turn your cells on in case I need to talk to you."

My arms and legs were almost completely numb. I could barely walk. Running, or fighting, was not an option. For the moment.

There were two SUVs outside. Lod got into one of them and drove away. We got into the other and followed.

I expected to see Lod's SUV parked outside his motor home, but when we arrived it wasn't there.

Bella marched me into Lod's rig, pushed me into a leather chair, then cuffed me to the leg of the end table next to it. She didn't bother with my legs this time. It was a lot more comfortable than being manacled to her kitchen table, but that was hardly intentional. She was no more worried about my comfort than a butcher about to slaughter a pig.

Bill got into the driver's seat and started the big diesel engine.

Bella leaned in close to my face with the butcher knife still in her hand.

"I'm going to take off the duct tape. I have some questions about this Beneath document. If you call out I will slit your throat. Do you understand?"

I nodded.

HE'S BLEEDING

Coop said.

They had us lined up against a redwood. Alex was between Coop and me, barely able to stand.

"He's lucky he still has blood," Carl said. "LaNae usually doesn't —"

His explanation was cut off by the arrival of an SUV. The lights were blinding. I couldn't see who got out from the driver's side, but he looked to be carrying a small briefcase.

Martin nodded at the case. "Is that mine?"

"As soon as you explain what happened."

"Larry," Alex said quietly.

"Hey, little brother," Lod said, stepping forward. "You should have stayed dead."

Alex said nothing.

Martin looked at us. "I'm afraid you boys aren't very bright."

"You're a Pod member," I said.

Martin shook his head. "Freelance. Batting cleanup. For money."

"So you weren't a cop?"

"I was a cop. A dirty cop, as it turns out. Got caught. Did some prison time. Got out." He nodded at Lod. "With a little help from my friends, or his lawyer friends."

"What about the others at Nehalem Bay?" I asked.

"Real cops. Probably law-abiding. Who's to say?"

"Talk to me," Lod said. "I'm the one paying you."

"They caught up with me four or five hours after you left Nehalem Bay. The older kid was looking for the girl. I followed them south. Kept my distance so they didn't get suspicious. Lost them in Lincoln City, where they exchanged their Ford Taurus for the camper. Picked them up again farther south."

"Why didn't you tell me they were following us?"

"You were hours ahead. You told me I couldn't use a cell phone. Too far away for the CB most of the time. When I got close enough to you, I figured they were monitoring your transmissions. Short of knocking on your door there was no way of telling you anything. They didn't appear to be a threat, so I just kept an eye on them. Until they got to Arcata, where I found Carl following them. How'd you get onto them?"

"We have more than one pair of eyes watching our backs," Lod said.

"Smart," Martin said.

"What happened in Arcata?"

"I lost them again. Flat tire when I crossed the California border. Bad spare. Took me hours to get it fixed. Had to check out every town and camping spot south of the border. I was trolling for them in Arcata and came across a bunch of cops at a parking lot looking at the boat and trailer. The camper was gone. It looked like the whole force was there. Dead woman in the boat. Saw Carl in the crowd looking a little forlorn and confused. Figured he was one of yours.

Walked up to him and told him I was working for you. Thought it best if we teamed up. He wanted to snatch and kill the kids right away. I figured it would be better if we found out what they knew before we killed them."

The good news, for us anyway, was that the police had found the digital recorder. The bad news was that we might not live long enough for it to do us any good.

Lod turned to Carl.

Carl looked uncomfortable. "LaNae and I went to Arcata like you asked. We couldn't find your informant, so we started driving around. LaNae kicked me out of the truck and told me to poke around the campus. That she'd find me later. Well, she didn't find me later. I started looking for her and came across the parking lot with the cops. You know the rest."

"The problem is that I don't know the rest." Larry looked at Alex. "Care to fill me in?"

Alex shrugged, then winced in pain. "I was unhitching the boat and the she-devil stabbed me in the shoulder. I grabbed an oar and hit her in the head."

"What about this digital recording I was told about?"

Martin must have told one of the people in the woods about it, and they had passed it on to Lod.

"According to the kids, it's for some FBI agent. They don't know where you're going, but they know where you've been, which is probably enough for the feds to run you down." Martin smiled. "And this is where I leave you. Thanks for the get-out-of-jail-free card. As soon as I get the money, I'm outta here."

"Of course. But you should have found a way to contact me."

Martin shrugged.

Lod held the briefcase out.

As Martin reached for it, Lod raised his other hand.

The muzzle flash lit up the campsite.

There was a spitting sound.

No bang.

Martin lay on his back.

Blank eyes staring at the moon up through the redwoods.

LOD HAD A GUN

in one hand. A laptop in the other.

Next through the door was Alex. He was holding a bloody towel to his shoulder, his skin as white as the leather chair I was sitting on. Pat came through next, followed by Coop, who gave me a broad grin even though there was nothing to smile about. Carl was last. He was carrying a shotgun and had to stoop to get through the door.

"You three at the kitchen table," Lod said. He handed the revolver to Bella. He looked at Pat. "The bullets."

Pat dug into his pocket and pulled out six bullets. Bella took them, flipped open the cylinder, and expertly loaded the gun.

"Carl's riding with you. I'd prefer to keep them alive, but if any of them causes you any problem whatsoever you have my express permission to shoot them, including Kate. The FBI is on its way. I always expected them to find us, but not this soon. When you reach our location give this computer to Bob Jonas. Tell him it was in Alex's pack. I want him to crack the passcode and find out what's on it." He glanced at his watch. "The feds are going to have satellites on us soon, so you need to get moving."

"And we can use our cells?" Bella asked.

Lod nodded. "The FBI knows where we are thanks to

these two, and that we've been using CBs, so we'll change it up."

Bella waved her gun at Alex. "What about him?"

"Once you get moving, you can patch him up. It would be a shame if he bled out before I got a chance to interrogate him. He wasn't hauling around that laptop for fun. I'll see you there."

I looked out the window. Lod climbed into the front of an SUV and drove away.

I looked at Coop. "I'm sorry you're here."

"I'm not," Coop said.

"You will be," Bella said.

She opened a cupboard and took out a first-aid kit.

Bill put the motor home in gear and pulled out of the campsite.

THE SATELLITE PHONE

If I could get it out of my pocket under the table without Bella seeing, and hit the redial button, I might be able to give Agent Ryan a pipeline to what was going on, providing she answered her phone.

Kate was cuffed in a chair a few feet away from the kitchen table. Coop was sitting next to me on a bench seat. Alex was in a chair across from us watching Bella lay out the first-aid supplies. She had already stripped off his shirt.

"Didn't think I'd see you again, Alexander, or is it Alex now?"

"Doesn't matter," Alex said.

"The wound is clean, but deep. How'd you get it?"

"LaNae Fay."

"She likes her knives."

Not anymore, I thought.

I slowly put my hand in my pocket.

"She's dead," Alex said.

Keep her talking. Keep her occupied.

"Bound to happen," Bella said. "How'd she die?"

"I hit her on the head with an oar."

"This is going to sting."

The phone was out.

Coop gave me a subtle nod.

I glanced at Kate. She could clearly see what I was doing from where she was sitting.

Bella poured a liberal amount of disinfectant onto a sterile pad and put it on Alex's wound. He jerked away from her.

"Don't be a baby."

I looked down at the phone. There was a volume button on the screen. I moved it down to zero.

"You need sutures," Bella said. "Maybe Lod will have the doc look at it."

"I doubt it," Alex said.

"I doubt it too, but you never know what Lod is going to do."

Bella wasn't paying any attention to me. Carl was in the passenger seat next to Bill with the shotgun resting between his legs. He had swiveled the chair around to face us, but he looked half-asleep.

"So I hear you've been working at the library for the past few years."

"That's right."

"Learn anything?"

"Guess not."

Coop and Kate were staring at me. I gave them both a slight head shake. They looked away.

I found the redial button.

I pressed it.

No sound.

Relieved, I slipped the phone under the cushion with the microphone semiexposed.

"Where are we going?" I asked.

"Shut up," Carl said.

I guess he was paying closer attention than I thought.

"They call it the Deep Two Point Zero," Kate said loudly.

"Shut up," Carl repeated.

"No," Kate said.

Carl got halfway out of his seat.

"Go ahead," Kate said defiantly. "There is nothing you can do to me that isn't going to happen to me anyway. Might as well get it over with now."

"Let them talk," Bella said. "It might be interesting to hear what they think they know."

Reluctantly, Carl resumed his seat.

"So what is this Two Point Zero?" I asked.

"They're going underground," Kate answered. "Again."

Which meant I was going underground. Again. I suddenly felt dizzy. I hoped Agent Ryan was on the line listening.

"I don't think it's too far from here," Kate continued. "Lod has been planning it for years. He already has people there. People I knew from New York. People I thought had been sent to the mush room, which by the way, doesn't exist, and never did."

"So everyone sent to the mush room is already there?" I asked.

"No," Kate answered.

I didn't need to ask what happened to them. They had no doubt been taken care of the same way Lod had taken care of Martin: brutally, without the slightest bit of remorse.

"I'm going to have to wrap the dressing to your shoulder to stem the bleeding," Bella said, ignoring us. "It's going to hurt."

Alex screamed, his eyes rolled up into his head, and then he passed out. Coop jumped up and caught him before he hit the floor. He glared at Bella.

Bella smiled. "It was either that or bleed out. By the color of his face he's already lost a lot of blood. Get back in your seat."

"We need to lay him down," Coop said.

"There's only one bed in here. Lod won't be happy if we get it bloody."

"Lod won't be using the bed, or the motor home, after we get to the new compound," Kate said.

Bella thought about it for a moment. "Fine."

Coop wrapped his arms around Alex's chest. I took his feet. He was surprisingly light. We carried him into the bedroom in back and laid him on the bed. As I was putting a second pillow under his head he opened his eyes and pulled me in close.

"Do you have my USB thing?" he hissed.

"The flash drive?"

"It's not a flash drive. It's a silver bullet. Do you have it?"

"I have it."

"Guard it with your life. We'll need it when we get into the Deep. I'm not as bad off as I look."

I was going to tell him about the satellite phone, but Bella interrupted me.

"That's good enough. Get back out here."

WHAT TIME IS IT

I asked.

Coop glanced at my wrist, saw that I was no longer wearing my watch, and caught on immediately.

"Ten after two."

"So, we left the park forty-five minutes ago?"

"About."

Are you out there, Agent Ryan? Can you hear us?

Bella was sitting on the sofa across from Kate. Carl was dozing in the passenger's seat.

"Lod has a copy of the document we gave to the FBI," Kate said, loud enough to be heard out on the highway.

Carl's head snapped up.

"How did he get ahold of that?" Coop asked.

Bella shook her head and chimed in. "Lod has people above in every walk of life. It's been that way from the very beginning. Not everyone went into the Deep. Some of us stayed above, and some of those became prominent leaders in government and business. I suspect many of them will be joining us in our new home soon, if they aren't there already."

"Why?" I asked.

Bella smiled. "Because a change in the weather is coming."

"What do you mean?" Coop asked.

"None of you will be around long enough to find out."

Bill slowed the motor home down and made a sharp turn to the left.

"What time is it?" I asked.

Coop looked irritated. "Fifteen minutes past the last time you asked me what time it was."

Did you hear that, Agent Ryan?

THE DIESEL ROARED

as we started up a steep incline. With my hand cuffed it was all I could do to stay in the leather chair. I thought we were going to tip. I looked over at Coop and Pat. They were holding on to the table. Carl nearly fell out of his seat. Bella was using both her arms to brace herself against the window frame.

"You sure this is right?" Bella shouted at Bill.

"Yeah," he shouted back to her. "There was a lightning cloud sign, and I can see taillights up ahead. It's a compacted gravel road, in good shape in spite of the rain. If we can get this rig up it no one else is going to have any problem."

Coop had taken off his coat.

I was startled by the tattoo coming out of his T-shirt.

He laughed, still gripping the table. "A phoenix rising from the ashes."

"Wait until you get to be sixty-five," Bella said. "Then see what that chicken looks like on your flabby, wrinkled skin."

"According to you, I'm not going to get to sixty-five."

Touché, Bella.

"That's a fact," Bella said.

I think we were all talking to get our minds off the terrifying angle of the motor home.

"I like the tat," I said. "I've always wanted one."

"What kind?" Coop asked cheerfully, as if he wasn't riding in a metal coffin to his own funeral.

"I don't know. Something light and airy. Maybe a mountain. Maybe a sunrise." I looked at Pat. "How about you?"

"Weirdly, I'm kind of with Bella on this one," Pat said. "Don't get me wrong. I like looking at tattoos. I just prefer to use ink for writing things down."

Bella stared at Pat. "Did you write the Beneath document?"

"We all wrote it," Pat answered. "It's epistolary."

"What's that?"

Coop gave his standard mini-lecture about epistolary writing.

Bella actually seemed interested in what Coop was saying. Coop didn't seem to care that she had a butcher knife tucked under her belt and a pistol in her right hand, with permission to murder all of us if she felt like it.

"I was never much of a reader," Bella said.

"It's never too late. Does this new Deep have a library?"

"I don't know. The compound in New York had a few books, but I wouldn't call it a library."

I'd known Bella my entire life, and I could see that she was struggling. She didn't want to like Coop, but she couldn't help herself.

"I don't get it," Bella said.

"What?"

"Your cheerfulness. Your calmness. Don't you know

what's going on here? Don't you know what's going to happen to you?"

"I don't think anyone knows what's going to happen to them," Coop answered quietly. "I'll admit that it doesn't look too good for us at the moment, but there's no sense in wasting whatever time you have left by being miserable about it."

"Carl!" Bella shouted.

Carl's head snapped up.

"Watch them. I'm going to sit up front for a while."

They switched places.

Carl was not nearly as charmed with Coop as Bella. He watched Coop through half-closed eyes, licking his lips as if he wanted to devour him.

"Sorry about your dog," Coop said.

Carl said nothing.

"I wish it hadn't happened."

Carl grunted.

"I'm sure you miss him. I know I would."

Carl's eyes opened a little. He gave Coop the slightest nod.

"Rottweilers have a bad reputation," Coop said. "I suspect you don't agree."

Carl shrugged. "Too much dog for most people," he said. "Hard to control."

"What do you mean?"

"Every once in a while they go nuts on you. You gotta deal with it right then. No hesitation."

"What about pit bulls?"

"Had one once." He lifted his sleeve, revealing an ugly scar. "He was a good dog up until he did this. We were walking above. He got this weird look in his eyes. Next thing I knew he'd latched on to my arm. Took a long time to shake him. He ran off. More like limped off. Never saw him again. Got Prince."

"Prince?"

"That's what I named my Rott."

I didn't know Carl well, but this was the first time I'd heard him have a normal conversation where he wasn't angling for something. He was just talking.

"No dogs here?" Coop asked.

"No."

"Do you think they'll be allowed in the new compound?"

Carl shook his head. "From what I hear it's nothing like the old compound. No need for guide dogs, Seekers, or guard dogs. One way in. One way out. And no reason to go out. It could be years, or decades even, before we see the light of day."

It was clear by his glum expression that he wasn't looking forward to it. Perhaps this was why he stole the money from my pack. Had he been thinking about leaving the Pod?

"Those are just rumors, Carl," Bella said from the passenger seat. "Lod will let us know how the new compound is going to work when we are all there. Not even I know the details."

It was interesting that Bella didn't want to talk to Coop, but she was still listening. The problem for Carl was that if

272

the new compound was everything he feared, once inside, he wouldn't be able to leave the Pod.

Coop must have seen that the direction the conversation was going was upsetting Carl. He turned his attention to me and changed the subject. Sort of.

"You said you wanted dogs. What kind? How many?"

"When did she say that to you?" Bella asked.

"In DC," I answered for Coop quickly. No point in aggravating Bella further by mentioning the notes. "I'd like to have a dozen dogs, but I'd settle for three. As to which breeds, I'm not sure. I like small dogs. I was very fond of Enji."

Carl nodded. "I liked that little basenji of yours too. Little dog, big heart."

"I hope she found a good home up top," I said.

"I heard the FBI rounded up most of the dogs and are holding them," Carl said.

"Where did you hear that?" Bella asked, back in the conversation. She couldn't seem to help herself.

"Lod told me."

"Whoa!" Bill said, slowing the motor home. "We're here."

BEFORE YOU ASK

it's five after three," Coop said.

"Thanks," I said, and started to get up from the kitchen table.

"Sit back down!" Carl said. "I need to zip-tie your wrists."

"Why?" I asked.

"Orders from Lod."

While they were talking about dogs I had this fantasy that Carl was actually on our side and that he would shoot Bella and Bill, jump behind the steering wheel, slam the rig into reverse, and get us out of there.

I guess I was wrong.

There were bright lights shining through the windshield. Carl was the first to slip on his shades. Bella and Bill followed next.

"It's a mine," Bill said, getting up from his seat. "Or it was a mine."

"What kind of mine?" I asked loudly.

Your last hint, Agent Ryan.

"How would I know?" Bill said. "They're waving for us to come out."

Bella and Bill picked up small identical blue backpacks from between the seats and slung them over their shoulders. I hadn't seen Bella do it, but I guessed she had slipped Alex's computer in her pack.

"Put your hands on the table," Carl said.

"What about Alex?" Coop asked. "I don't know if he can walk. We can't help him with our hands tied."

Carl seemed to falter for a moment, then shook it off. "Nah. Gotta tie your hands. I'm in enough trouble with Lod as it is."

I wanted to grab the phone, but I couldn't. Carl was too close and Bella was looking right at me.

Carl zip-tied our hands in front of us. I figured this was a compromise. He could have tied our hands behind our backs. Kate wasn't so lucky. Bella freed her from the table, then recuffed her with her hands behind her back.

Carl handed his shotgun to Bill, then went into the bedroom. A minute later he came out with an unconscious Alex cradled in his arms like a sleeping baby.

"Is he okay?" Coop asked.

"He's alive," Carl said. "Let's go."

Bella stepped outside first, pistol in hand, followed by Kate, Coop, me, Carl, and Bill carrying the shotgun.

Dozens of rigs were parked close to one another in a huge gravel parking lot.

It was drizzling and foggy.

Floodlights on tall stands lit the night.

The rumble of portable generators was deafening.

A woman carrying a clipboard walked over to talk to Bella.

"I heard you were bringing company. Their names?"

"Coop O'Toole. Pat O'Toole. Kate Dane, who you already know. And Alexander Dane."

"Lod's little brother? I thought he was dead."

"He will be soon."

The woman wrote the names on her clipboard. "Just follow the road up to the mine entrance. People will meet you inside and tell you where to go."

"Is Lod here?"

"Not yet. He'll be the last down. He's making sure everyone gets inside safely. I think we'll be sealed up in less than an hour."

I turned around and saw more headlights coming up the road behind us.

What I hoped to see were flashing police lights.

We started up the road toward a black rectangle cut into the side of a rock wall.

"You going to be okay?" Coop asked.

"Probably not," I said.

Up ahead, a line of people wearing backpacks were disappearing into the dark hole as if they were being willingly devoured. My heartbeat increased. My mouth went dry. I glanced behind. Bill was smiling like he was heading toward heaven's gate. In front of him, Carl (still cradling Alex) was frowning like he was heading toward the gates of hell, which for him was an eternity with no dogs allowed. Behind us was another group, and behind them another, with more rigs pulling into the lot. None with flashing lights.

I was going into the Deep.

Again.

The entrance looked much bigger close up than it had from the parking lot. I took some solace from this, until I stepped through the opening.

The cavern beyond was cold and dark. Something brushed my cheek. I reeled backward and slipped. Coop caught me before I fell. No easy task with his wrists bound.

"Easy, Lil Bro."

"Something flew past my —"

"Bats," Kate said. "There are millions of them hanging on the ceiling."

With her acute night vision, she could probably see them clearly.

"Millions?" I asked. "Bats are nocturnal. Why aren't they outside hunting?"

"Hibernation," a man said from the darkness. He turned on a flashlight with a red beam. "We're trying not to disturb them. If they fly out into the cold they might starve. Not enough insects to support them this time of year."

"Then why did you build the Deep here?" Kate asked.

He looked down at a clipboard. "Ah, you must be Kate Dane." He looked at Coop and me. "Our hostages."

He said this cheerfully, as if he were welcoming us to a fun party.

"Hostages?" I asked.

He ignored my question.

"For your information, Kate, the bats didn't show up here until last fall, years after we created this cavern. We've been very careful not to disturb them. Your early arrival to the new compound put a serious kink in our plans for these bats. We had planned for you to arrive in the summer so we could shoo the bats from here at a time when there would be plenty for them to eat as they search for a new roost."

He shined the red flashlight behind us. There were gigantic sliding steel doors big enough to seal the entire cavern off to the outside world.

"We know that the feds are going to show up here eventually."

My hope was they would show up in about one minute.

"Our plan is to open the doors sometime this summer and set the bats free. The doors are soundproof, bombproof, and hermetically sealed. The bats should be just fine until we can let them out. Lod has a profound love for all of our wild brethren."

This guy was in his early thirties. Kate didn't appear to know him. I doubted he had ever met Lod. I wondered what he would have thought of his beloved Lod if he had seen him shoot Martin Holds in the forehead.

"So we are hostages," Kate said.

"That was probably too harsh of a word. And I haven't introduced myself. My name is Dexter, but everyone here calls me Doc. I'll be escorting you below. You and the boys will be put in our holding cube. I think you'll find it comfortable. Your friend Alex will be taken to the infirmary so I can treat his shoulder."

"You're a doctor?" I asked.

"I'm a nurse practitioner, which is as close as we'll have to a doctor for a long time."

"We had a doctor in New York," Kate said.

"He's here. I just met him. He says he's too old to practice medicine. He'll be advising me when I need him."

Dexter looked at me. "I understand that you have claustrophobia."

"Not really," I said.

"Oh, that's good news. But I was going to say that there is nothing here that should trigger an episode."

"Except that we're standing in a dark cave," I said.

"Light and fresh air is just a few steps away. We installed blackout doors so as not to overstimulate the bats. Follow me."

We followed him.

He opened a door. On the other side was nothing but blackness.

"Wait," he said.

He closed the door.

"I know you've all been above for several weeks and have gotten used to the light, but you might want to put on your shades. The new Deep is brighter than the old one. Ready?"

I was more than ready. The tiny vestibule we were standing in was beginning to get to me.

Dexter opened the second door.

It was bright, especially after the darkness of the cavern, but not overly bright. What shocked me, and by the look on their faces, the others as well, is what the light revealed. It was as if we had stepped through, not a door but a portal, into a completely different place. We were standing in a long hallway. The floor was smooth seamless cement. The walls were painted white. The temperature was perfect. The air smelled fresh. Lights, inset into the ceiling, ran ahead for as far as I could see.

"Of course no one can imitate the sun," Dexter said. "But these are full-spectrum lights. The newest thing. I understand that your old compound was a bit on the dim side."

I could see now that Dexter was wearing a sky-blue jumpsuit. He was well-groomed. Clean-shaven. Styled hair.

We looked like a group of castaways compared to him.

He had a holster with a pistol strapped around his waist.

A nurse with a gun.

I looked back. There was another set of steel doors as thick as my arm was long.

Dexter must have noticed.

"Four sets of doors. Everything here is operated by a centralized supercomputer. It is impossible for anyone to get inside without clearance. The third set of doors is just down this passageway. Follow me."

We followed Dexter.

MY WRISTS HURT

from being behind my back, and Bella locking them too tight.

The third door was like the others.

Massive.

We walked down another passageway to a freight elevator large enough to park our motor home inside.

"How about taking Kate's handcuffs off," Coop asked. "What could she possibly do down here?"

He'd be surprised, but I appreciated him asking.

"The cuffs stay!" Bella snarled.

Bill pushed me into the elevator with the shotgun.

Coop stood behind me. He held my hands. His hands were dry. I was amazed at how calm he had been through this ordeal.

The elevator doors closed with a hissing sound.

"Going down?" Dexter joked.

Bella and Bill laughed.

Coop, Pat, and I did not laugh, or smile. Nor did Carl, who looked grim, as if he were feeling the same dread that I felt.

Hostages, Dexter had called us.

I suppose that was better than *corpses*, but what the word implied was that Lod knew the FBI would find him and that he would need hostages.

Lod plans for the worst and expects nothing to go smoothly.

There were only two buttons. Up and Down. No stops in between. Dexter pushed the down button.

I'd been in an elevator only once in my life. The Empire State Building. I was nine years old. We'd been on one of our rare daytime forays above. Lod met a man on the observation deck on the very top of the building. He handed the man a duffel bag. I was thinking more about the view than about why Lod was up there. I'd seen Lod pass briefcases to people a hundred times and never thought about what he was doing. I realized now that he was passing money to people. The elaborate security with Shadows and Guards was not for him. It was to protect the dead presidents he was delivering to people helping him above.

My ears popped. We continued our descent. I looked at Pat. He was almost as pale as Alex.

Down.

Down.

Down.

Finally the elevator began to slow, then came to a gentle stop.

"A thousand feet," Dexter said. "Three hundred and four point eight meters."

The doors hissed open.

Another short passageway. At the end of the passageway was the final set of doors. But this set — more massive than the previous doors — was closed.

Dexter led us over to them. "We're being checked out, or

checked in, depending on how you look at it. It'll only take a moment."

I searched the ceiling and walls for cameras. I didn't see any.

Dexter laughed. "You won't find the cameras. I've looked. We're using some kind of fiber-optic gizmo. The compound is riddled with them. Controlled remotely by our central computer. I hear there isn't a blind spot inside the whole structure. We have microphones as well. Everywhere. We can hear a pin drop on a pillow. Just kidding about that, but don't try having a private conversation. That won't work out for you. We're totally open down here."

Dexter was totally ignorant.

I'm sure Bella and Bill knew this too. So did Carl. Lod's private quarters would not have cameras and microphones. The Originals wouldn't have them either. And there would be a very private room somewhere in the compound where no one was allowed except Lod and the Originals.

The steel door slid open.

A group of fifty or sixty people were there to greet us.

They were smiling.

They were clapping.

They were wearing different colored jumpsuits.

Bob Jonas was wearing a red jumpsuit.

We stepped through the entrance.

The door slid closed behind us.

"Welcome," Bob said. He shook Bella's and Bill's hands. He totally ignored the *hostages*, and looked at Carl. "We have a wheelchair coming for him."

The wheelchair appeared, pushed by a woman wearing a sky-blue jumpsuit like Dexter's. Carl sat Alex in the chair. He was barely conscious.

"This is where I leave you," Dexter said. "I'll get Alex patched up, then bring him over to your holding area."

They wheeled him away.

Bob looked at Bella. "I think you have something for me."

Bella pulled Alex's computer out of her pack and gave it to him.

"Whoa!" Bob exclaimed. "An RS32X. There are only a dozen of these in the world. It'll be fun messing with this thing."

"Where do we go?" Bella asked.

"Someone will take you and Bill to your new quarters." He looked at Carl. "You'll be billeted in the Guard and Watcher barracks."

"Watcher?" Carl asked.

Bob pointed at the television monitors, which were hanging everywhere, flipping from one video feed to another. "I guess everyone here is a Watcher to some degree, but we do have a control center where the serious watching takes place, and where we can manipulate the cameras if need be. You'll be splitting your time between watching, guarding, and listening."

The compound was similar to the Deep in New York. There were five levels in a horseshoe shape overlooking a huge common area, which was filled with people in colorful jumpsuits milling around looking for people they knew in plain clothes, and introducing themselves to the ones they didn't know. There were probably a hundred and fifty people, but room for three times that many. The new compound was five times brighter than our old compound. There were plenty of chairs and tables. A lot of people were eating, getting plates of food from the cafeteria, bringing them out to tables in the commons to chow down. There were more children than we'd had in the New York Deep. A couple dozen of them, from what I could see. All of them, boys and girls, were wearing pink jumpsuits.

A man and a woman in brown jumpsuits came over to us.

"You must be Carl," the man said. "I'm Sam and this is Tina. We'll take you to the Watcher barracks as soon as we get these three situated. Lod just sent a message saying we could remove their manacles now that they're in the Deep."

Carl unlocked my cuffs and cut Coop and Pat's zip ties. There was no point in trying to get away. Where would I go?

The door hissed open again, letting another group of people inside. I knew every one of them.

More clapping and cheering.

The door hissed closed.

I rubbed my sore wrists.

"I don't see any dogs here," I said to Tina.

She smiled. "Thank God there are no dogs allowed." She looked at Carl and shuddered. "Can you imagine what that would be like?"

Carl didn't answer.

He could imagine it, and I don't think he liked it.

CANARY YELLOW

I guess that's what hostages wore.

Kate looked good in the yellow jumpsuit.

Coop and I not so much.

They made us take showers before they escorted us to the holding area, which was a transparent cube on the third level. By transparent I mean see-through on all four sides. People walking on the balcony could see us. People walking to their apartments on the back side could see us. People down the short hallways on the left and right side could see us.

The cube was twenty by twenty feet. Twenty feet tall. Cement floor with a four-inch drain in the center. Two sets of bunk beds made out of stainless steel bolted to the floor. A square stainless-steel table with four stools around it — all bolted to the floor. A stainless-steel toilet and a tiny stainless-steel sink in the corner. A flat-screen TV hung down from the ceiling, showing live surveillance video of the Deep 2.0, including the inside of private apartments, and the shower room (men's and women's) where we had just taken showers.

I'm not sure they showed us taking showers, but about every twenty minutes Coop, Kate, and I showed up on the screen sitting around the little stainless-steel table. I'm not sure why, because anyone could go up to the third level and see us live, which three kids had done five minutes after we arrived to stick their tongues out at us.

Kate was glued to the surveillance monitor as if she had never seen one before. "Everyone appears to be color-coded," she said. "The Originals are all wearing red jumpsuits. But these video feeds are bogus. They're showing people only what they want them to see. No video of the infirmary where they allegedly took Alex. No Guard and Watcher barracks. No Originals' apartments, at least I haven't seen any red jumpsuits in any of the apartments. No surveillance control room, where all these feeds are coming from. Lod is blocking things he doesn't want people to see. He's only showing things that suit his purpose."

"What is his purpose?" I asked.

"Only Lod knows," Kate said.

"I suspect that Alex knows," Coop whispered almost inaudibly.

I'd forgotten they were listening as well as watching us.

"Did they take the flash drive from you?" Coop whispered.

"I have it," I whispered back. I'd managed to palm Alex's silver bullet when they took our clothes. I hoped the little box it was stored in was waterproof.

Kate got under the stainless-steel table.

"What are you doing?" I asked.

"Looking for bugs. Found it! Well, them." She emerged with four tiny microphones trailing severed wires in the palm of her hand. "I'm sure they'll replace them, but for the time being we should be able to talk at the table without being overheard if we keep our voices down." She looked at Coop. "Are you wearing tap shoes?"

Coop grinned. "Didn't have time to change them before we got kidnapped."

"Are you really as calm as you appear?"

"Did you ever read *An Inland Voyage* by Robert Louis Stevenson?"

"No."

I had, and I knew what was coming. Coop's favorite sentence in English literature.

"There's a line in the novel, and it goes: 'Quiet minds cannot be perplexed or frightened but go on in fortune or misfortune at their own private pace, like a clock during a thunderstorm.'"

"So, you're a clock?" Kate asked.

"Ticktock, ticktock."

"And you understand what's going on here? Lod is going to kill us."

"I think he *wants* to kill us," Coop said. "We'll see if it works out for him. Hope it doesn't. In the meantime, I'm not going to get upset about it, which doesn't mean I'm not going try to get out of this situation. Trust me, I'd do anything to save you and Pat and myself. It's just that I think a lot better when I'm not angry, or frightened. How about you?"

Kate was smiling, shaking her head in wonder.

"Welcome to Cooplandia," I said. "It's kind of a combination of the Land of Oz and Hogwarts."

Coop laughed. "I haven't heard Cooplandia in years. We had these twin sisters, the Floreses, who used to look after us. Poor women. Felt sorry for them. They said that they lived in the United States but that I lived in Cooplandia with a population of one."

Something changed on the monitor.

Lod was on the screen. He was stepping from the bat cavern into the first passageway. In front of him a group of people was heading toward the second steel door. He looked up at the camera and gave it a thumbs-up.

"Last group," he said. "We are all safe."

A cheer went up from the commons.

"Seal it!" he said.

The doors began to close.

The cameras followed him down the passageway through the second door.

"Seal it!"

The second set of doors began to close.

He stepped through the third set of doors.

"Seal it!"

A thousand-foot elevator ride and one more set of doors.

Agent Ryan was too late.

She probably didn't even know where we were.

"Watch," Kate said. "There will be plenty of room in the elevator, but Lod won't join the last group. He'll wait for the empty elevator to come back up for him and make his grand entrance all by himself."

Kate was right. The elevator doors closed with the last group aboard as Lod made his way slowly down the passageway.

"So, quickly, what's the story with this flash drive and the computer Bella gave to Bob Jonas?" Kate asked.

It didn't take us more than a minute to tell her about the laptop and the drive because neither of us had any idea how Alex had intended to use them.

Up on the monitor Lod was stepping into the elevator. The camera zoomed in on his finger pushing the down button, then back to his somber thoughtful face. He had a Bluetooth device in his left ear and a keycard hanging from a lanyard around his neck.

The cheering for the final group died down and a hush fell over the crowded commons. I walked over to the balcony and looked down. Everyone was staring through the open steel doors down the passageway. They had wheeled in a small stage with a microphone stand on this side of the massive doors. As soon as they saw Lod, they began to cheer again.

Lod smiled, nodded, and waved, pausing to shake the hands of the Originals dressed in red. He mounted the steps to the stage.

Kate and Coop joined me.

"I remember this," Kate said.

Coop and I looked at her.

"My grandfather's notebooks," she said. "I saw a sketch of this stage with the steel door behind it. He's been planning this moment for years. It's unfolding just as he imagined it."

She went on to tell us about Lod's notebooks as the crowd continued to cheer.

Lod held his hands up in the air.

The crowd quieted.

"Seal it!"

"It's like remembering bits of a story I read long ago," Kate said.

The doors began to close.

This was a horror story.

THE FBI

is almost here," Lod began. "Sooner than expected, but not entirely unexpectedly. We knew they would find us. In fact, we wanted them to find us. We are going to use them as a conduit to tell the world why we are here. Do not be afraid when they arrive. This is not a hiding place. It is a refuge. They cannot get inside. They will try to negotiate with us. What they will discover is that we are not here to negotiate. We are here to save the earth. To get people back on the path they should have never left. It could take months, maybe even years, to level the playing field above, but it will level, and when it does we will emerge and help those who have survived.

"There are no secrets in the Deep. You will hear and see me speaking to the FBI on the monitors. Do not be afraid of some of the things I will be telling them. I will be lying to them just like they will be lying to me. You have all read their lies in the newspaper articles. How I planned to bury those left behind in our former quarters. How I planned to use sarin gas to kill people above . . ."

I wondered what he would have said if Alex hadn't managed to disarm the gas.

" . . . I have never harmed another human being, except in defense of the Pod. You are my family . . ."

Lod glanced up at the third level and paused.

". . . my new family. My own brother murdered one of our most loyal and valued Pod members, LaNae Fay, a few hours ago. My only granddaughter, Kate, along with two coconspirators betrayed us to the FBI."

He shook his head sadly, then wiped away tears, or acted like he was wiping away tears.

We hadn't told Kate what had really happened in the alley all those years ago during the blood moon. She didn't know that she had *two* very weird grandfathers.

"Of course we apprehended them. I only wish we had caught on to their plan to destroy us sooner. They are confined in our holding cube."

Everyone turned their heads and looked up in our direction. I actually felt a tinge of guilt, which was ridiculous because we hadn't done anything wrong.

"After the perpetrators have served their purpose, the Originals will meet and decide their fate."

Our fate was already decided, but I was glad to hear that we would be around until we had served our purpose, whatever that meant.

"While we wait for the FBI, I want all of you to return to your assigned duties. And remember, there are no mediocre jobs in the Deep. Every job is important; every job is necessary; every job makes it possible for us to live another day."

I guess this final sentence was aimed at the people who mopped floors, emptied garbage cans, and cleaned toilets.

Everyone broke into applause and more cheers. The camera zoomed in on Lod's smiling face.

Kate pointed. "There's Bella and Bill."

They were in their red jumpsuits, smiling, shaking people's hands. Whatever magic Coop had worked on Bella appeared to be gone.

I walked over to one of the bunks and sat down. Every muscle and bone in my body hurt. Coop and Kate joined me on their own bunks.

I lay down trying to keep my eyes open.

It didn't work.

I KNOW WHO YOU ARE

Lod's booming voice said over the speaker.

That woke us up.

We jumped out of our bunks and hurried over to the monitor.

The screen was split. Lod was on the right side of the monitor sitting at a desk. Agent Tia Ryan was on the left side, standing.

It was light outside.

It was raining and misty.

"How long did we sleep?" I asked.

Coop shrugged.

"It must have been several hours," Kate said.

Agent Ryan was wearing a blue FBI Windbreaker and baseball cap.

Milling around behind her were dozens of policemen, FBI agents, patrol cars, helicopters, ambulances, fire trucks, and by the look of their gear, SWAT teams.

A lot of blue and red flashing lights.

I hadn't seen Agent Ryan since Coop blew up the neighborhood, but she looked pretty much the same.

"Can I call you Larry?" Agent Ryan asked.

"No. You may call me Lawrence. Or Doctor Dane."

"I'll call you Lawrence."

"Fine."

Agent Ryan pointed behind her. "As you can see we have come in force."

"I expected nothing less."

"Are you going to come out on your own, or are we going to have to come in?"

"We are not coming out, and I doubt you are coming in."

"Why is that?"

"Because the steel door your technicians are examining is almost impregnable. I say almost because I'm sure you'll figure out a way to drill through it. But that will take several weeks, if not months. On the other side is a large cavern. Inside the cavern are about a million hibernating bats. I know that's not an issue for the FBI, or the federal government. You don't care about bats. You don't care about any of our wild brethren. But we do, and so do a huge number of other enlightened citizens. We erected this outer door, at great expense, in order the protect the bats. If you make too much noise with drills or explosives it will disturb the bats. They will fly around in the cavern until they drop from the air, dead of starvation."

Agent Ryan continued to stare at the camera. She didn't seem to be overly concerned about disturbing the bats.

"But the bats are not your only problem. Beyond the first steel door are three more steel doors just as formidable as the first. My engineers assure me that if you use explosives on any of them this entire hillside will collapse. If we use explosives to stop you, which we will, this entire hillside will collapse. If explosives are used, our engineers' best estimate of your reaching us is around three years at a cost of five hundred million dollars."

Lod seemed to be enjoying himself.

Agent Ryan not so much.

"If you're thinking that we will come out long before you begin killing bats and collapsing the hillside, you are wrong. We're happy right where we are. We have decades of experience dwelling in the Deep. We have enough food, water, and supplies to last us for at least thirty years. Long after I'm dead."

"If you collapse the hill the bats will die," Agent Ryan said.

"Collateral damage," Lod said. "Which will be on you."

"How many of you are there?" Agent Ryan asked.

"As of right now, three hundred and thirty-three, but that could drop by four people soon."

"Why?"

"Hostages. Hold on a moment." Lod reached for something out of view and the picture on the monitor changed to a shot of Alex walking down a hallway with Carl. He was wearing a canary suit and had his arm in a sling. Carl was dressed in gray.

I was relieved he was alive and able to walk.

The picture changed to us wearing our canary suits and looking up at the monitor.

"I assume you recognize them," Lod said.

"The boys. I've never met Kate or your brother, Alex."

"He used to insist that people call him Alexander, but I think he's mellowed in his old age."

"What happened to his shoulder?"

"He was stabbed by his murder victim."

"LaNae Fay."

"Yes. That's a capital offense."

"You are not a country or a government."

"That depends on your viewpoint, Agent Ryan."

"How about letting the hostages go as a gesture of goodwill."

"I feel no goodwill toward you whatsoever. And I'm certainly not going to open the doors to let them out so your SWAT team can come in. I should mention that there is only one way in and one way out. One front door. I know this won't stop you from looking for a back door. I'm just trying to save you some time. The other thing you're looking for is our power source, thinking that if you cut it, the doors will magically open for you. They won't. We are operating off the grid. A combination of generators and batteries. I regret that we are using fossil fuel, but there is no way around that. It would have been nice to use solar, but we knew that you would find the panels and destroy them. So there was no choice."

"How much fuel do you have?"

"It will outlast our food supplies."

"Back to the hostages. I think we've identified all of the cameras in your surveillance system. We haven't found any blind spots. We could back all our personnel and vehicles off. Say a half a mile. We couldn't possibly breach the opening at that distance before you close it again."

Lod shook his head.

The door to our cubicle opened. Carl pushed Alex inside, but not viciously. He gave us a look, which I couldn't read, and a slight nod before closing the door and locking it with the keycard around his neck.

Kate rushed over to him. "Are you okay?"

"I'll be fine. Nurse Dexter did a pretty good job patching me up. He gave me pain meds and antibiotics." He pulled a couple of bottles out of his pocket.

"Lod, I mean Larry, is talking to Agent Ryan," I said.

"I've been watching it. Everyone is watching it. This place has come to a standstill." He looked at Kate. "Did you find any blind spots?"

She shook her head. "Full coverage as far as I can tell."

"Bugs?"

"I yanked out the ones around the table."

"Did they give my laptop to Bob Jonas?"

"Yes," Coop answered.

Alex gave us the slightest smile. "Good," he whispered, then in a normal voice said, "Let's hear what Larry has to say to the FBI."

Agent Ryan was talking.

"I can assure you that if your brother is guilty of murder we will prosecute him to the full extent of the law."

"He will be prosecuted, but not by you."

"What are the others guilty of?"

"Kate is guilty of treason, and the two boys are her coconspirators. It was a close-run thing. You almost caught up to us before we got inside. It wouldn't have mattered. I would have sealed this place whether the last of us made it here or not, and that includes me. Sacrifices have to be made."

I felt something tapping on my leg. I glanced down. Alex had his hand open. He leaned close to my ear.

"Do you have the drive?"

I nodded.

"Give it to me. Subtly. Smile like I just told you something that was humorous."

I smiled.

"You appear to know a good deal about how the FBI functions in these situations," Agent Ryan said. "So you know I can't give up on the hostages. How about you and I having a one-on-one conversation . . ."

I reached into my pocket, slowly, casually, and wrapped my hand around the little box. I leaned over to Alex and whispered, "The box got wet in the shower."

Alex smiled and whispered, "Waterproof. Give it to me."

". . . you must have a cell phone, or a landline. Let's talk about this privately and see if we can work something out."

"We don't have a landline, or a cell, down here. And I guess you haven't looked at your cell lately. You don't have a signal either . . ."

"He did it," Alex said under his breath. "He figured out how to take out the US without hurting his precious wildlife."

I pulled the little box out of my pocket and handed it to him.

"In fact," Lod continued, "no one in the United States has a cell signal. All the smartphones and watches just got stupid. I took down the cellular network nationwide."

Agent Ryan turned around and looked at the people standing behind her. The cameras followed her gaze. Several of them were fishing their phones out of their pockets, look-ing at them, and shaking their heads.

"It's not surprising there isn't a signal up here," Agent Ryan said.

"No signal anywhere in North America," Lod countered. "While you were checking your signals I took out cellular in Canada, Nova Scotia, New Brunswick, oh and here goes Iceland and Greenland as well. The talking heads on the television are screaming about it right now. Make a call on your sat phone. Call the FBI office in DC. Call a landline. They'll verify it. But make it quick."

Agent Ryan nodded at one of the other agents. He hit a button on his sat phone.

"No GPS in cars," Lod continued. "People are going to have to actually figure out where they are going on their own. Paper map companies are going to be happy. If people want to talk to someone they are going to have to find them and talk face-to-face . . ."

I looked over at Coop. He was expressionless, but I sus-pected he wasn't very upset about this.

". . . because after I take out the sat phones, landlines are going out next. I never did like the phone company."

The agent on the sat phone looked at Agent Ryan and said, "Cellular is down nationwide."

"Call our New York office," Agent Ryan ordered.

Lod grinned. "Too late. Sat phones are down. That was a tricky one."

Agent Ryan looked back at the guy with the sat phone. He shook his head. "It's out."

Agent Ryan was clearly shaken and trying to hold it together. "What do you want, Lawrence?"

"You mean my list of demands?"

"Yes, what do you want?"

"I get it," Lod said. "You thought we were negotiating. I am not negotiating. There is nothing you or the government has that I want or need. I'm just telling you what's going to happen as a courtesy. As soon as I'm finished and send this video off to the press, I'm going to take out the Internet. By the way, I should mention this: The cellular network and the Internet are not coming back anytime soon, if at all. This is not immediately reversible. It's not like I threw a switch and all you have to do is turn the switch back on. It doesn't work that way, as you will soon find out."

"People will die."

Lod nodded. "A lot of people, but more important, at least to me, most of the corporations are going to go down, along with the government and Wall Street. I've tapped into most of the power grid. Remember that unexplained brownout on the East Coast three months ago? That was us. Washington, DC, will be the first to go, then state governments, then cities."

"To what end? There will be anarchy."

"That's exactly what we need. A new start. We need a population of people and a governing body that care more about the earth than they do about what they can take from the earth. I have no idea how it's going to turn out. It will be interesting to watch from the Deep."

"And I suppose you want to be the leader of —"

"Oh," Lod interrupted. "In the excitement of the moment, I forgot to mention something. We do have sarin gas, explosives, and if you get this far, weapons. It's only fair that I tell you that if you somehow manage to breach what we consider our sovereign territory, any part of it, including the first door, we will defend ourselves. You've been warned."

"Let's talk about —"

"Good-bye, Agent Ryan. And good luck on the new planet Earth."

I LEFT COOP

Pat, and Alex. We were watching the monitor from the table.

I wanted to see the celebration through the window.

People were dancing, cheering, high-fiving.

Lod had sketched this scene in one of his notebooks.

The charred pages were coming back.

Coop walked up and put his arm around me. "Are you okay?"

"Yes," I said, but I wasn't sure. "My grandfather sketched his future and it has all come true."

"What do you mean?"

I told him about Lod's little notebooks.

"How much do you remember?"

"The sketches and notes are still coming back to me. Faster, now that we're here . . . now that it's too late. I'm so sorry to have gotten you and Pat into this."

"I got myself into this," Coop said. "I followed you into the Deep. I followed you here. I'd do it again. I have no regrets."

Coop kissed me.

"I don't have any regrets either," I said. "Not now."

He grinned.

I grinned back.

"Hey, you two!" Alex said from the table. "If you have

some spare time, why don't you join us so we can figure out what we're going to do."

Coop and I walked over to them hand in hand, smiling.

Pat was smiling too.

"Glad to see you're all deliriously happy," Alex said. "But we need a plan of attack. I'm open to suggestions."

"I'm kind of stumped," Pat said. "I've never been locked in an inescapable glass box before."

"Don't worry," Alex said confidently. "We'll get out of the cube. What I'm worried about is how we get back up top."

"Those doors are formidable. I'm not sure how we..."

I tuned them out. Seeing the celebration had somehow unlocked a secret memory compartment inside my head. In it were all the notes I had ever seen. It was as if I were leafing through a photo album. Image after image... *Motor homes. Steel doors. Surveillance room. Infirmary. Barracks. Apartments. Kitchen. Cafeteria. Holding cube. Lod's private quarters... They all made sense...*

"There's a back door," I said.

"What?" Alex said.

"A back door," I said. "Another way out."

"How do you know?" Coop asked.

"Lod's notebooks. In one of his sketches there's a shaft with a ladder leading up to the surface. It's inside his private quarters. I might not be remembering it perfectly, or maybe some of the sketch was burned. But in my mind the shaft appears to end before it reaches the surface. I guess that doesn't make sense."

"It makes perfect sense," Coop said. "It's a dead ender. Remember those, Pat?"

Pat nodded at him like he knew exactly what Coop was talking about.

"What is a dead ender?" Alex asked.

"When you're tunneling it's hard to tell where you are up on top," Coop explained. "We popped through in the wrong place several times. You can't leave a hole that people will fall into. You don't want them to know that you're tunneling under their property."

"And you don't want to block your tunnel with fill," Pat added.

"Right," Coop agreed. "So you cap the hole a few feet underground with a piece of wood, or something. That way you don't have to use a lot of fill to top it off. We made our caps three feet below the surface, or about two big wheelbarrows full of dirt. We'd disguise the surface scar with lawn turf, or whatever landscaping they had on top. I'd guess Lod's dead ender is a lot deeper so no one can find it above."

"I'm not surprised he left himself a way out," Alex said. He pointed at the cheering crowd on the monitor. "A lot of these people are new to the Deep. They're happy now, but after a year or two that could change. They might want to see the sun, and Larry holds the key to the sky."

"The keycards on the lanyards," I said. "We have to get ahold of one."

Alex shook his head. "Not just any card. Larry's card. Dexter is not only a good nurse, he's a talker. He told me that his keycard opens only a few doors. The Originals' and the Guards' keycards open more doors, but not all of them. Larry's keycard opens every door in the Deep. He personally programs all of the keycards and has been doing it since they started locking doors down here, which was about two years ago. Dexter said they had to send an authorization request directly to Larry. If it was approved, and a lot of times the requests were rejected, a reprogrammed keycard would arrive in the mail."

Pat said, "So all we have to do is get out of this cube, find Lod, subdue or kill him, take his keycard, break into his apartment, find the back door, scale a thousand-foot shaft, then dig our way through the several feet of dirt and rock to the surface."

"Gravity should take care of the dirt when we bust out the cap," Coop said. "We'll just have to make sure we don't get scraped off the ladder when the load falls."

I looked at Pat. He seemed to have gone several shades lighter in the past few seconds. "Are you okay?"

"Yeah, Lil Bro. You look a little pale."

"I'm fine," Pat said.

I WASN'T FINE

My claustrophobia had come roaring back.

Cold sweat trickled down my side.

I did not want to climb a thousand feet up a dark cramped shaft.

"You're sure you're okay?" Kate asked.

"Perfect," I lied.

I was mad at myself. It was ludicrous for me to go all claustrophobic over something that hadn't happened yet, and probably wouldn't happen because we were locked in a glass cage like a quartet of zoo monkeys.

"So how do we get out of here?" Coop asked.

"A big glass cutter," I said.

Kate laughed. She had a good sense of humor.

Alex not so much. He didn't even crack a smile.

"Larry dropped by the infirmary just before he delivered his manifesto to the FBI," he said. "He told me that when he was finished, he was going to drop by the cube and pay us a visit. That might be our only chance. He never really needed hostages. The only reason he told the FBI about us was to get into Ryan's face."

"What do you think he'll do?" Coop asked.

"He's going to murder us," Alex answered. "Maybe not today, but —"

Kate slapped the table in frustration, startling us. "He's thought of every contingency! I should have left the Deep a long time ago and turned him in."

"He hasn't thought of every contingency," Alex said calmly.

"Like what?" Kate asked, still angry.

"Me," Alex answered. He opened his hand revealing the flash drive.

It was flashing red and green.

Flash drives have no power. They get their power from the computer they're plugged into.

"That's not a flash drive," I said. "What is it?" I asked.

"Actually it is a flash drive," Alex said. "With a little something added. Did you try it on one of the computers in the library?"

"I tried it on two computers. It killed both of them."

"The silver bullet," Alex said. "My invention. I knew that Larry was doing something with computers in the Deep. Something that would eventually hurt people." He looked at Kate. "I was hoping that you might one day be able to get into the Original room in New York and insert this into their main computer, or server. Larry has been using his own server for years now. I wanted to take his system out." He put the device on the table and spun it. "And this little baby would have done it. Inside is a nasty malware virus that I came up with."

"And you named it the silver bullet," Coop said. "Like in that Stephen King story."

Alex shook his head. "I named it after the Brothers Grimm story 'The Two Brothers,' in which they use a silver bullet to kill an evil witch."

"What about the laptop you didn't tell us about?" I asked.

"Just like Larry has contingency plans, so do I. In the event that I wasn't able to insert the silver bullet into their system, I set up a way to do it remotely." He pointed at the flash drive. "There is a battery, receiver, and transmitter in the drive. The flashing red-and-green light means that Bob Jonas is trying to crack the code on my laptop. When he does crack it, and he will, the silver bullet will enter their system through their Wi-Fi signal."

"I didn't think that was possible," I said.

"Just because nobody has done it doesn't mean it's impossible. When the light turns a steady green, I push this little button on the drive, and the server and computer will go down along with everything that is tied into them."

"How does that help us?" Kate asked.

"It probably won't help us, but it will stop Larry from doing any more damage like shutting down the power grid, which I'm certain is on his agenda. It's all part of his plan to level the playing field. I'm sure he's already streamed his interview out with the FBI. He'll make sure that it airs on TV and the Internet before he pulls the plug. He wants everyone to know he took down the United States. We are almost completely dependent on technology now. That's what he was waiting for in the Deep. Lawrence Oliver Dane's day has finally arrived."

I looked up at the monitor. The live video stream cycled through. Commissary. Private apartments. Cafeteria. Commons. Gym. Public shower. Commissary . . .

"No cube," I said.

"No witnesses," Alex said with tears in his eyes. "Larry is on his way. I didn't want any of you to be here when this happened. That's why I left you two in Arcata. My plan was to go to the park, plant the laptop, get Kate, and get out. It wasn't a very good plan. That's one area where Larry is much smarter than I am."

He looked at me.

"If you hadn't taken the bullets from the gun and the drive from my backpack I would be dead right now. They would have shot me and found the laptop and the remote."

He looked at Kate.

"If you hadn't followed Bill and Bella, we would still be in Portland. Probably sitting in some hotel room eating Voodoo Doughnuts, watching Larry on the television, wishing we had been smart enough to stop him."

He looked at Coop.

"And you. You went into the Deep. You followed your desire, oblivious to the risk, and saved my granddaughter."

"Granddaughter?" Kate said with confusion and shock.

Tears were flowing freely down his cheeks now.

"Your mother, Rebecca, was my daughter. She —"

Blinds began lowering outside on all four sides.

"They're here," Alex said.

THE DOOR OPENED

Carl stepped in first.

Lod second.

The door closed.

Kate, Alex, and I stood up from the stainless-steel table.

Coop weirdly decided that it was time to take off his tap shoes.

Carl frowned at him. He was dressed in a gray jumpsuit with a gun belt around his waist and a two-way radio hanging from his pocket.

Lod had a silenced pistol in his hand, and a two-way radio clipped to his belt. He was wearing a white jumpsuit. The only white one I'd seen in the Deep 2.0.

Lod looked at Alex. "What did you think of my manifesto?"

"Succinct," Alex answered.

Lod smiled.

"Is the Internet still up?" Alex asked.

"For ten more minutes. Then we'll start taking it down. Because of all the servers it's a little more complicated than the cellular system. No matter, we'll be taking out the major power grids soon. Major cities first, then smaller communities. You should see the television feeds. The panic has begun. There are hundreds of people on their way here right now hoping to join us. Others are coming because they don't think the government is doing enough to stop us. Vigilantes. There will be blood in the streets when the two groups meet."

"And what do you think other countries will do when the US crumbles?" Alex asked.

Lod shrugged. "We'll have to see how my compatriots fare in other countries. This takedown is not happening just here."

Coop stood holding his tap shoes by the laces. One in each hand. I was certain he would tie the laces together and string them behind his neck. I had seen him do this a thousand times. But now? What was he thinking?

"There will be blood in here as well. This is not really a holding cube. It's an execution cube." Lod walked to the center of the cube and pointed down at the drain. "Easy cleanup. I thought of everything. I've sealed off the stairs and the elevators so Carl can drag your bodies out of here quietly. It's just Carl and me. Everyone else is down below celebrating. The only decision that remains is what order. The boys first, obviously. Pat, then Coop. My quandary is should I kill you next, or Kate? Have you told her?"

"About Rebecca?"

"So you have told her. Good. That makes the decision easy. You'll be number three." He looked at Kate. "And you will be last. I guess there is something to gene hardwiring. You became a traitor just like your mother."

"You didn't think of everything," Alex said. "No one can. Not even you."

Lod gave him a sarcastic smile. "Really? What am I missing, brother?"

"The laptop."

"Nice hardware. Your passcode was weak though. Bob had no problem cracking it. He's playing with the laptop right now, looking at the software as we speak. Says he can't decipher it. But he will."

"No, he won't." Alex held up the remote.

"A flash drive is no good without a computer."

"This one is a little different."

Alex flipped it over. It was no longer flashing. The green light was bright and steady.

"It's tied into that laptop. It's a switch. It will kill everything you worked for. All I have to do is press it. There will be no restarting the computers or your servers. Ever. You can't get new equipment because you can't leave here."

Lod raised his pistol and pointed it at Alex.

"Go ahead," Alex said. "The last thing I do before I die is press the button."

Lod pointed his pistol at me.

"Go ahead. You're going to kill us all anyway," Alex said.

I couldn't have disagreed more. I wanted those few minutes.

"You're bluffing," Lod said.

Alex shook his head. "You know better than that. I don't bluff."

"Carl! Get on the radio. Tell Bob to shut down everything right now!"

Instead of grabbing his radio. Carl pulled his gun.

"I asked you to pull your —"

Two things happened at once.

Kate dashed forward and kicked Lod's pistol out of his hand.

Coop threw a tap shoe at Carl's head. It would have hit him and knocked him out if he hadn't caught it with his free hand, moving as fast as a cobra.

"Shoot them!" Lod screamed, holding his wrist.

Alex pressed the silver bullet. There was a momentary flicker of the overhead lights.

"Shoot them!"

Carl walked over and picked up Lod's gun. "If I'm going to shoot anybody it will be you."

Kate kicked the legs out from under Lod, who fell to the ground, looking up at her in rage and pain.

"You killed my parents. If you try to get up, Carl won't need the gun."

Carl tossed the tap shoe to Coop.

"That would have hurt."

"Sorry," Coop said. "I won't do it again."

"You better not."

The lights were still on.

"You'll never get out of here," Lod said. "The exit doors are computerized. And you just took the computers out. Nice going."

Alex ripped Lod's lanyard off his neck, walked over to the door, and swiped it through the reader. The door clicked open.

Lod laughed. "Not the interior doors, you idiot. The *exit* doors."

"What about the back door in your quarters?" Kate said.

Lod's smile disappeared. "There is no back door. You're stuck here with me until the end of time."

"Of course you are lying," Kate said. "You have always lied to me."

"Tie him up," Alex said.

"Why?" Lod shouted. "I think Kate broke my leg."

"Good," Kate said.

Carl tied him up with the keycard lanyards.

LOD'S APARTMENT

was almost an exact duplicate of the one we lived in under New York City. The only real difference was the bank of computers that took up an entire wall.

All the screens were black.

We searched for the back door.

I went into the bedroom. It was exactly the same as Lod's New York bedroom, down to the bedspread and the walk-in safe built into the wall.

The combination has to be different.

But it wasn't.

I pulled open the heavy door. The shelves were filled with stacks of dead presidents, guns, and little velvet sacks of precious gems, just like the safe in our former apartment.

With one important exception.

"I found it!" I shouted.

Everyone rushed into the bedroom.

At the back of the safe was a small door with an electronic lock.

Alex gave me Lod's keycard. I swiped it. The door clicked open.

Behind the door was the shaft I'd seen in Lod's notebook. It was lit all the way to the top.

"I'll wait here," Alex said. "My shoulder. I'll never make it to the top."

"I'll wait with him," Pat said.

Coop found a small shovel and pick. "Remember these, Lil Bro?"

"Yeah, but I'm going to still wait with Alex."

Carl shook his head. "We're all going. No one gets left behind. I'll carry Alex on my shoulders."

"You can't do that!" Alex protested.

"I could do it forever, old man," Carl said.

I looked at Pat. "This looks a lot easier than the Deep."

Pat said nothing.

"I can pop the cap myself," Coop said, grabbing the pick and one of Lod's flashlights. "You can decide after I clear the hole. Everyone stay away from the shaft until I give you the all clear."

I gave him a hug. "Be careful. I'm . . . Well, just be careful."

Coop grinned and started up.

I GRABBED THE SHOVEL

"What are you doing?" Kate asked.

"Going up with Coop."

"But I thought —"

"I can't let Coop pull the cap alone. It's dangerous."

"I'll go," Kate said.

"I'm his brother. It's my job. We've done this kind of stuff before."

Before she could stop me, and from what I'd seen her do to Lod, she'd have no problem with that, I started to climb.

It was just as bad as I thought it would be.

A dark, damp shaft with slimy rungs and moldy air.

There were lights, but most of them were burned out.

Coop was at least fifty feet ahead of me, climbing fast, with the pick somehow slung over his shoulder.

I stuffed the handle end down my jumpsuit. It wasn't very comfortable with the shovel end slapping me in the face with every step, but the slaps did help keep my mind off my claustrophobia.

Breathe in.

Breathe out.

Don't look down.

Don't look up.

One slimy rung at a time.

"Lil Bro, is that really you?"

I looked up.

Coop was three rungs above me, shining a flashlight in my face.

"It's me. How about getting the flashlight out of my face."

"Sorry." He clicked it off.

"Thanks."

"Well, I'm glad you're here. I'll probably need some help with the cap."

"We're at the cap?" I was so relieved.

"Uh, no. We're maybe a quarter of the way up."

My heart sank.

"Let's climb," Coop said.

Breathe in.

Breathe out.

Don't look down.

Don't look up.

"It's like old times," Coop said.

"We never dug a thousand-foot vertical shaft."

"Yeah. But we wanted to."

That was true. We'd talked about it all the time. Our plan at one point was to go to Africa and start a diamond mine.

"What do you think Mom and Dad are doing?" Coop asked.

I knew what Coop was doing. He was trying to keep my mind off the climb. And it was working, to some degree.

"I don't know what they're doing," I said. "I miss them. I hope they've gotten back together. They may not have been the best parents, but we weren't the best kids. They made a good team."

"As soon as we get out of here we'll call them . . . Well, I guess we can't call them. The phone system is out."

"We can Skype them."

"What's that?"

"Never mind."

Breathe in.

Breathe out.

Don't look down.

Don't look up.

"What do you think of Kate?" Coop asked.

"I think Kate is wonderful. I saw the kiss."

"Yeah, that was pretty spectacular."

"It wasn't that spectacular."

"You weren't there, Meatloaf."

"Close enough to see it wasn't spectacular."

Breathe in.

Breathe out.

Don't look down.

Don't look up.

"We're here," Coop said.

I was out of breath, sweating, wheezing, but I was happy.

"What's the setup?" I asked.

"Simple but clever. It's a hinged manhole cover. The hinge is on the opposite side of the ladder. When I knock the hasp free the cover should bang open to the opposite side and not decapitate us."

"That's a plus."

"Ready?"

"No, take your time. I'm really comfortable here."

"I doubt the dirt is going to drop right away. I'm sure it's compacted and we'll have to chip it out a little at a time. But get a good grip on the ladder. Legs and arms just in case. Cover your head."

I heard steel on steel as Coop used the pick on the hasp.

"I just about have it," he said. "Get ready. We're almost —"

Clang!

This was followed by a loud *whoosh*. It felt like I was being dumped down a garbage disposal. My eyes and mouth and nose filled with dirt and rock. Something hit my back. It wasn't dirt or rock. It was softer. Warmer. I let go of the ladder with one hand and reached out.

Something grabbed it, nearly wrenching my arm out of my shoulder socket. I hung on with all my strength.

The dirt passed.

The air cleared enough for me to squint down at what was threatening to pull me to my death.

It was Coop, covered with dirt, dangling by one hand, grinning.

"Hey, Lil Bro, look up. It's the moon."

KEEP PORTLAND WEIRD

the sign reads above the grassy area where we have set up our evening picnic. There are signs like this all over Portland.

It's been over three years since the Deep 2.0.

When we got everyone out the back door, we stumbled down to the command center.

Agent Ryan came out of a trailer.

"Looks like you boys have been digging again."

"Kind of," I said.

She looked at Coop. "I thought I told you to quit digging."

"Well, I was digging up, not down. I think there's a difference."

Agent Ryan looked at Kate. "You must be Kate."

"Yes, ma'am."

"Where's your grandfather?" Agent Ryan asked.

"He's in the . . ." She looked at Alex. "He's in the Deep, and he's here." She slipped her arm through Alex's arm.

"I'm sure there is an explanation for that," Agent Ryan said. "But I meant Lawrence Oliver Dane."

"He's tied up in a cube," Kate said. "I broke his leg."

"Good," Agent Ryan said. "I'm sure the prison doctor will set it for him."

The agents and SWAT teams swarmed down the shaft like invading hornets. They brought laptops and servers to reboot the Deep 2.0.

They didn't lose one person.

Or bat.

There was a media blitz.

Court trials.

A worldwide sensation, which Coop and I and Alex and Kate were able to avoid for the most part.

One thing Lod did accomplish is that he forced everyone, individuals and governments, to rethink our dependency on technology. That's not what he had in mind. But there it is.

Lod, Bella, Bill, and all the other Originals are in prison.

They won't live long enough to get out.

Everyone talked except for Lod.

It's said that he hasn't uttered a single word since they found him in the cube.

I graduated from high school and moved to Portland.

Mom and Dad joined me. They live across the street from us. Dad has become a gourmet cook. His refrigerator is now used for food. He may be the only Nobel laureate teaching cooking classes out of his home three days a week. Mom has set up a foundation that gives free flying lessons to those who can't afford it. She believes that everyone has the right to fly.

Kate has a lot of dogs now. Dozens of them. She and Coop started a dog-training facility and boarding kennel.

Kate is out with the dogs right now. Six of them in a sit-stay exercise in the field where we are having the picnic that Dad has prepared.

Carl is helping her.

They gave him immunity for all he did for us, and for the world actually.

He lives in a small apartment above the kennel.

He has a dog. Not a Rott. Not a pit bull.

A standard poodle.

It's the smartest dog Kate has ever known.

Alex lives in the attic of the house Mom and Dad helped us buy next to the kennel. His room is lined with books. He works for Powell's City of Books part time.

I'm going to Portland State University, majoring in English.

I'm thinking that I might want to teach.

Or maybe write.

Or maybe both.

And Coop?

He's still tapping. I can hear him now.

Tap . . . tap . . . tap . . .

There is a bridge on the other side of the field where Kate and Carl are training dogs. Coop is under it right now.

Tap . . . tap . . . tap . . .

He spends his free time teaching tap to kids.

It's getting dark out.

The moon is full.

Tap . . . tap . . . tap . . .

In an hour the lunar eclipse will begin.

Tap . . . tap . . . tap . . .

We missed the last blood moon fourteen months earlier.

We were at the hospital.

The tapping stops.
Coop walks across the field toward me.
He is carrying a baby in his arms.
She is fourteen months old.
Her name is Rebecca.

ACKNOWLEDGMENTS

A huge thanks to my editor at Scholastic, Anamika Bhatnagar, who caught a ton of things I missed in the rough draft. Whew! And thank you, once again, to the Fabulous Phil Falco, who designs these books. Thanks also to Ellie Berger, David Levithan, Ed Masessa, Robin Hoffman, Lizette Serrano, Emily Heddleson, Antonio Gonzalez, Charisse Meloto, Saraciea Fennell, Rebekah Wallin, Erica Ferguson, Megan Peace, Adelle Pica, and everyone else in the Scholastic family. But the biggest thanks, as always, goes to my wife, Marie, the kindest person in the room, every room, always.

ABOUT THE AUTHOR

Roland Smith is the author of numerous award-winning books for young readers, including the Cryptid Hunters series and the Storm Runners trilogy. For more than twenty years he worked as an animal keeper, traveling all over the world, before turning to writing full time. Roland lives with his wife, Marie, on a small farm south of Portland, Oregon. Visit him online at www.rolandsmith.com.